The Danger in Desperate Bonnets

Ladies Most Unlikely
Book Two

D1617245

Jayne Fresina

A TWISTED E PUBLISHING BOOK

The Danger in Desperate Bonnets
Ladies Most Unlikely, Book Two
Copyright © 2016 by Jayne Fresina

Cover design by K Designs
All cover art and logo copyright © 2016, Twisted E-Publishing, LLC

ISBN-13: 978-1540707420
ISBN-10: 1540707423

Melinda Goodheart is a young woman with a vivid imagination and a very determined plan for her future. With no expectation of finding a husband—she's been described as an *"ungainly, robust girl with big feet and the grace of a plowhorse"*—Melinda has opened a small hat shop called Desperate Bonnets.

Hoping to stay out of trouble and spread simple happiness with the help of her uniquely designed hats and bonnets, she is quite content without a man anywhere in her sight.

But Melinda has the demands of her father—impoverished baronet, Sir Ludlow Goodheart—to deal with before she can get on with her life. And he has his own plan for her future. As if that's not enough obstacle, there is also her lazy, scapegrace brother; a bumbling, over-eager suitor; a fantasy highwayman who keeps wandering into her thoughts; and, finally, that "dullest man on earth", Heath Caulfield, a Bow Street Runner who always seems to be rescuing her.

Whether she needs it or not.

If only all these men would stop meddling, and insisting they know better, this "Lady Most Unlikely" might finally be able to get on with her own adventures.

Dedicated to all the quiet heroes.

Chapter One

1813

An Introduction in Mid-Air.
(Well, one must begin somewhere)

Dangling from a drainpipe could be a distinctly drafty business, she discovered. It was also a pastime far from ideal when dressed in her Sunday best. However, if such measures were necessary, Melinda Goodheart was your girl. Few pupils at the Particular Establishment for the Advantage of Respectable Ladies would claim to be made of stronger stuff, and certainly none could prove it.

As she clung to that rusted, cast iron pipe and felt one shoe begin its slow, tantalizing slip from her foot, knowing her own weight would not be far behind it, her predominate concern was not for herself, but for whom or what she might land upon when she fell. Hopefully she would not leave too large and unsightly a stain on the pavement, scar some poor child for life, or frighten a horse.

"Oh, do take care, Melinda," shouted her new friend Georgiana Hathaway who, being ten months older, thought herself a decade wiser. Clutching the window ledge from the warm safety of their bedroom interior, the young lady added gravely, "You might fall! Do hold tightly!"

"Your counsel, dear friend, is invaluable," the amiable maladroit replied from her chilly perch. "How lucky that you are here to advise, for it had not occurred to me to hold on. No, no, being of simple

brain, that was the last thing I had in mind to do."
Barely was the last word out than another bracket
gave way and the drainpipe tilted ominously away
from the building, exhaling a low groan that vibrated
through her fingertips.

It was, she mused, inevitable that she should
meet her end in so undignified a manner. Everybody
had warned her.

"Of all my pupils you three are the very worst,"
Mrs. Lightbody, the school headmistress, frequently
assured Melinda and her friends. "You are this
academy's biggest failures, with no accomplishment
or talent among you. Not for anything but mischief,
that is."

All of it quite true, Melinda would agree, nodding
solemnly.

But this ready concurrence by the miscreant
made Mrs. Lightbody even more scarlet and fuming,
and when she added, as she invariably did, "You are
the most unlikely to make good matches. You'll be
three debauched old ladies huddled together,
probably living a life of crime, not a decent husband
between you," it meant nothing to Melinda. The
words were merely hot air and as hollow as the threat
they sought to impose.

At the age of fifteen, seldom sparing a moment
to consider anything that was not immediately before
her, she could only reply with great warmth, "Thank
heavens. Whatever would I do with a decent
husband? I'd only get him dirty and worn. Look how
merciless I am upon my shoes!"

Melinda saw herself not as a delicate flower of
England waiting to be plucked, but as a brave Sir

Galahad with spears of sunlight sparking off her armor, a champion of the downtrodden, rescuer of desperate princesses. Or even princes, if the need arose.

Or even— as was the case on the day Melinda rode that rusty drainpipe— a savior of lost bonnets.

As she was fond of saying, one has to start somewhere.

Ah yes, bonnets. Has any item ever been more innocent in nature and yet more likely to get a young lady into trouble? The hat at the very root of Melinda's problem today had earlier been thrown by somebody leaning out of the window and tossing it up, with all their spiteful might, to the frosty roof. There it was held custody by two curious pigeons who pecked at it, and each other, with increasing violence, while little Emma Chance, to whom this hat belonged, had burst into a fresh round of hiccupping sobs whenever a flicker of windblown ribbon was visible over the edge of the gutter.

"Mrs. Lightbody will be furious," the poor girl had lamented, clutching at her dress with fingers that probably already felt the sting of a fiercely wielded cane. "She says that to lose one's possessions shows carelessness and disrespect."

"Nonsense." Melinda would not let any friend of hers suffer the wrath of Lightbody. If there was one thing she could not abide, it was to see a small creature being picked upon, and nobody was ever more eager to right a wrong than she. "I'll get your bonnet back for you." She had already assessed the breadth of the window ledge and the proximity of the gutter, her heart beating excitedly.

"Oh, do take care, Melinda," Georgiana then exclaimed, while comforting Emma with an arm around her. "I know you mean well, but really...I could lend her one of my bonnets for church today, and Mrs. Lightbody will never know."

Of course, Georgiana, who had a devoted elder brother to send her beautiful gifts from his travels with the navy, would not understand how it was to have so few nice possessions and even fewer fond relatives who cared to give them.

No, Melinda's mind was made up immediately and the hat must be rescued. It might not be entirely practical, but it was a matter of principal.

Do not think she embarked upon this mission completely without fear, however. She was forced to concede that it did look to be a very long way to the ground. Once galloping forward in battle, however, one could hardly turn about and charge away again without exhibiting a less than flattering view of one's backside. So once she had climbed out onto the ledge there was no retreat.

Her plan had been to reach the fluttering ribbons and pull the lost bonnet loose. But a most inconsiderate winter wind had suddenly blown the ribbons farther away from her stretching fingers, soon making it apparent that this would, by no means, be an easy task.

Unfortunately, as Mrs. Lightbody liked to point out, our heroine was an "ungainly, robust girl with big feet and the grace of a plow-horse." In all honesty, Melinda found that description rather more flattering than it was meant to be— she loved those solid, steady and gentle horses—but this was certainly a time when she wished she was less the lumbering oaf and more of a willowy, light-footed creature with long elegant, dexterous fingers.

Balanced precariously on the ledge, she had suddenly heard a bloodcurdling scream and, thinking somebody must have been trampled in the street by a coach and four, she glanced down, only to see a cluster of people on the pavement below, pointing up at her. After a moment's contemplation, realizing they thought she meant to jump to her death, she had smiled and waved down to the growing crowd.

"Good people, please do not fear! I am retrieving a hat."

Apparently they could not hear. Her gestures must have convinced them that she was unhinged, for another wave of screams drifted up to her.

For pity's sake, had they never seen a girl on a ledge before? If they had ever witnessed poor Emma's sore, beaten fingers they would understand the dire situation and shout their encouragement. Because those wailing cries of apprehension were not helping at all.

Carefully she had inched her toes along the ledge, trying to ignore her audience. The wind built up again, plucking at the edge of that ribbon, teasing her with it.

"I've got it! I've got—"

Alas, what she hadn't got was more ledge and when a gust of wind from behind blew her skirt hard against her legs, challenging her balance, hasty requisition of the rusted drainpipe had become necessary. It rattled in protest and then gave a low creak, signifying a definite reluctance to be part of her scheme.

Even then, the rhythm of her heart thumping like battle drums in her ears, Melinda had determinedly reached once more for the hat. This time the startled pigeons took off in a flurry of discontent and grey feathers, giving up their claim. But before she could celebrate, the drain shook, grumbled a somber dirge, and began pulling away from the building.

So that was how she got there, slowly dropping through the air while the weathered old pipe, struggling under her weight, bent toward the pavement. Inch by shuddering inch. And as the quickening breeze pummeled her gown and froze her fingers, her friends continued to offer their advice, which, while well-intended, was neither useful, nor particularly uplifting in the circumstances. Indeed, some of it bordered on the bizarre with offerings such as, "Try to land on your feet, Melinda dear," "Bounce just before you land," and "Fall slowly."

Although she muttered a hasty prayer, Melinda feared she had little credit with the Almighty. It was certainly doubtful that He would listen to her pleas, since she was such a wretched girl, inclined to daydreaming in church, watching folk in the other pews and making up lurid stories about their lives. Hardly likely to put her on His good side.

She imagined her headstone beside all the other Goodhearts whose bones and boots were deposited in the parish churchyard at home:

Here Lies Melinda 1798-1813
She meant well and managed ill

Hopefully they would plant her next to Grandmother Ethelreda, who had shared her love of good causes, rhubarb pie, and hide-and-seek—particularly the hiding part. Melinda had once remained hidden for almost an entire day before she realized that her brother had long since grown bored with the game and had, in fact, left the house for a ride, having supposedly forgotten she was hiding at all.

As she dangled above the street her shoe finally slid completely from her foot and tumbled toward the ground, caught mid-air by the gloved hand of a passing gentleman who, previously paying no attention to the scene unfolding above, was now obliged to stop and see what held the gawping crowd so deeply enthralled.

"What on earth—?"

"Perhaps you would be so good as to keep my slipper, sir," she shouted cheerfully, "until I have made my descent, one way or another. It is from a very good pair, and I should hate to misplace it or see it destroyed in a puddle. Or have a horse ride over it."

The downpipe shifted again as more brackets and nails came loose.

"Keep your slipper? The fate of your shoes, young lady, would appear to be the least of your difficulties." His stern gaze followed her overhead as she swayed from left to right and back again, like a pirate flag.

"I comprehend your concern, sir, but one can never be dispassionate about pretty footwear. Especially when there is a distinct lack of those

11

delights in one's possession."

At that moment Melinda's icy fingers finally lost their grip on the pipe and she followed her shoe through the air. Fortunately the gentleman was there to break her fall too, having remained riveted to the very spot where he previously caught her slipper.

"Good God!" he wheezed from somewhere under her petticoats.

As he set her back on her feet, she heard the ominous snap of stitches, followed by a cool breeze through her chemise under one arm and knew the seam of her sleeve was torn. Nobody in the school had more torn sleeves than Melinda, and she was recently punished for it by being made to wear a sign around her neck that said "Miss Goodheart is a very poor seamstress, a reckless gesticulator and hard on her garments."

Not withstanding all these acknowledged failings, today she was victorious, Emma's lost bonnet reclaimed and her mission successful.

"Thank you, sir, for breaking my fall and saving me from a most ignoble end," cried she. "One day I shall repay the favor and, when you are in need, I'll save you in return."

Still winded, clutching Emma's bonnet to his chest, the fellow gasped out a bemused breath. "I sincerely hope that service is never required. For both our sakes." He paused, catching another gasp of surprise as she gripped his gloved hand to help her balance on one foot and replace her shoe. "Were...were you breaking out or in, might I ask?"

"Neither, sir. I was rescuing the hat for a friend. I would have thought that was obvious."

"Indeed. For what other purpose would anybody be dangling from a downspout?"

"Desperate situations require extreme measures, do you not think?"

"And a bonnet is a desperate situation?"

Men were generally too thick headed, of course, to understand the importance of peripheral adornment, but she had no time to explain further or even treat him to a scornful remark. Melinda now heard Mrs. Lightbody's less-than-dulcet tones demanding to know what was going on— locked away in her study with the gin bottle, the headmistress had missed most of the excitement— so our heroine hastily took Emma's hat from the gentleman's grip and bobbed a curtsy of sorts. "Goodbye then, sir."

With his heels together, he gave a neat, quick, shallow bow. "Might I suggest you stay off rooftops and away from those *Desperate Bonnets* in the future?"

He smiled. It was as if he didn't want to, but couldn't help himself. For that brief moment he was almost handsome. Then sadness, like the shadow of a raincloud, passed over his face and he turned his back.

"But sir," she called after him, "were you not going that way?" She pointed over her shoulder in the direction he'd been walking before she fell onto his head.

"Ah." He spun around on his heel. "Yes. You got in my way, didn't you?" The man seemed annoyed rather than thankful to be reminded. With a brisk nod, he marched by her again and he did not look back.

Melinda was so distracted watching him pass that

she tripped over the step and banged her cheek on the door frame. The resulting bruise was 'oohed' and 'aahed' over with great respect for almost a full week.

And so, you see, the Desperate Bonnets were all *his* fault. He was entirely responsible for putting the idea in her head.

* * * *

She would, many years later, write to her friend,

Some romances might be described as whirlwind. They might be stormy with passionate declarations and littered with tortured embraces stolen by moonlight. They generally, of course, involve an innocent, fragile maiden and a wicked rogue, who suddenly reforms his debauched ways at one glance of her limpid eyes.

But for me it was very different. No cupid's harp sang in my ear, no clouds were rendered apart by lightning, no breathless recognition seized my bosom, no delirium of star-crossed, self-sacrificial love sent me to the charnel house. And he was no rake seeking my love for his redemption.

No.

Mine is not that sort of romance.

My awakening took place on the slowest of meandering, rainy dawns. But it leaked upon me with steady persistence so that I could not fall back asleep again.

It was years before I saw him a second time and more years still before I saw him a third, or thought of him as anything other than the dullest, most frustrating of men. In truth, I believe he wishes I still thought of him as such, for the idea of becoming anything more thrilling and beloved in my vivid, lust-filled mind quite terrifies the poor fellow. Look how hard I am on my favored slippers!

14

But good things come to those who wait, and ours is a story of Patience and Virtue.

Neither of which, incidentally, were mine...

Chapter Two

Two years later.

The first thing Melinda Goodheart would want you to know about her is that she never, in the whole course of her life, planned to cause any trouble.

The second thing you *should* know is that this declaration was usually the opening line penned in any letter she wrote. Because any letter she sat down to write during the first seventeen years of her life was either an explanation, an apology, or a confession. And decorated with a great many blots of ink between the misspelled words, where she was too eager to get her thoughts down and too impatient to mend her pen.

The third thing you *must* know is that despite an unfortunate arrangement of facial features, which, so it had been said, sometimes appeared "devious" and "conniving", she was not the sort of girl who did anything in a deceitful way. If she disliked you, she made no effort to hide it, and if she liked you then she was the most loyal of friends.

But this, alas, brings us full circle back to the first item in the list above. For due to that unwavering devotion to friends and causes, and an indomitable sense of justice equaled only by her courage— which had politely been described as "undomesticated"— Melinda invariably found herself in the thick of that chaos she never planned. She was a girl who went along with the conspiracies of others, especially if she was convinced of a wrong to be righted, and that made her daring, dauntless spirit an invaluable tool to those friends who *did* plot and scheme.

Too often ruled by her temper and driven by a desire for thrills and escapades, she might be mistaken for a stupid girl. Occasionally she even mistook herself for one. But is there anyone amongst us who has never been a fool?

On this morning, where we join her story again, we find our dear, affable scant-wit admiring a display in a jeweler's window on Sackville Street, while waiting for her friends who were both off on errands of their own.

Harmless enough, one would think.

Innocently minding her own business, and with both feet on the ground, she was certainly not anticipating any excitement. It was far too early in the day, she wore only her second best bonnet— made over in her own design— had appointments at the cobbler to mend her boots and the stationer to post a letter, and it was a Friday, which meant fish for dinner. On this day of uninspiring tasks surely nothing of any rousing significance *could* happen.

In the words of Mrs. Lightbody, headmistress at The Particular Establishment for the Advantage of Respectable Ladies, "When one's day is laid out with dull routine, there can be far less opportunity for Wicked Temptation and Wayward Curiosity to sneak their way in."

Mrs. Lightbody said this often— complete with emphasis for capitalization— while looking directly at her least promising pupil, although what she thought Melinda could do, single-handedly, to stop something so ancient and ubiquitous as Temptation was anybody's guess.

As for Wayward Curiosity, that too was widespread and not all Melinda's fault. In a boarding school full of overheated, intellectually stifled young women, it took no more than a spark to ignite the dry wood of their breathless, depraved imaginations. Even a visit from the chimney sweep, who was certainly no Adonis and had an unfortunate susceptibility to boils, had been known to cause an avalanche of heaving bosoms, and Melinda could find herself swept up in the turmoil just as easily as her fellow pupils. Wild romances were a specialty of her imagination, along with lurid tales of horror. Quite frequently they were one and the same.

But she waited patiently for Mrs. Lightbody's theory about tedious errands to do its work and keep her out of danger. Perhaps there was still hope for the "stupid, blundering girl", and she might yet transform into a lady of manners and elegance, one who let nothing divert her from the importance of being terribly dignified.

Alas, even with the best of intentions, Melinda seemed destined to fail. Distractions inevitably lured her from the righteous path and directly into the doorframe, even when her friends did not.

But surely today would be uneventful. It had started well enough.

Of course, she could not afford to purchase anything from Gray's jewelry shop, nor did she have any secret lover urging her to pick out a trinket. But it didn't hurt to look, did it? Despite possessing very few pretty things, and having no illusions of being one herself, Melinda could still take pleasure in the sight of beauty. There was nothing more comforting than to stand looking at the calm, complacent luxury in Gray's window while devouring a warm muffin from a street vendor.

Besides, she could always imagine there was a handsome gentleman waiting to dress her with diamonds.

When she screwed up her eyes, she could see his dashing, masked reflection beside hers in the window, as he held her arm and whispered in her ear. He had to be masked, of course— an obligation of the highwayman's life. That thin silk barrier was all that came between them when his naughty lips brushed her cheek with a kiss. In public too, as only a bold scoundrel who defied the rules ever would.

Suddenly she felt something tug her wrist. Rudely forced out of her daydreams, she spun around to spy a young man, slight of build and quick of hand, running away with her reticule.

The gall of it! Was no place sacred these days, not even the window of Gray's?

Ladies of Mayfair did not run, nor did they scream loudly and colorfully in the street. Melinda, on this particular morning, did both. Elegant society, quite possibly, had never seen anything like it. Not since the day she dangled from a drainpipe.

The lanky young man she chased along the pavement was just as startled as the onlookers they passed. When he looked back to see her making good ground, he tripped and almost stumbled to his knees.

"Come back here at once!" she yelled. "How dare you!"

People fell aside, staring in astonishment as she lifted her skirt and ran faster. So intent was she on catching the villain, that the sound of other steps gaining upon hers went unnoticed. As did the deep, anxious voice of someone advising caution.

She reached out and, with a final burst of speed, caught the robber by his coat collar. By then she was traveling much too fast to stop with ease and tripped forward, crushing her captive to the pavement. He was white, sweaty, and squirming like a landed fish, his eyes bulging.

"Oy!"

"Oy? I'll give you *oy*, you despicable little thief!" Melinda retrieved her purse from his filthy grasp and then set about squeezing his nose between her fingers, much as she did to her brother when he once ripped all the woolen hair from her doll's head and threw it down the privy. "I'll teach you to steal from me, boy!"

Before she could proceed further with her punishment, however, a stiff, gloved hand swooped out of the sky to hover briefly upon her shoulder. "Madam, what are you doing?"

"I would have thought that was obvious."

"If you please, I'll take charge of this offender."

Still sitting on the stunned robber's chest, she looked up. "But he's mine! I caught him."

The other man withdrew his gloved hand at once, as if it had been stung. He was plainly dressed, but smart in a blue coat, and holding his hat under one arm. Although only somewhat out of breath, he now ran that stung hand over his front, as if worried something in his very staid and tidy appearance may have become dislodged in the pursuit.

Melinda continued to administer the nose

20

twisting in which she specialized, until the interferer's hand stiffly tapped her shoulder again.

"I cannot be certain where you come from, madam," he said in a somber, quiet voice. "But here in London we are not lawless savages with everybody dispensing their own punishments as they see fit."

"For pity's sake, what are you rattling on about? Speak up, do!"

He cleared his throat. "As I said, madam, you may leave him to me."

"Why should I? I don't even know who you are. You could be in league with this thief."

"In league with—?" His eyes widened and then narrowed quickly. With a rigid squaring of the shoulders, he replaced his hat, stood tall and replied, "I am an officer of Bow Street, madam, entrusted by the magistrate to keep the peace and apprehend criminals. As it happens, I was nearby and saw you give chase. Now you may release the perpetrator into my custody. And please make haste, there are larger crimes and criminals at hand requiring my attention."

"Then since you're so taxed, why can't I deliver his just deserts myself and have done with it? It was *my* purse he tried to steal. Kindly step aside and allow me to box his ears. That will be quite sufficient." She didn't want to send anybody to their hanging over a few shillings.

"Madam, in a civilized world the general populace cannot be left to administer their own justice. Particularly wo—" Their gazes collided again, and something in her eye apparently caused him temporary amnesia regarding the end of his sentence. Perhaps he anticipated that she might turn her

21

pinching fingers to *his* nose instead. But, after a brief pause, he bravely resumed his trail of thought. "Particularly women, who are ruled by their emotions and lack the ability to keep a level-head."

"So now you are in haste to take charge *and* all the acclaim, when it is entirely due to my fortitude and rapidity of foot that he was apprehended!"

"Madam, I could have caught him myself, had you not got in my way. When you leapt after him I was obliged to worry about your safety first, instead of the thief's capture."

"Well, I'm sure I didn't ask you to fret about me. I'm only the *general populace*!"

"As a gentleman it is my duty, madam. When a lady is in need of rescue, I do not have to be asked."

Meanwhile, the captive, probably fearing— and with good cause— that he had been forgotten, resumed his squirming and yelling, until Melinda quickly gripped his nose again. "Hush, villain! I ought to shake you upside down and see what else drops from your pockets that does not belong to you."

The gentleman in the blue coat leaned over and muttered, "Madam, as much as I admire this desire to take matters into your own hands, you obstruct the course of justice, not to mention the miscreant's breathing. Unless you plan to sit on him in the middle of the street all day— and I should point out that it looks like rain— I suggest you turn him over to me. I'll let the Chief Magistrate know that you are to be commended, if you care to leave your name." Not waiting for more argument, the officious fellow bent down, gripped her arm firmly, and hoisted Melinda to her feet.

Thus, breakfast at Gray's, usually a delightful quarter hour of soothing reflection — and cake—was utterly ruined, and although she knew the purse thief was to blame, this arrogant man surely deserved some measure of her ire. Especially when, due to his unwarranted handling of her person, a line of hasty mending under her arm gave way. The snap of tearing stitches caused his brow to ripple in further contempt, while she suffered considerable mortification. Who did he think he was? At that moment, only her best impression of the school's patroness, Lady Bramley, could serve to show sufficient outrage.

"Unhand me, sir! Fie upon your impudence! Now you've torn my spencer."

Still holding her arm in a very tight grip, and not looking at all concerned or sorry, he muttered, "Madam, you are fortunate a torn seam is all you suffer. Running through the streets like a hoyden you might have suffered far worse. You are clearly in want of restraint and rational thought."

"And you are a presumptuous, jumped-up little man, who has let an ounce of authority go to his head and inflate it." That was often the way of it with these Bow Street Runners. Everybody knew that most of them were crooked, out for reward money rather than any interest in justice or preventing crime. As Lady Bramley often remarked, a woman was better off arming herself with weapons than she was relying upon a man to save her from villains in the street. This one looked cleaner, better groomed and more respectable than the usual "Charleys", but his patronizing demeanor had immediately got her temper up.

"Madam, I suggest you moderate your tone and go quietly about your business, before I arrest you for disturbing the peace."

Oh, Mrs. Lightbody would like that, wouldn't she? The headmistress had predicted that her most troublesome charge would end her days in Newgate prison.

But Melinda, shaking off the man's hand, announced with fearless aplomb, "I, sir, am the daughter of a Baronet. I have friends in high places."

His expression remained blank and cold, utterly annoying to look upon. She'd never seen such a dreadfully plain and boring countenance. It forced her to continue, as if a busy flow of words and indignation might eventually make a mark upon his stoic, flinty features.

"I am a student at the Particular Establishment for the Advantage of Respectable Ladies."

"You don't say." Even his soft, unemotional voice annoyed her. To Melinda it seemed as if he quite naturally expected everybody to stop whatever they were doing and strain themselves just to hear what he said. As if his words could be nothing but earth-shattering. Clearly he'd never had to shout for attention in his life.

"So you see, you poor, misguided, self-important fellow, I have connections of consequence in this town." She paused grandly, but there was still not a flicker of interest on that slab of granite he called a face. "*I* have taken tea with Lady Bramley. Twice." It might have been a class with nine other girls, learning to converse without offending anybody or indeed

24

saying anything meaningful at all, and how to sip rather than slurp, but what did that matter? He needn't know the details and she was determined to impress him somehow, although why on earth she cared for his opinion was quite beyond her.

Slowly he nodded, his lips working tightly together. He reached into his coat and offered her a handkerchief.

"What, pray tell, am I to do with this?" she exclaimed.

Finally a glint of amusement showed in his eyes, but it was at her expense, as she discovered when he lowered his voice even further to let her know, "Perhaps attend to the muffin crumbs, madam. All over your face."

* * * *

A woman running down the street after a pickpocket— and catching him no less— was, in his experience, unheard of. Unless she was a gin-soaked hussy or an angry wife chasing a feckless husband home from the tavern, most women kept their ankles well out of sight and would never risk unladylike perspirations stains. Especially not in this part of town.

But Heath Caulfield had taken note of this young woman earlier, as she stood outside the jeweler's window, probably picking out expensive gems for some foolish suitor to bankrupt himself over. At first glance he had taken her for just another pampered, idle, upper-class miss, whose only concerns revolved around which style of sleeve was in fashion.

However, something about this woman soon

struck him as out of place. And disturbingly familiar.

Being an observant fellow, he'd noted that the hem of her gown required mending, and the silk flowers on her bonnet, excessive in number and an... interesting... collusion of color, looked rather beaten and bedraggled— as if a confused and pugnacious squirrel had got in amongst them. In one hand she had held a muffin, which she enjoyed in large, unapologetic mouthfuls, without a care for the appalled glances of passing pedestrians, or for the crumbs tumbling down her front. Her cheeks were freshened pink by the air, and when she raised a hand to rub her misty, yearning breath from the window, he saw that her spencer had been sloppily mended at the seam under the sleeve, the repair tackled with a markedly different color and breadth of stitch.

Deeply enthralled by the window display and enjoying her little feast, she had seemed utterly unaware of anything else happening around her. A wide-eyed victim, waiting to be taken advantage of, he'd thought bleakly. Better keep an eye out.

So, fortunately for her, he had.

Not that she was grateful.

"Surely you know the danger you put yourself in by attempting to confront a robber alone, madam? You must not to be so impulsive in the future. Anything might have happened to you."

Although he spoke in earnest concern, her eyes sparked with skepticism. "Such as? Do I look like a helpless, fading lily to you?"

"Madam," he assured her with grave trepidation, "you are a female." There was no other way to put it, unfortunately.

26

Her brows, which had seldom been still for the past few minutes, now arched high. "I *am*? Well, goodness, why didn't anybody tell me? Do you mean to say, I've been walking about all this time with a false sense of grandeur? With an over-blown, pig-headed sense of self-importance? As if I'm a man?"

"I believe you know what I mean to say, madam."

"I haven't the slightest idea. I daresay, being a *female*, wracked with unhinged passions, barely capable of sentient thought, and not entrusted with powers by the Bow Street Magistrate, I lack the ability to understand your deliberately nebulous insinuation."

He exhaled a fraught sigh. "Must I explain to you," he replied, with as much equanimity as he could muster, "the peril that can befall a member of the fairer sex in this town, especially when she is left untended and happens to be of a venturesome, foolhardy spirit? What if you were injured in the pursuit? What if this man you chased had a weapon? What if he was not working alone and you found yourself surrounded by his accomplices?"

"*Left untended?*" she scoffed. "I am not a pork loin on a spit."

"I didn't mean to suggest that you were."

"I am not a helpless, naive child, who has lived all her life cosseted within the confines of a silk purse. Nor am I an idiot."

He said nothing to that, merely looked.

Apparently something about his countenance was enough to raise her hackles again. "I am *seventeen*."

"Ah, the very zenith of wisdom. Of course."

She scowled. "Naturally, when I gave chase I

considered the possibilities." After faltering briefly, she thrust his handkerchief back at him, as if she'd like to choke him with it. "Perhaps not as swiftly as I might have, however," she conceded.

He tried to soften his tone, for she was, after all, young and somewhat amusing. Remembering how he was at that age, Heath knew it unlikely that she ever made concessions of any size, so this one must have hurt. "Then you will have the belated good sense to leave this matter in my capable hands."

Although he thought he had softened his words, her expression told him otherwise. He should have known not to bother. Umbrage seemed second nature to this woman.

"I still do not see why your hands are more capable than mine," she exclaimed. "You're just as likely to run into trouble as I am, especially if you go around trying to help women who do not care to be helped and then tearing their clothes in the process."

"My hands are more capable than yours, madam, because I'm a man, I am considerably older than you, and I am not subject to sentiment or prone to acts of impulse."

"How awfully dull and drear your life must be."

"At least my seams are intact. Literally and figuratively."

Again she hesitated. Then, arm clasped tightly to her side, she exclaimed, "I had better absent myself from your company, sir, before I am obliged to cause a scene."

"Another one?" he inquired, bemused.

She adjusted the wilted rainbow of flowers on her bonnet— an act which merely resulted in their droopy heads nodding just as sadly in the other direction— and marched off, her reticule safely clasped in both hands. He realized, too late, that she hadn't left her name.

The Particular Establishment for the Advantage of Respectable Ladies? Never heard of it. Sounded like some sort of masquerade for a criminal enterprise, he mused. Perhaps she was at the window of Gray's that morning measuring the place, and its contents, for a potential robbery. Wouldn't put it beyond her.

She was certainly fast on her feet. And colorful. The sort of woman who might be used to cause a diversion. Look how long she'd managed to keep him talking and completely preoccupied while any manner of crime could have taken place behind his back.

And even as he thought that, Heath turned on his heel to find the cutpurse gone— flown at some point during his debate with the troublemaker. She had utterly distracted him.

He would bear that in mind the next time he saw her.

From first sight he'd known there was something suspicious about that woman. Something peculiar.

For future warning he would remember the curious gold flecks in her eyes that made it seem as if fireflies, gone astray from another continent, hovered and danced there. He also filed away in his memory the crooked line of her querulous mouth— all too ready to insult him— and the worn-thin material at her elbows which suggested a great deal of sullen arm propping. Not to mention the mending under her sleeve, a line of stitches made in clumsy haste by somebody far too impatient to find matching thread.

Just as those lively, glowing lampyridae he saw in her eyes were out of their customary climate, she too was out of place in Mayfair. Indeed, she was, he suspected, out of the ordinary for anywhere on the planet. He wouldn't be surprised to find she'd fallen out of the sky.

And that was when he remembered where he'd seen her before— clinging to a drainpipe.

Where else? As she would say, it should have been obvious.

Chapter Three

Four years later still.

The air smelled of old, damp carpet and hot, dead flowers, with a greasy, pervasive tone of burning tallow. He was glad he hadn't eaten for several hours or else the undigested food might have come up into his throat.

An overly-powdered woman drooped against him, rubbing her body along his side, rather like a cat hoping to be fed. Or scratching a flea bite.

"What's a nice, polite gent like you, doin' 'ere?" she murmured drowsily. "We don't see many of your sort around," she added. Her eyes were very dark, the pupils eerily expanded until they almost filled the iris. "You smell better than most. I wager you taste nice too. My name's Ivy. What's yours?"

Heath carefully removed her limp, clammy hand from his thigh, while leaning as far away as he could from the protruding curl of her questing tongue. He was quite certain that every woman in the place nurtured a virulent fever. Probably of an as yet undiscovered type, extremely contagious and incurable. "I'm here on business, madam. No time for pleasure." He scratched one eyebrow with his little finger, discreetly shifting a few inches away from her.

"What business can a man like you 'ave in this 'ouse?"

"I'm here to dispose of the pests, madam."

"Pests?"

"Rats in particular."

She blinked and leaned against him again. Heath

31

began to suspect he was the only thing holding her upright on that small sofa. She stuck to him and laid claim, crawling up his unwelcoming side with the determination of her namesake on stone. "You don't look like no rat catcher."

"That is to my advantage. The rats don't see me coming." As he continued this conversation with the feverish, sticky ivy plant, Heath kept an eye on the other figures around the dimly lit parlor. There were three gentlemen— all intoxicated— and a variety of highly decorated women, one of whom thumped never-ending noise out of an old pianoforte, which was in dire need of tuning. No one paid much attention to Heath. He preferred to be in the background, nondescript, able to come and go from a room with nobody noticing his arrival or his absence.

Only Ivy had singled him out and cornered him on the small chaise. She ran a fingertip down his cheek and he bore it bravely, although it was all he could do not to get out a handkerchief and wipe his face. "Pity you can't spare a moment for me," she whispered.

He winced, realizing he'd suddenly run out of space to retreat on the sofa. "I am a pest inspector licensed by the city of London, madam, and on duty. I take my work very seriously."

Fortunately, at that moment, one of the bedroom doors finally opened and a tall, spare fellow stepped out into the parlor. He was still adjusting his garments, smoothing down his oily hair and laughing with the two plump-breasted, scarlet-cheeked women in his company.

Heath stood, relieved to finally brush Climbing

Ivy's tentacles from his side. "Mr. Percival Archibald Clipper?" he asked softly.

The fellow turned, stumbling against his much shorter partners. "I might be. Who the devil are you? What do you want?" he slurred. Evidently nobody had called him by that name for some years and it took him by surprise. He was, of course, better known in these parts as Archie the Clip, due to his habit of cutting pieces off his victims when they failed to repay their loans the very minute he decided they were overdue.

Heath put out his hand to help steady the tilting man. "I am here to inform you, sir, that you've won a lottery."

"A lottery? What bleedin' lottery?" But his eyes perked up, widening, the prospect of an unearned windfall always appealing to one such as he.

"The Seven Dials Scenic Development Lottery, sir."

"Eh? But I don't remember purchasing a ticket."

Heath gave a humble, apologetic smile. "No, sir, it's not that sort of lottery. The ticket was purchased in your name when you were born. Presumably by your mother or father, or some other relative to mark the occasion of your birth. They never mentioned it to you, sir?"

"Never knew my father and my old ma died long since."

"Well, if I could ask you to come with me, you'll have to sign for the money. It is such a large amount, we keep it in a secure place, of course, and I'm not allowed to turn it over to you without the proper forms in order."

"I never 'eard of no lottery."

"We don't advertise the winner, sir, until we have the lucky fellow's permission in writing. Some folks prefer anonymity."

Archie frowned, shaking off his companions and tilting closer to Heath, looking him up and down. As he did so, a curved knife dropped to the stained carpet between them. He didn't seem to notice, possibly too drunk. Heath stooped to retrieve the weapon.

"This must be yours, sir," he said with a quick smile, passing it back to the villain, handle first. "Wouldn't want to lose that beauty, sir."

Archie grabbed the knife and, as he looked at the man who had casually, and apparently naively, handed it to him, his eyes slowly lost some of their innate suspicion.

"Will you come then, sir?" Heath yawned, tipping back the brim of his hat with one thumb to scratch his head. "I only get paid my fee when I locate the prize winner, you see. You do want to claim the winnings, do you, sir? Some men would run from the responsibility of so much money, and I wouldn't blame you for it. Life will change. Can't say I'd know what to do with it myself. The quiet life is for me. The quiet life and a bit of kidney pie now and then." He yawned again. "So if you'd rather not—"

"Oh, I'll take my winnings! I want what's coming to me," the fellow exclaimed, pulling up his braces. "I won it, didn't I? It's mine. Somebody signed me up for it. 'Bout time I got a bit of luck come my way."

"Yes, it is indeed. Time you got what's coming to you." As ever, polite and mindful of discretion, he gestured to Archie's breeches and suggested he might like to finish buttoning the fall before they went outside. He even handed the man his hat and coat, brushing down his shoulders for him, by which time Archie was already mentally spending his winnings and in a very genial mood. The drink helped, as did his evening of sport, which is why Heath had waited so patiently. Even the most cunning of criminals had moments when they let down their guard, places where they felt most at ease. The trick was simply to find out where and when, and then to sit and wait for an opportunity. Tonight, Archie was a man on top of his world, unaware of the tumble to come.

"How much did I win then?" he wanted to know.

Heath lowered his voice, "I think we'd best not discuss it here, sir...among these folk, if you understand. Wouldn't be...prudent."

"Aye." Archie sniffed, eyes gleaming with excitement. "Quite right. Can't trust nobody around here. Not these common types. And wenches blab worst of all."

So he let himself be escorted out of the brothel and into the waiting hackney carriage. Later, witnesses even described Archie the Clip as whistling and laughing as he stepped up into the dark interior. Observers could only say that he was followed into the carriage by the somber, nondescript figure of an unknown man— a man with the sort of face nobody ever remembered. A man pulling a heavy pair of iron bracelets out of his coat.

* * * *

"I am impressed, Caulfield. To take on a man like

that, all alone, to walk into his lair and bring him out. That takes considerable courage. Reckless bravado, some might call it."

Heath gave a brief smile, although it made his cheek sore where Archie had succeeded in landing the first of two hard punches before he was cuffed. "No, sir. I am never reckless. I study my prey, learn about their weaknesses. I take my time and weigh the danger before I take steps."

Sir Nathaniel Conant, Bow Street's Chief Magistrate, assessed him with sharp eyes across the desk. "And all by yourself in that hackney carriage, you succeeded in disarming one of the most slippery, artful and elusive sharkers in London."

Heath shrugged and set Archie's knife on the desk. "I've wrestled for Eton." A picture flashed through his mind, of all the trophies he'd collected for a variety of sporting events throughout his school and university career.

He'd always thought it most symbolic that sports prizes were empty cups, because the person he'd wanted to impress in the beginning— his father— could not care less about his achievements. After a while, Heath had given up on that, in any case, and competed just to please himself. At a time when the rest of his life was still very much under his father's tyrannical thumb, he had drawn some satisfaction from that sense of control winning gave to him.

And all those years of hard, disciplined training served him well now. Archie the Clip— a man with a soft belly, a drink-ravaged liver and, in all probability, body organs wracked with syphilis— was no match for him in the tight space of a hackney carriage.

Heath waited on the edge of his chair. "Is that all, sir?"

Apparently not. The magistrate, stood and began to pace with both hands behind his back. "You know, of course, Caulfield, that Bow Street was crippled with scandal in recent years."

"Yes, sir."

"Our reputation has been sullied by a wretched few, but with those bad apples removed from the barrel, we can look to future progress. We must improve the public's perception of our officers."

"Indeed, sir."

Matters had come to a head in the year 1816, when many officers from Bow Street and the City Patrol were accused of bribe-taking and corruption. Over the subsequent three years, reformers had struggled to make effective change, but Sir Nathaniel Conant's health was failing— he had remarked upon the likelihood of his imminent retirement on those grounds— and Heath knew the man must be anxious to see improvement while he remained at the helm.

"We need hard-working, educated, dedicated young men like yourself, Caulfield, to help gain the public's trust in us. So we have decided to promote you."

"Ah."

The magistrate waited, head tilted, brows raised expectantly.

"Ah...um. Thank you, sir."

After another pause, the elder gentlemen chuckled drily. "Try to restrain your excitement, Caulfield."

"Yes, sir."

Heath Caulfield had always been a serious soul, even as a child. If asked, he would have described himself as a cautious pessimist, because to march through one's life with too much optimism struck him as a certain way to hard disappointment. And to show outright enthusiasm for anything was likely to leave a man looking foolish. He usually kept to himself and did not expect to be singled out for any special attention. Had hoped not to be.

But there was, it seemed, no escaping Sir Nathaniel Conant's shrewd eye. "You are...unusual, Caulfield. You get things done without fuss, without fanfare. You *think* differently to other men. And you have a patience few can boast." Conant sat and rested both forearms on his desk. "I *like* you, Caulfield. I like the way you work."

"Uh. Thank you? Sir." He rubbed his tense thigh muscle and cleared his throat.

"We intend to put your mind to work on cases where those particular talents can be most useful— the more substantial criminal schemes and organized frauds whose perpetrators have eluded us. These unresolved cases are a thorn in our breast, a deadly canker infecting the streets of our great metropolis."

"Yes, sir." He understood that Conant wanted these old cases cleared before he must retire. Once more Heath prepared to leave the chair seat, shifting his full body weight to both feet. "Will that be all, sir?"

The magistrate studied him intently across the desk again for a moment, before he said, "We were surprised, Caulfield, to learn about your father."

The temperature of his blood cooled a few

degrees. He dropped back into the seat. "My father?"

"We understand he is —"

"Disapproving of the path I've chosen. Yes, sir. But his opinion will not affect my work or interfere in any way."

"And you do not wish to be addressed by your title?"

He felt the blood drain to his feet, every part of him recoiling from the suggestion. "No! *No*... thank you, sir." He could not abide the discomfort of other people suddenly changing the way they treated him. For this reason he used only his first and middle names.

"So you've taken lodgings near Covent Garden. Quite a difference for you."

A strong wave of anger brought the blood back, heated it and almost lifted him up out of the chair. "Difference in what way, sir?" he asked, jaw clenched, fighting his temper and the sick feeling in his stomach.

"Covent Garden is hardly comparable with the magnificence of Beauspur Rising. By all accounts His Grace's estate is—"

"My lodgings are more than adequate, sir."

"And so here you are, earning a guinea a week and living among the working classes?"

"Every man should work for his money. A man's worth should be measured, not by the title he was granted merely for being born, but by what he achieves in his lifetime. At least," he hesitated, suddenly self-conscious of his voice, afraid he might have spoken to angrily, "that is what I believe, sir."

Conant nodded slowly.

"Besides," Heath added in a calmer tone, "I find my living arrangements most advantageous. I see things, hear things...all beneficial to policing the district, sir."

"But if His Grace knew you resided near the Seven Dials, surely—"

"A third son is always superfluous in a family such as mine, sir, so I chose to make my own way in life. After university I joined the cavalry and after my discharge I came here, keen to find occupation and purpose." Glancing down at his gloved fingers, he added, "I would prefer to achieve something worthwhile, sir, on my own merit. That is why I'm here. I want to make a positive difference in the world while I am in it."

"A noble cause, Caulfield, and I can make no quarrel with it." The magistrate got up and offered his hand across the desk.

If he noticed anything oddly stiff about the younger man's grip through his right hand glove, he was gentleman enough not to mention it. As they walked to the door together, he passed Heath a bulging file of papers in a worn leather satchel.

"Your first investigation, Caulfield. A villain we've named the 'Cuckoo'. Fellow pushes his way into the life of wealthy, idle young rakes and widows about town and quickly empties their pockets, their bank accounts and then their houses of any valuables. He—"

"He's back in England?"

"Yes. He returned a few weeks ago it seems. You are familiar with this character?"

"I have followed the trail of ruin he leaves in his

40

wake for... some time now." Almost seven years to be exact, although the name "Cuckoo" was only known to him for three of those years. Heath had some personal unfinished business with the villain. A fact he kept to himself.

The magistrate continued, "Most recently he absconded in daylight with horses, a carriage and sundry property from the estate of Lord Hastings during a large house party."

"Sundry property, sir?" It was often the smallest detail that left the most important clue.

"Shirts, breeches, boots, even a few wigs. Odd things. As if he merely took what was at hand. A rather sloppily committed crime for the 'Cuckoo', who is usually far more subtle and patient, less impulsive. We suspect he grows careless."

"Or perhaps he merely wanted to humiliate Hastings." Such a blatant and reckless crime, in Heath's experience, was often unplanned and spurred by opportunity. This daylight robbery had an air of the schoolboy prank about it.

"A few days ago, the 'Cuckoo' was seen in the company of a gentleman identified as a Mr. Lindley Goodheart, Baronet's son and general wastrel about town. Likely to be the next victim. They are thought to be traveling together, although for how long I cannot say. The 'Cuckoo' occasionally goes into hiding, as you know, but he is soon bored with that. I have accumulated a ledger of statements dictated to my clerk by the many aggrieved souls ruined by this villain. Make a study of it, Caulfield."

Heath took the file of papers under his arm. "Thank you, sir."

"I believe you have the ability to corner this slippery fellow, but take care. Look about you. I would not like to be the one who must face the Duke of Ormandsey, over his youngest son's grave."

Clearly the magistrate still failed to believe that he was truly unimportant to his father. "Godspeed, Caulfield."

Heath took the leather satchel back to his room on Charles Street, above the busy 'Crown and Beehive' tavern, where, by candlelight and oblivious to the rowdy noise below, he quickly devoured the contents of each victim's complaint, absorbing every detail he could possibly need about the various incarnations of his prey. Unfortunately every description differed. The villain was an accomplished chameleon, frequently changing his name and his appearance.

Pausing his study for a glass of wine, he went to the small window and peered out on the noisy cobbled street below. Sometimes he imagined one of the young women wandering by was his sister, Clara. It was impossible, of course— thankfully; he knew she was safe now in the home of Mrs. Oliver, the caring parson's widow who lived in Chiddingfold and had once raised other children like his sister, born deaf and mute. There, in that comfortable house, Mrs. Oliver was teaching Clara a form of language with her fingers, and the last time Heath visited his sister she was much improved in health, looks, and happiness. It was a vast relief and very different to how he found her when he first came home from war in 1812 and discovered his little sister abandoned by both her family and the man who had seduced her away from them— the man who, at the time, had called himself John Croft, and who he now knew as the "Cuckoo".

For weeks Heath had searched London, desperate to find Clara. Eventually he located her living in a Whitechapel hovel where she had given birth to, and lost, an illegitimate child. In a fog of laudanum to ease her pain, she barely knew her favorite brother at first, but he took her away with him and repaired her as best he could. He had written to his father, hoping Clara might be forgiven and taken home to Beauspur Rising, but the letter was returned— supposedly unopened, although it had been resealed— and that was the last time he ever attempted contact with the Duke. Since then Heath had paid a monthly fee and expenses for his sister to live with Mrs. Oliver, where she was treated, at last, with the kindness and empathy her own family had always lacked.

No, Sir Nathaniel Conant could not know how much anger and hatred Heath held in his breast, not only for the "Cuckoo" who seduced his sister in an attempt to get his hands on her dowry, but also for the man the world called his father. The man who had simply cut his own daughter's moorings rather than be in any way associated with a scandal.

In the past, Heath had fought for his father's attention, and then for the glory of his king, but neither man knew or cared whether he lived or died. Now he was done with the futility of all that. Instead he fought for what mattered, for his beloved sister and for anybody in want of a champion.

* * * *

43

A story about the capture and arrest of Archie the Clip was featured in the next issue of *The Hue and Cry* police gazette.

When it was suggested that a piece might be added about Health Caulfield, as somebody of whom Bow Street "can be proud", he immediately rejected the idea. He did not want to be brought to the public's attention, especially not while he was trailing the "Cuckoo". But those in power were intent upon it, their eagerness to be *seen* as reformed in the public eye far greater than their patience for actual improvement. Although *The Hue and Cry* was generally used to give notice of criminals wanted and crimes committed, certain powerful people had concluded that the publication could benefit from the addition of better news— something in which the public could take heart. They saw Heath as their ace in the pack, a figurehead for their new reforms, and they cast his protests aside as being nothing more than misplaced humility.

"The criminal element will know they're being watched," he was told, "and the innocent public, visitors to our great city, can take comfort in the knowledge that our finest men are alert and on the streets among 'em."

Heath was extremely doubtful of this theory. He could not see himself as being a deterrent, but rather a target. A large, pudding-faced target.

When this ill-advised plan was enlarged to include an article in *The Gentleman's Weekly* newspaper too, and somebody by the formidable name of Lady Thrasher was dispatched to interview Heath, he was glad of an excuse to avoid her. On the trail of the elusive "Cuckoo", he had far more important things to do than participate in a silly piece of flotsam for *The Gentleman's Weekly*.

Let the reformers of Bow Street find another face for their mission. He preferred *his* to remain anonymous and forgettable.

First, however, before he left London to follow his prey, Heath had an important errand to discharge.

Chapter Four

She saw his face squinting through the window between a straw bonnet and a muslin turban. Strictly speaking, she did not see his face exactly, just parts of it, for the September sun was exceptionally bright that afternoon and it sliced through the glass like white-hot angel's wings, fallen to earth and half blinding to any human who looked upon them.

But there he was, intruding upon the intense beauty of those heavenly feathers by looming over her window, his shadow making a dirty smudge that hovered back and forth. A bit of a nose, an ear, the edge of a jaw. Melinda knew it was a man, from the shape of his silhouette and his restless fidgeting.

By her count, this was the fifth time he'd glanced in, apparently unable to decide whether to enter the premises or not, as if the sight of so many bonnets and hats of all sizes gave him severe indigestion. And itching feet.

Or perhaps she was to blame. Gentlemen, if they looked at her at all, often surveyed Melinda with a mixture of vexation, fear, and a desire to be gone. For when a young lady reached a certain age and remained unmarried, she was treated like a barrel of gunpowder with a lit fuse.

Pausing in the process of winding a roll of grosgrain ribbon, Melinda waved, thinking to encourage the smudge inside before he left a mark on her glass— which she had just cleaned. He promptly disappeared again beyond the window frame.

What did he think she was going to do to him?

Perhaps he was a robber and she should arm herself with a hatpin.

Well, whatever his purpose, if he didn't make haste he would be out of luck. With a long and tiring journey ahead of her tomorrow and no more scheduled customers today, she was soon to close for the evening.

At last, as she stacked hatboxes, she heard the door open and hesitant steps enter.

"Er...hello?" he muttered dubiously.

"Good afternoon, sir." She had just set a ladder against the shelves, and prepared to take the hatboxes up out of the way. "What is it you wanted? Eye of newt, toe of frog? Scale of dragon, tooth of wolf?"

"I beg your pardon?"

"I saw you hovering, sir," she explained over her shoulder, "like Macbeth before the witches' lair. You must brook your disappointment for I am completely sold out of evil spells. There has been a great demand of late."

He cleared his throat. "Evil spells?"

"Hats, however, I have in abundance. That and impudence, so I am told."

"Impudence?" He sounded concerned.

"Don't mind me, sir. I talk altogether too much and seldom say anything worthwhile. I suppose that's what they mean, isn't it?"

"Is it?"

"That I speak up without being asked and have the sheer gall to imagine anybody is interested in what I have to say. But in truth it is not any form of conceit. It is more a case of thinking aloud out of habit. It rather makes me an open book. One most

47

people want to snap shut and throw against the nearest wall." She chuckled; he did not.

His somber presence cast a mantle of shadow inside the small shop, just as it had over her window display. Something about his cautious manner felt distantly familiar. At that moment she was simply too busy and distracted to give him much thought, however, and had spared him no more than the briefest of glances.

With much on her mind that afternoon, the last thing she needed was a diffident, indecisive customer, and a man, of all things. Men knew nothing about bonnets, and Melinda did not have a spare moment to educate him.

* * * *

It was her.

He'd thought as much when he first saw the sign, "*Desperate Bonnets*", hanging over the window. Remembering that strange conversation, many years ago, with a young lady on a drainpipe, curiosity had got the better of Heath and lured him inside the little shop.

He knew it could not be a coincidence, and he had to see for himself what became of her. But his visit was also practical. As it happened his sister's birthday would soon be upon them, so he had decided to have something sent to Mrs. Oliver's house before he left town. He would not want Clara to think he'd forgotten her, and he had no idea how long he'd be gone.

"I'm looking for a bonnet," he muttered, "for a young lady. I have her address here and—"

"What sort of bonnet?"

"I'm afraid I know nothing of fashion and...and fripperies. Or bonnets. Or young ladies."

"Then you're in rather a fix, aren't you?" He heard a smile in her voice, although she was hidden behind a stack of hatboxes. "But it shows much in your favor that you are, despite your fears and doubts, willing to enter this terrible place of *fripperies* on her behalf. I'm sure she'll be very impressed." The tower of boxes moved as she backed up and bumped into the shelves. "What sort of young lady is she?" With one foot she felt for the first rung of a rickety ladder. "Fair or dark? Or a redhead like me? Is she short or tall? No-nonsense or decorative? Does she prefer flowers or fruit? Feathers or beaded trim? Is she a carefree spring sprite, a bright summer bloom, a lustrous autumn goddess of the harvest, or a sultry winter princess? Is this a bonnet for a special occasion or everyday use?" He could see only one coppery curl bouncing around the curved edge of a hatbox.

"I...do not...I hadn't thought." Suddenly he felt the faceless wooden heads crowding in upon him, turned expectantly in his direction and whispering. Even without lips. "Nothing too expensive. I'm not made of money." He looked around at the array of fanciful trimmings on display— ostrich plumes, peacock feathers and wax fruit— a gaudy abundance that made him think, for some reason, of a Roman orgy. Excess, frivolity and... debauchery. The air was heavy with scent, the shop over-brimming with femininity. He felt slightly drunk.

And he'd just caught a glimpse of one silk-clad ankle.

Was it hot in there? Must be. A bead of sweat tickled his brow and his shirt felt too small and tight. As he turned stiffly, he bumped into a faceless wooden head and it rocked as if filled with silent, mocking laughter.

"Something simple and...and practical," he growled, taking off his hat to wipe his forehead.

"Oh, dear! Are you sure you're in the right place, sir? Why not buy her a besom broom, or some headache powders instead?"

Although she spoke with a jovial tone, the sarcasm did not go unnoted. Heath worked his jaw for a moment, resisting the urge to flee. "It's just a hat, isn't it?" he murmured. "Won't any one of them do?"

From behind her boxes, she exhaled a dramatic sigh. "That is precisely the trouble. Men never take bonnets seriously." There was a pause, but he still could not see her behind the tilting tower of hatboxes— only her fingertips, as they tapped impatiently. "A woman would never go out with *just any* bonnet upon her head, sir. Describe the lady to me, if you please. I must have something to go on."

"Well, she's not very tall. Older than you, perhaps. At least she looks older."

"What color are her eyes?"

"Er... like mine...a murky shade of brown."

Her fingers ceased their tapping. "And her hair?"

"Mousy, I suppose."

Aha! Heath belatedly remembered that he had a miniature portrait of his sister and fumbled to retrieve it from his waistcoat pocket.

* * * *

Melinda was vexed and yet amused. She knew men were notoriously careless when it came to noticing the little things, but one would have thought a gentleman might describe his lady love in more glowing terms than short, old, and mousy. "If you wait a moment, sir, while I put these boxes up, I'll show you a few ideas. Usually a lady comes in person and tries on various shapes and trimmings to find what suits her face."

She heard him move closer. "Madam, allow me to help."

"No, no, that's quite all right."

"But madam, that ladder looks unsteady."

"I suppose it has passed its best years and is missing a few rungs, but aren't we all?" she replied cheerfully. "There is a way to balance it, and I have mastered the art. It seems disloyal to buy a shiny new one when this has served me so well."

Apparently he was incapable of leaving her to manage this task, for his gloved hands suddenly attempted to wrestle the boxes from her. "Please, madam, you might fall."

It always raised her hackles when a man stuck his nose in where it was not required, but she remained polite. Which she would not have done a few years ago. "Really, your concern is unnecessary. Do let go."

"Madam, I insist."

"No, sir, it is—"

As he tried again to take the boxes from her, she pulled back. The ladder swayed on its uneven legs and as she felt the rungs slip away under her feet, Melinda dropped her boxes to stretch for the shelf. She missed, ripped the under seam of her sleeve, and found herself, quite unexpectedly, laid over the stranger's shoulders like a rolled length of carpet, and clutching his ears for balance. Fortunately his shoulders had some width to them and, apparently, some strength, for he stumbled only a little under her clumsy weight before he righted himself.

"Pardon me, madam."

"I did tell you I could manage."

He tried to set her down on her own two feet, but now there was a further tragedy. Melinda wore a pinafore over her dress that day, as she did whenever at work in the shop. The pinafore contained many useful pockets in which to hold sewing tools, and somehow the gentleman's gloved hand became caught and trapped in one. The resulting tussle finally sent them both to the floor, among ribbons, spilled boxes, feathers, wires and tulle, where Lady Bramley found them two seconds later as she swept into the shop. Immediately Melinda's kind patroness assumed some attack was taking place and proceeded to beat the gentleman with her parasol, her high-pitched, outraged shouts completely obscuring their attempts to explain.

Lady Bramley had little time for men, even when her mood was bolstered by a stiffener or two of sherry; she considered most of them a waste of her air and, these days, suspected all— even her long-suffering butler— of harboring criminal intentions. Since the death of her husband, who had been one of the very few males she could tolerate, Lady Bramley much preferred the company of dogs, and frequently stated this fact.

But in the midst of raising her parasol again, she suddenly exclaimed, "I know you, do I not, young man?"

"No. No!" he sputtered. "Certainly not!"

The poor customer, having taken the brunt of her ladyship's assault, grabbed his hat from the counter, ducked his head as if he feared further beatings, and made a hasty exit, cursing under his breath about "a fool's errand" and how he should have known better. The door slammed in his wake.

"Where is that girl I hired to help?" Lady Bramley demanded breathlessly of Melinda as the walls rattled in his wake. "You should not be left alone in this shop. Anything could happen! There are vagabonds about in the streets at this hour, as I have warned you before."

"Your ladyship, I appreciate your concern, but I am quite capable of defending myself. The streets are not overflowing with villains awaiting a chance to molest unchaperoned women in hat shops." She brushed down her pinafore and tidied her hair as best she could, aware of Lady Bramley's intense appraisal. "That gentleman came in to buy a bonnet for his young lady, and he made the mistake of trying to help me with some boxes. A slight mishap ensued. It was all quite innocent." She paused. "And you look at me, your ladyship, as if nothing I ever do is innocent. You know very well that I never set out to cause any trouble."

Lady Bramley pursed her lips and pointed with her parasol. "I have not forgotten your school days, young lady, when you and your friends took it upon yourselves to create havoc at my garden party."

Melinda turned away, hiding her smile as she tucked a loosened lock of hair back under its pin. "Your ladyship, I am one and twenty and, I *hope*, improved somewhat since those days."

"Hmph. Miracles, my dear girl, do not come to pass in so little as two years. Not even when *I* am in charge."

"I suppose not." She hoped the lady wouldn't see that she'd torn her sleeve again, or else there would be another lecture about the unseemliness of waving one's arms around in public. *Miss Goodheart is a very poor seamstress, a reckless gesticulator and hard on her garments.* She sighed and removed a stray feather from the front of her pinafore.

"As for Nancy, I sent her home because her mama has not been well and she needed medicine from the apothecary before he closed for the evening."

"And the errand boy, Joseph? Where is that wily young rascal?"

"He was not needed this afternoon, which was just as well. There was much feverish anticipation in the air about an impending pig race and the consequent consumption of strong ale. With such entertainment on the horizon I had no hope of keeping his attention."

"Then you should have bolted the door and closed the shutters when they both left."

"But I was expecting you, your ladyship, and would not want to leave you locked out if I was up a ladder when you arrived." She reached for the book of accounts so that the lady could cast her stern eye over the figures. After eight months of business, *Desperate Bonnets* was almost making a profit. She would soon be able to repay Lady Bramley for the lease on the shop. "Now, you have not forgotten I go home tomorrow in response to my father's summons, your ladyship?"

"Of course I have not forgotten. I am not so far into my dotage that time has rendered holes in my immediate memory. But why does your father so suddenly call you home, Miss Goodheart? He has shown little interest in your well-being these last few years."

All innocence, she replied, "It is indeed a great mystery, your ladyship."

But it was not truly a mystery at all. She knew why her father suddenly called her home after seemingly forgetting about her since she finished at the ladies academy. Melinda simply did not care to say the reason out loud. And she also knew that her father was about to be bitterly disappointed in her, yet again. All things considered it was a subject she would rather avoid completely.

It was then that she noticed the miniature oval portrait on the counter and the square of folded notepaper on the floor. The nervous gentleman must have left one behind and dropped the other when he departed in haste.

Leaving Lady Bramley to review the ledger, Melinda rushed to the door and looked out, but the fellow was gone, lost in the crowd along the pavement. In all likelihood she would not have known him anyway, since she only glimpsed a little of his face peering through the window.

Hopefully he would return for the portrait once he realized it was missing.

She looked at it again. The small frame embraced the head and shoulders of a dainty young lady with a somber face, sad blue eyes and lips so faded they barely formed a shape. The notepaper contained a name, "Clara", and an address in Chiddingfold, Surrey.

"*I'm looking for a bonnet,*" he had said, "*for a young lady. I have her address here...*" The girl in the portrait certainly looked as if she needed a new bonnet to cheer her spirits, poor dear. Obviously not a wife, or he would not require the address written down.

Melinda's imagination immediately went to work on their sorrowful tale. They must be forbidden lovers, separated by feuding families. That would account for her sad face and his gloomy, nervous disposition. They had known one another from childhood and sworn to marry against the wishes of their parents. Now they saw each other in stolen moments and exchanged gifts as discreetly as possible. It was obvious.

How very unfortunate for Clara that the gentleman had not completed his mission today, but he was so uncomfortable in the shop that the point of Lady Bramley's determined parasol had been enough to chase him out again. Apparently mortified and easily discouraged, he had not even stayed to collect the little portrait. No wonder he had not yet got up enough gumption to steal poor Clara away from her cruel relatives and instead clung to this faint facsimile for company.

Men. What exactly did they ever achieve?

St. Paul's Cathedral. Well, yes, she supposed Sir Christopher Wren deserved some credit, but in all probability there was a woman somewhere who cooked his meals and poured his port, and without whom he would never have finished the project.

Hargreaves invented the 'Spinning Jenny', but it was his daughter who gave him the idea. And the Montgolfier brothers had supposedly invented a hot air balloon, but they were only two of sixteen children in the family and Melinda was quite certain they had a lesser known sister without whom their invention would never have got off the ground. Did books mention her? No.

Women were always in the background, waiting to be noticed.

Like miserable, faded Clara, who waited behind the hedges of Chiddingfold, watching for her timid lover.

Feeling somewhat responsible herself for the gentleman's sudden departure, Melinda decided to see to it that his young lady got her bonnet. Such things were often left up to the women to resolve, of course.

She would make one tonight and deliver it tomorrow since she changed coaches there at The Crown Inn. A most fortuitous circumstance. It would seem as if fate had put this duty in her hands.

But her mission was not entirely selfless. Any excuse for a little delay in going home was more than welcome, naturally.

Chapter Five

It was a small cottage with an orderly, well-tended garden and a painted gate. There were hollyhocks, old-fashioned roses, and a gravel walk, even tidy hedges of privet and boxwood, just as she'd imagined.

A lady came to the door in a plain grey day-gown and a mob cap. She smiled very pleasantly, but seemed confused when Melinda presented the hat box "For Clara".

"There is a Clara here, is there not?" Oh dear, had she jumped into too many conclusions, as was her habit?

"Yes, there is, madam. I am her guardian, Mrs. Oliver. But I'm quite sure she has not ordered a bonnet."

"Oh, but this is a gift from a gentleman."

"A gentleman?" The lady paled and raised a hand to her throat. "What...What gentleman?"

Aha! Her supposition about a forbidden love affair seemed likely to be quite true. There was definitely a fearful gleam in the woman's eye.

"He came into my shop in Mayfair yesterday to order the bonnet, but I'm afraid he dashed out again before he could give his name. The gentleman left this address behind, however, so I decided to deliver it myself." She looked around the grey lady's shoulder and into a tidy, narrow passage. A console table by the wall held a vase full of late blooming roses with big blousy heads and beside it stood a hat stand— empty and rather bereft.

After a moment of apparent consternation, the lady stepped aside and asked Melinda to come in. "Since you have gone to all this trouble, and come all the way from Mayfair, you had better see Lady Clara yourself, madam."

Lady Clara? Her curiosity roused, she walked into the foyer, passed the lonely hat stand, and followed the woman into a small, sunny parlor. There, by the window, a thin girl with fair hair in a braided knot at the nape of her neck, sat before an easel, skillfully painting a watercolor of the cottage garden. She had her back to the door and worked calmly, quietly. The window was ajar and through it a soft breeze floated into the parlor, gently moving a curl by her cheek on its way through. On the mantle, above a gently glowing hob grate, a clock ticked away to a tidy rhythm. A budgerigar tweeted merrily in a domed cage by the window, and a tortoiseshell cat lounged with sultry disinterest along the back of a Queen Anne sofa, only the very tip of its tail occasionally twitching to show that it still lived and that it might, when it felt like it, get up and menace the bird. But only if it had naught else to do.

It was a peaceful, restful scene—the very picture of a proper young lady, quietly at her work, practicing an approved accomplishment.

Everything Melinda herself had never managed to achieve.

To her surprise no words were spoken, and the girl at the easel did not even turn when the door opened. But Mrs. Oliver walked around Melinda and put herself beside the easel, where she quickly began to make signs with her fingers. The young girl set down her paintbrush, stood and turned to see who had come.

Although clearly flustered and surprised by a visitor, she gave a curtsey far more graceful than any effort of Melinda's.

"This is Lady Clara Beauspur, madam," her guardian explained, those busy hands still for a moment, the fingers, in crochet half-mittens, spread against her grey skirt. "I have told her about the bonnet."

"Good afternoon, Lady Clara. My name is Miss Goodheart. I manage a millinery shop in Mayfair, and a gentlemen came in yesterday to order a bonnet for you. He left without giving his name."

The girl looked as if she had stepped right out of her faded portrait, or drifted rather, like an elegant ghost. Making no move toward the offered hatbox, she stared wide-eyed, while Mrs. Oliver once again signed with her fingers. This time Lady Clara responded with similar gestures, but hers were curt.

"I'm afraid she cannot accept such a gift, madam. It would not be proper. I'm sure you understand."

Melinda was annoyed with herself. Of course she should have known there would be an objection. The young lady was clearly being kept away from her unsuitable lover, just as she'd suspected, and the poor thing dare not take the bonnet while in the presence of her guardian. Charging forward like a bull in a china shop, Melinda had been too eager with her good deed as usual, believing in the power of love and desperate bonnets to set things right.

At the advanced age of one and twenty, she really ought to stop doing this, she thought. But something about that melancholy gentleman had left her feeling unsettled, wanting to help.

Again Clara signed with her fingers.

"She would like to know how you found her address, Miss Goodheart."

"The gentleman left it behind. I believe it fell out of his coat when I landed on him."

"You...landed... on him?"

The other two women exchanged startled glances.

"There was an incident... perfectly innocent. Suffice to say, he meant well and managed ill, much as I often do." Melinda shrugged listlessly. "I suppose that's why I felt sorry for him." She set the hatbox down on the small round table by the window. "You might at least try the bonnet on," she addressed Lady Clara directly. "I have always found my spirits cheered tremendously by a new bonnet, and your gentleman did put himself to great trouble, merely to enter my shop. I watched him hesitate outside for a good half an hour, before he plucked up his courage and stepped over the threshold." She sighed, shaking her head. "What is it about men, do you suppose, that makes them so dreadfully stupid when it comes to shopping? I do not think I have met one who has mastered the art. Do not ask them to choose between two or three items. One might as well tie them in a blindfold and spin them about, as expect any reasonable consideration of the choices. No, no, a man is better off being told what he likes and having it presented to him. Goodness knows what he would end up with if he was left free to roam the streets without a woman's guidance. This is especially true, I find, in the matter of bonnets."

Lady Clara's expression had changed slowly from puzzlement to astonishment to amusement, while Mrs. Oliver, having attempted to keep pace with this speech, finally gave up and waved her fingers in surrender.

"She cannot hear, you know, madam. Lady Clara has been deaf from birth. Nor can she speak."

"Well, that had occurred to me. I am not completely without powers of reasoning. But I'm afraid I talk rather out of habit and I usually have much to get off my chest. I must speak on the gentleman's behalf. He seemed so very lovelorn and despairing—"

The young lady made a quick series of signs to her guardian, who then translated. "She says she understood. Your face speaks eloquently for you, madam."

"Excellent! Then will she at least try the bonnet on?" Melinda took the little oval portrait out of her reticule and squeezed it into Lady Clara's hand, fearing it might be snatched away. "He left this behind when he departed in a hurry."

Clara looked at the portrait and then smiled slowly. Her eyes lightened, as if with relief. She signaled to the other lady who, once again, spoke for her.

"Lady Clara wants to know whether you found this gentleman... handsome, Miss Goodheart."

"Oh very," Melinda lied brazenly. "I thought him the most handsome fellow I'd ever laid eyes on."

"And... did you like him?"

"Very much or I would not be here. You are

lucky to have such an admirer." She would have lowered her voice to a whisper then, but she needed the other lady to hear and sign for her. It was rather awkward, but she had come here to do a good deed and leaving a mission only half complete was not in her nature. "Even if he is not rich— and he told me himself that he is not— there is so much more to life than money. Love should never be thwarted by mercenary intentions. Money is made every day and lost just as frequently, but true love, once found, is forever." She looked at the lady in grey. "Please tell her what I said, madam, for the sake of love."

Mrs. Oliver complied, looking faintly amused herself now, and Lady Clara's smile broadened further. She gestured in reply.

"Her ladyship wants to thank you for the bonnet. She will accept it after all. She knows the gentleman to whom she gave the portrait. He is not a stranger, so it is quite proper."

"Oh, I am glad! I wanted to make amends. He seemed so very sad, and it was my fault that he left in humiliated haste."

"After you landed on him?" muttered Mrs. Oliver wryly. "Must have stopped his heart."

"Yes, I did flatten him rather. Naturally I felt very badly about it. That's why I brought the bonnet myself. But after I got here I feared I might have overstepped."

She stopped, for the young lady was making quick hand signs again for her guardian.

"You did not overstep, madam," Mrs. Oliver passed along to Melinda. "Lady Clara was, in fact, hoping to hear from the gentleman, as it has been sometime since she last saw him. She has been concerned about his welfare."

"Oh?"

"Lady Clara worries about his health as he works so hard and plays so little. She waits patiently for a visit, but he can so rarely get away."

"I am only sorry he could not bring the bonnet to you himself. I know he wanted to."

"She says it is a pity, indeed. But her heart is warmed by the gift and her mood is improved to know that he thinks of her still. As she so often thinks of him with great fondness, waiting here for his return."

"Well done, Lady Clara! Your loyalty is admirable. If you love him, stand up to your family. Surely they care about your happiness most, when all is said and done." Melinda felt this most strongly, because she hoped her own father would be understanding when she went against his wishes.

This was, once again, repeated by hand signals to the young lady, who answered with a high, timid laugh. She gripped Melinda's fingers tightly and nodded. A curious look came into her eyes. And then she signed again.

"Will you stay to tea, Miss Goodheart?" said her faithful translator.

"Thank you, but sadly I cannot, as I am on my way into the country and must catch the stagecoach." The idea of remaining longer in that peaceful, pretty cottage was tempting, for she had a hard journey ahead of her and few delights at the end of it, but her difficulties must be faced.

"Where do you travel to?" the young lady wanted

to know, her eyes filled with sudden longing.

So she explained that she was going home to the village of Kingsthorpe in Buckinghamshire.

Lady Clara signed passionately, "I do wish I could see more of the world."

Her guardian quickly gestured a reply, which was not translated for Melinda, and the young lady looked down with a sad sigh. But she recovered a moment later to smile again and sign a warm goodbye.

"Please do call in again one day. You have greatly cheered our spirits."

Melinda left the Chiddingfold cottage feeling as if she had made another friend in the world, and that was a satisfying sensation. If she had succeeded in bringing two lovers together, all the better. It was always her dearest hope that her bonnets would spread happiness in some small way. A person had to make a difference in the world, however they could.

* * * *

"Clara," he strode into the parlor, hat in hand, "I have come to tell you that I must go into the country and I do not know for sure when I'll return. I know it is your birthday soon, and I had planned to buy you a—"

He stopped so abruptly that Mrs. Oliver, walking behind and translating with her fingers, stumbled into the back of him.

His sister, with a cat curled up in her lap, was seated by the fire and pouring tea. Beside her on the sofa there was a striped hatbox.

"Bonnet," he added, perplexed.

Mrs. Oliver explained, "A young lady delivered it,

your lordship, not much more than an hour ago."

Heath frowned at the box and then at his sister, so discombobulated that he did not even correct the elder woman's use of "your lordship".

Finally he managed a terse, "What young lady?" Of course he knew already. Who else would be so bold? Clara looked up at him expectantly, more color on her face than usual and a hint of amusement pulling at one side of her mouth.

She signed with her fingers and lifted the box lid to show him.

Mrs. Oliver translated, "Isn't the bonnet pretty... in an unusual way?"

Heath, however, had learned enough of the language to know that his sister had signed the word "woman" not "bonnet". It was impossible to confuse the two gestures. Mrs. Oliver, in her usual fashion, was being cautious and keeping on his good side. Sensible and discreet. Which is why he had liked her enough to hire her in the first place. In truth, he did not like many people at all, so Mrs. Oliver was a rarity.

Clara signed again, repeating her question, which was once again carefully edited by her guardian.

"The *bonnet*," he answered carefully, "is certainly...unusual."

His sister had developed a small, rather disturbing streak of mischief when it came to his non-existent love life, but as long as he pretended not to understand everything she meant he didn't have to answer it, did he?

She wanted to know where he was going in such haste and he told her, via Mrs. Oliver.

"I am on my way to a village called Kingsthorpe in Buckinghamshire." He could not tell her why he was going there, which evidently frustrated her.

He knew she found the confines of that cottage, with only her guardian for companionship, trying sometimes. But it was, as he always reminded her, for her own good, her own safety. And his peace of mind.

Before he left that day, she thanked him again for the bonnet.

"How clever and brave of you, brother, to purchase a bonnet. It must have been no easy task for you," Mrs. Oliver translated.

"I've wrestled for Eton," he murmured darkly.

Chapter Six

Our heroine had known many wretched moments in her one and twenty years, and it would be a challenge of titanic proportion to pick any as the most disagreeable and uncomfortable, but her journey over the following two days certainly ranked among the top three.

At least she was not on the outside of the stagecoach, where tree branches whipped and snagged along the roof, threatening to dislodge luggage and the few unfortunate travelers who, unable to afford the relative comfort of a seat inside, clung to the back of the bulky vehicle like fleas to a dog's wet, swinging tail.

Despite his hapless passengers' pleas for mercy, ranging from polite whimperings of "Gracious" and "For the Love of Saint Pete" to howls of unbound despair, the coachman had no care for the fate of these flung-about souls— those outside or in— as he raced his horses along the bumpy road and under the low cover of trees. In all likelihood he did not hear anything above the creaking and cracking, for with his hat pulled down, his oil-skin collar pulled up, and his one good eye shut against the rain, he steadily, and with great volume, exhaled his own tuneless cacophony of sounds in the rough form of a drunken lover's serenade. Like the rain, his song had not let up since the journey began.

And that felt like a very long time ago.

Melinda had no idea how many hours they'd all been stuck in that tooth-rattling death-carriage. In fact, it could be months or years. It could be that wars had been fought and lost, civilizations tumbled, and a cure found for the common cold since they first set off. It certainly felt that way.

She looked at her fellow sufferers. Surely the fashionably attired gentleman opposite was not so wrinkled and grey-haired when they first set off. Once, he was a merry member of their group and had playfully teased Melinda, the way gentlemen of a certain age always did to young ladies, speculating that she must be running away to join her soldier beau and that her protests to the contrary made it all the more certain.

Allowing her wicked mind and imagination free rein, she had soon made up a story about his life. He was a man with several wives, she decided— five or six who had no idea of each other's existence. A romantic fellow who enjoyed the act of falling in love and did not like it to end, he kept the excitement alive by moving from wife to wife and avoiding ennui. Yes, she had his character drawn within the first five minutes.

At first, even when his foot was stepped upon in the crush and his ear poked by the point of an umbrella, his stock of good humor had not deplenished. Rubbing his hands together and winking at Melinda he had exclaimed, "How cozy we shall all be, crammed in together like pickled cucumbers!"

But now, several hours later, her jolly bigamist was a very wilted cucumber, weariness pulling the corners of his mouth downward, not a single jest left to share, his witty banter exhausted somewhere since the last change of horses. Even the cheerful wink was lost, abandoned between the eighth and ninth knocking adrift of his hat, when a stray porkpie crust — to which nobody would lay claim—accidentally hit him in that merry eye.

Beside him, the miserable, screaming, kicking child, squirming astride the lap of a haggard mother, had surely been nothing more than a rosy-cheeked babe in arms, gurgling sweetly and contentedly when they left the last toll gate behind. Melinda remembered thinking what a darling little angel it was. Before it's beady eyes opened and sleep was forgotten. For anybody.

Yes, they had all aged considerably during this hellish journey.

Suffering a cramp in her knee, Melinda attempted a stretching movement, but since there was no space into which she might extend her leg beyond an inch in any direction, this was as little effective at relieving discomfort as putting a compress on a severed head. The only physical exercise for her confined limbs came about whenever they arrived at a steep incline and all the passengers were forced out to walk uphill for the sake of the horses.

Until then she was firmly stuck between a large, frequently weeping lady with a basket on her knees and an elderly, deeply sun-browned fellow who, in addition to possessing the boniest elbows Melinda had ever encountered, also held claim to the worst breath. It reeked of onions and rotting beef— an aroma that did not become any more tolerable, no matter how often he burned her ears with another huffed apology for squashing her, or the utterly unqualified, and many times proven erroneous,

70

assurance that they would "soon be there now".

He must be an old sailor, she surmised. Once press-ganged into service, he spent several years at sea until he participated in a mutiny and slaughtered the Captain. No doubt he was still evading justice. With breath like that nobody would ever venture close enough to capture him.

The soggy-eyed lady on her right, Melinda concluded swiftly, had birthed fifteen children, of whom only one survived and he was soon to meet his end on the gallows. That basket on the woman's knee was probably filled with baked goods to be enjoyed by her imprisoned son at his last meal. It was all his reprobate father's fault, obviously. The man was never around to provide a solid example of manhood and thus the boy turned to crime and left his poor mother to sob her eyes swollen on a public stagecoach.

Melinda sighed and shook her head. Men: what were they good for?

St. Paul's Cathedral, hot air balloons and sandwiches. To say nothing of war and the French Pox.

The carriage rattled onward, bruising more parts than it was ladylike to think about.

Adding insult to injury, a spiteful trickle of rain water seeped in from a hole in the badly patched roof. Whenever the overloaded coach tipped violently to the right, that dripping leak increased its flow to a bitterly cold stream that splashed directly onto Melinda. She could have no warning, no way to prepare or save herself, because that mischievous sprinkle landed somewhere different each time, depending on the severity and duration of the tilt. Only one thing could be counted upon— that it sought out her person, and hers alone.

Suddenly the carriage lifted and dropped violently, something cracking loudly beneath her feet.

This was it. The end must have come.

All forward motion ceased abruptly— apart from that of bodies shot about in one last frenzy.

There followed a scream, a shout, and the carriage door was ripped open.

"Ladies and gentlemen, I beg patience for the interruption, but with your kindly cooperation this shall not take long." A wide-shouldered figure stood there, filling the frame of the open door. "Hand over your valuables and make haste with it, if you please."

For a moment nobody spoke or moved. It seemed as if they were all too stunned.

"Ladies first," he bellowed heartily, waving the muzzle of a pistol into the coach interior. "One at a time will do. Out you come!"

Although the child opposite had finally stopped its noise, the mother now began, wailing that they were all about to be shot dead where they sat, and that she had foreseen such an occurrence in her tea leaves not two days before. Meanwhile, Melinda's neighbor with the wide basket and the equally capacious backside, forgot her own sniffles and boldly declared that the robber would have to come and take her purse with his own hands if he wanted it, as she would not pass it over and she absolutely refused to step out into the rain in her new bonnet.

She must have purchased that spectacular feathered bonnet to wear at her son's hanging, thought Melinda. It would certainly make her stand out in the crowd.

While the other female passengers refused to leave the carriage, our heroine saw that shaft of rain-dappled daylight as a beam sent down from heaven. Fresh air and space in which to stretch out her tortured limbs! Before anybody else could make a move, she scrambled up from her tight seat, so desperate to get outside that she might have trampled violently upon the face of any other passenger who tried to reach the opening first.

She did not anticipate much assistance from the robber, for he surely had other things on his mind than helping her down, but to Melinda's surprise he gripped her right hand in his left and steadied her as she took the leap.

"I'm afraid I haven't any valuables," she declared, breathless. "But you're quite welcome to search me, sir."

Looking up into his masked face, she found a pair of deep blue eyes watching her with warm curiosity. His gloved fingers still held hers. "I'm sure you possess something of worth to me, madam."

The light rain that fell around them now seemed much less bothersome than it had been when spitting on her through the carriage roof. Sifted by the canopy of gold-edged leaves that shivered and danced over their heads, it was gentle, not much more than a damp, refreshing haze. Beads of water dripped to the brim of her bonnet and then her nose as she tipped her head back to look up at him. "I really haven't anything you'd want. If you knew me, sir, you'd know it to be true."

73

"Ah, but you are wrong, madam, for there is something I can steal from you." He tugged the scarlet kerchief from his mouth to reveal a strong, square jaw, marked with a slight cleft, and slender, beautifully carved lips already curved in the brazen smirk of a confidant scoundrel.

"Oh?" She caught her breath as he leaned over her and that smile widened.

"A kiss, my sweet maid."

But as he lowered his lips to hers, Melinda struck him firmly in the filberts with her knee and, at the same time, relieved the wheezing, sputtering fellow of his pistol.

"Stand aside, villain," she exclaimed. "For pity's sake, what are men good for? You are all so wretchedly predictable." Then she turned her pistol to aim at the coachman who had finally ceased his drunken song. "Get down from there at once, you blackguard. I am commandeering this vehicle with no further ado."

A cheer rose up from within the carriage and she felt the hot flush of pride as she fired that pistol into the air with a flourish.

"Well, I think *that* one shook a tooth loose!" a fellow passenger abruptly complained. "What do they spend the toll money on, I wonder? For sure it cannot be the mending of the turnpike road itself."

Melinda opened her eyes to find that she was still confined inside the stagecoach. Even now that the wheels had rumbled to a halt temporarily, her bones ached from every hard bounce already suffered, and there was no highwayman demanding a kiss, no pistol in her possession, no respite from the discomfort of this journey.

The gentleman beside her appealed for help in finding his missing wooden tooth and everybody set to the task of reluctantly looking for this treasure, but they had a hard mission for the daylight waned rapidly and within the carriage it barely kept a foothold.

When the door opened, there was no handsome, lusty highwayman standing in the damp, fading light, but an ordinary, unremarkable fellow in a dusty coat who slicked his wet hair back, tucked a hat down over his brow and then, much to the other passengers' horror, stepped up to squeeze himself onto the seat beside the wilted gentleman cucumber.

Melinda could barely make out the peevish syllables of a half apology that spat forth reluctantly from the new arrival's lips, but she gathered that something had happened to his hired vehicle, which required him to join the stagecoach for the remainder of his journey. He was, evidently, no happier about this occurrence than they were. Barely had the door closed than they were off again in their swaying torture chamber. There was no time for introductions— not that anybody was in the mood for one.

The drenched and dour newcomer sat with his arms crossly folded, legs uncomfortably bent, and head bowed. The brim of his hat kept most of his face hidden in shadow. On his lap he held a small pile of tattered books, tied together with a leather strap. Apparently they were too precious to be left with his luggage on the outside.

She ought to be able to make up a story about him, Melinda thought. Something to provide new entertainment.

Suddenly he raised a hand to tip his hat back and although the coach interior had darkened considerably in the last half hour, she could see his eyes, peering directly at her with a quietly fuming gaze. A gleam of surprise temporarily smoothed out the line between his brows and then he looked away, turning his head to stare through the small, rain-spattered window. Rain water glistened as it dripped from his hair and trickled beneath the collar of his coat, which must make him very uncomfortable.

He had seemed about to say something, but then changed his mind. Snakes of grey shadow slithered across his profile and hid it again, as the carriage wheels rolled forward.

Did she know him? No, surely not. He was perfectly uninteresting. She found her lively imagination stymied. What use was he to her, if she could not even bring herself to make up a salacious story about his past?

Glum, she sank wearily between the toothless, murdering mutineer and gallows-mother.

There would be no handsome highwayman with a chiseled jaw in her future. If there were, he would not want to kiss *her*. Melinda was the sort of girl that young men occasionally found useful and amusing company, but the moment a prettier face passed by they forgot her completely. And there were many prettier faces.

Melinda had nothing to offer but a strong (and improper for a female) handshake, an excellent shot, a fearless nerve for adventure, and a colorful imagination— although that last probably counted against her. As a certain, mean-tempered, vengeful old headmistress had often remarked, "That fictional world you create in your devious, wicked mind, Miss Goodheart, bears no resemblance whatsoever to your shabby truth and, if you don't put an end to these fancies, they will send you to swing from a gibbet one day. Or worse."

At the time she was not entirely certain what could be "worse", but as her friend Georgiana had said, it probably had something to do with men. It usually did.

Now she was on her way home again for the first time in two years— the last visit having taken place just after she finished at the Particular Establishment for the Advantage of Respectable Ladies and shortly before Lady Bramley invited her back to London for further tutelage under her wing. Melinda had been intensely grateful for that opportunity and could not get back to London quickly enough, gleefully embracing the reprieve from her father's expectations.

For her, therefore, this journey home again was not unlike the progress of a tumbrel taking the condemned to Mademoiselle Guillotine.

"Soon be there," the elderly mutineer on her left lied yet again— this time with a lisp, since nobody had found his missing tooth.

Rain rattled across the carriage roof, another cold leak hit her in the face, and that naughty child's foot thumped her squarely on the shin.

The newest passenger had just checked his fob watch, and then he shot Melinda another glare— sideways, this time. His lips closed a little tighter. As the coach tilted to the right, allowing a fresh whisper of light through the small window, she caught the glimmer of an almost imperceptible anger, a flame he did his best to snuff.

"Do I know you, sir?" she asked. It wasn't proper to address him, since there had been no introduction, but Melinda decided the uncomfortable proximity made etiquette a moot point. After all, she knew all about the state of her neighbor's gumboils and his arthritis, so a civil inquiry across the carriage did not seem beyond the bounds of acceptability in the circumstances.

He blinked before his face vanished again into the folds of shadow. "Highly improbable, madam." And from his tone it was not only improbable, but the most ludicrous suggestion anybody had ever uttered in his lofty presence.

But even his voice seemed to jolt her memory.

Soon after that, clutching his treasured books, he twisted his full body away to stare out of his window again, thereby removing any possibility of her attempting further conversation.

Melinda looked around the stout lady on her right and peered out through the other window. She thought back to her first journey in the opposite direction six years ago, when her brother Lindley had escorted her to Mrs. Lightbody's academy, dumping her on the doorstep like a sack of dirty laundry, with a note from her father pinned to the inside of her coat. Lindley, no doubt, had a card game in want of his presence that day and could not spare a moment longer to see his little sister safely settled in.

Not that it mattered. Melinda was never a timid girl and probably could have managed the journey to

London entirely on her own, even at fifteen. She had never been a child who relied upon others to protect her. But her father had insisted Lindley travel with her to London— yes, Lindley, who would likely hand her over to the first villain who came along if the fee was enticing enough.

How innocent her life was in those days, she mused. How excited she had been to travel the stagecoach to London back then. Leaving from the crossroads in the middle of the night had added to her delight, of course, for the one stagecoach that passed Kingsthorpe for London only approached the sleepy village in the depths of the evening, sometimes did not stop at all, and was always later than expected. That thin, twisty sliver of road joining the village to the turnpike had only been carved out within the past two decades, and twenty years, in that part of the country, was recent enough to make it still eyed with suspicion as an ambitious, new development that might bring unwanted strangers to the area. Not to mention the encouragement of local folk to try their luck in the sin-ridden streets of London.

But Melinda, at fifteen, was not afraid to travel. Back then, during that first journey, embarked upon in the dark of night, Melinda's world was a box of adventure waiting to be pried open by her clumsy hands. She did not know how quickly the time would run out, letting the lid of that box fall shut again to trap her fingers.

She often missed the laughter and the pranks of her school days with Georgiana and Emma. She even missed the outraged, gin-slurred rants of Mrs. Lightbody.

"Of all my pupils you three are the very worst. A bad lot. Destined to go down in infamy. Mark my words, the three of you will come to no good. You are this academy's biggest failures. By far the most unlikely to make good matches."

However, when in the company of her friends — her fellow "Ladies Most Unlikely"— the most important thing had always been that they did *not* fit in with the other girls, for that was their bond from the beginning. Together they fancied themselves buccaneers, destined for a life of daring exploits, unstoppable, heroic and defiant in the face of society's rules.

But those years of lawless piracy— enjoyable as they had been— were not the experience for which her father had paid thirty guineas a year. Or rather, *promised to pay*, since, according to Mrs. Lightbody, he had rarely settled a bill.

When Melinda last went home, two years ago, Sir Ludlow Goodheart had expected to see his only daughter transformed into an elegant, accomplished young lady. An *engaged* lady. But she had let him down on all counts. Lady Bramley's invitation, therefore, had been gratefully received by them both and after she had returned to London, Sir Ludlow wrote to his daughter.

"We'll take no less than seven or eight thousand a year. Don't you give him so much as a hand to kiss if he's a second son— unless the elder boy's on his deathbed, or got a limp wick. A few bad habits you can put up with. Fortunately, you're not squeamish like some girls, even if you aren't the prettiest. A fellow in his last years with no conversation and a face that makes dogs bark will suit our needs well enough. That's the sort what's too thick and slow to get the first choice

and, if he's over forty, he'll be desperate for an heir before he meets his maker."

Melinda was supposed to find this prize of a suitor with Lady Bramley's help, her own limited charms and the sum of five hundred pounds— left to her by her mother, who once took great care in making her father promise that the money would be used solely for their daughter's dowry and nothing else. In her mother's day five hundred pounds had been worth more, of course, than it was today. To Melinda it was more symbolic and sentimental than anything else— a reminder of her mother's love and concern.

Apart from the money, the only other item at her disposal was a set of jewelry, including a string of pearls left to her by Grandmother Ethelreda Goodheart. Her father liked to claim that those pearls and the jewelry that came with them once belonged to Anne Boleyn, but then he liked to claim a lot of things when he'd enjoyed a jug of his homemade wine in the evening. In any case, the value of this necklace "heirloom" was severely reduced after Lindley pried a large stone from the clasp and never replaced it.

Despite all this, Sir Ludlow Goodheart remained an optimist.

"I've seen some unsightly clodhoppers catch themselves a rich husband, my girl," he had written to her, *"so there's no reason why you cannot."*

But Melinda knew she had as much chance of success in this endeavor as she had of prying pleasant conversation out of that grumpy gentleman with the tight lips and the dusty coat. Desperate for entertainment, she mischievously began to wonder what might happen if the inhabitants of this carriage were the last people left on earth. Which of the men present would she choose for a mate?

Dusty coat was the youngest man in the carriage and probably the most healthy. Pity his face was not much to look at— indeed, he did his best to vanish into the worn shadows and now that his eyes were closed, feigning sleep, his features were even less distinguishable from the gloom. His fob watch was gold, his boots good leather and well soled, but in need of a polish. He clearly had enough coin at hand to pay the extra ten shillings for an inside seat, but there was nothing else that suggested wealth. He was probably a tradesman of some kind, moderately well-off, but new money. Her father would not approve a lack of lineage — "We Goodhearts are one of the oldest families in this 'ere country and don't you forget it!"— but in Melinda's eyes a small degree of happiness and equality in marriage were more important commodities, and even rarer, than a spare aristocrat with a convenient fortune.

Dusty Coat might never be in love with her, she reasoned— probably best if he wasn't, for there was something about soppy, romantically inclined men and poetry that made Melinda want to shut herself in a dark cupboard with a rhubarb pie and never come out again— but at least a practical marriage would save her from her father's disappointment. And she could keep the fellow's boots polished for him. She might even work toward putting a more cheerful expression on his dour face.

Oh dear, it would be a marriage made in despair and destined for disappointment, but there was no other possibility and she must make the best of it or else die an old maid. Most matches were made on far less logic.

The other male passengers were completely out of the question. Even if her father thought she should overlook a man's advanced years and infirmity, Melinda knew she could not tolerate an aged flirt in a frilly cravat, or a fellow with wooden teeth. Not even if he had twenty thousand pounds secreted under his mattress, and a deliciously bloodthirsty past.

No, her only reasonable choice of the three was Mr. Highly Improbable. Quite typical of her luck. Mr. Highly Improbable for a Lady Most Unlikely.

His behavior suggested he would be most comfortable in a dimly lit library, surrounded by ancient tomes and the cobweb-laced busts of dead playwrights. Yes, she could imagine him stooped over a cluttered desk, reading one of those books with a magnifying glass to his eye, snapping at anybody who destroyed the tomblike quiet.

Now, he kept his eyes closed, hiding from her. Melinda supposed it was survival instinct— his version of a dark cupboard and rhubarb pie.

Poor fellow, if he knew what she planned for their future he would probably expire on the spot.

Suddenly she laughed, as was her tendency in the most bleak moments. Something to do with the release of anxiety in the body, she supposed. A chord stretched until it snapped.

The other passengers all looked at her and, finding her laughter infectious, some smiled. Not their newest comrade, however. He resolutely kept his eyes shut and his lips fastened in that unrelenting line.

Must be the sort of person who held onto his chords no matter how much stress they were under.

Chapter Seven

Rather than wait for the official stop in the village of Kingsthorpe, Melinda alighted at the crossroads, taking her chance when the coachman made an impromptu stop to relieve himself behind the hedgerows.

Curiously enough, clearly not being a local man, Highly Improbable chose to disembark at the same time as Melinda. But despite the relief he must have felt from unraveling his body again and breathing a lung full of that fresh country air, his mood did not improve. Even the weather had stopped sulking, for the rain ceased and the sun, suddenly over-compensating for its earlier absence and just in time to set, spread frothy layers of petticoat in a belated, but brilliant display across the sky. Yet her traveling companion remained unimpressed, as if a persistent raincloud hung over him, unseen and unfelt by anybody else.

As they waited for their luggage to be untied from the top of the battered, groaning vehicle, Melinda made another attempt at friendly conversation, remarking upon her own joy at finally setting feet upon the ground again.

"I began to lose hope of ever reaching the end of my journey," she confessed genially. "I feel as if I've been tossed up into the air like a handful of spillikins."

Even though his eyes were hidden in the shadow beneath his hat brim, which he had once again tugged forward and down over his brow, she sensed him slyly looking her up and down.

"However," she added with a breezy sigh, "I've been told that terrible experiences, such as these, all serve to shape our character. In which case, my character is worn away to a rather sorry nub and considerably bruised by now."

Still nothing.

He clutched that pile of books as if he feared she might try to snatch them away.

"You must be very fond of reading, sir." When he scowled at her, she pointed. "All those books."

Ignoring this, apparently tired of waiting for their inept coachman to reappear from behind the hedge and untie their belongings, Mr. Improbable suddenly set down his books, leapt up the side of the coach, scaled it with the agility of a spider, and tugged their luggage free.

Melinda forgot what she had been about to say next. Her unsuspecting future husband cut an astonishingly well-hewn figure of strength and vitality against the brilliant, gilded cloth of sunset.

Her trunk was lowered to the grassy verge first, followed by his box, which was much smaller and tidier.

Melinda thought she heard him snap a terse complaint to the coachman about his reckless driving, and then he jumped down in the nick of time before the horses were off again, the carriage wheels churning in the soft ground and flicking wet mud up the front of his breeches. He took a hasty step back, saving the toes of his boots from being flattened, but the soft mud did its damage. Some of it even got onto his unshaven chin and the bridge of his nose.

It didn't seem fair to laugh— not when he'd kindly retrieved her trunk for her. Instead she felt the necessity of making a comment to clear the tension. "I always say, sir, that when it seems as if nothing more can possibly go wrong, one should take heart in humor. The day will come when one can look back and chuckle heartily at an event which, today, feels so wretched. I find a positive prospect and a little imagination tremendously helpful."

He was breathing heavily, seething with stifled anger, as if he might, any moment, explode into little pieces.

"One simply has to laugh sometimes," she added.

Exhaling a steamy huff of disdain, brushing furiously at the front of his coat with a gloved hand, he muttered, "Only if one has a disorder of the nervous system."

That remark dropped between them like a spiked portcullis, he stormed off, carrying those old books over his shoulder and dragging that small trunk behind him. Well, there went her chance of a last-minute, convenient husband— and his chance of getting his shirts washed weekly and boots polished daily without charge.

Still, if his miserable face drooped any further he could polish those boots with his own lips.

Melinda watched him go, wondering if he knew how far he was from the village. Well, let him find out for himself, complete with his muddy chin, since he had rebuffed her attempts at convivial conversation. He could take his broad shoulders with him too, because they were not so impressive after all.

That was the last time she'd choose *him* for a

husband!

A few moments later, Davy Rimple came by with his cart, as Melinda knew he would on market day, and she was able to acquire a seat beside him for the final two miles to her father's house. The cheerful company was very welcome, and it bolstered her spirits to see *somebody* pleased to have her home again. She knew the reception from her father would be very different.

* * * *

The front door was ajar— a fortunate circumstance since the bell rope came away in her hand after one tug. No servants emerged to help Melinda with her trunk as she dragged it over the threshold, but two goats, a pig, and several chickens did greet her arrival. Briefly interrupting their untended ramble around the rush-strewn floor of the hall, they had soon assuaged their curiosity about her, discovered she had no treats to offer, and trotted off again.

Although it was still daylight outside, the interior of the old manor house was dark, the thick, stone, fourteenth-century walls containing few windows— those that existed being small, almost an afterthought, and heavily-leaded. A thin, misty haze floated in, here and there, just enough to keep one's knees from cracking on furniture, but the greater glow of light shone at far end of the hall, where the wide-open mouth of a fireplace belched out all the heat in this part of the house. This is where her father sat, slumped in a high-backed wheelchair, one foot bandaged and resting up on the fender, a clay jug by his side.

"Who's that?" he demanded. "Who comes? Friend or foe?"

"It is only me, father. Friend. Mostly."

"*Who*? Speak up!"

"It is me, father. Melinda." She sighed. "Your daughter."

He muttered a low curse. "You? Back again, eh? Well, girl, I can't get a look at you all the way down there. Come closer!"

As she passed the long trestle table, Melinda caught a glimpse of rotting fruit, crusted with flies and maggots. Next to that, a small brown mouse currently enjoyed a half loaf of moldy bread. The little creature evidently felt quite at home there, for it turned to look at her, twitched its nose once, and then resumed its repast with no further ado.

"Where is Hattie?" she asked, drawing closer to the fire and her father's chair.

He sniffed, screwing up his face and hunching his shoulders. "That ol' trout upped and left, didn't she? *Good riddance* as I said to her when she marched out. Can do well enough without her interference. I reckon she were out to poison me anyway."

Melinda's heart sank. The one merry face she could always count on was Hattie Rimple, her father's cook and housekeeper for more than twenty years. Over time Sir Ludlow had managed to insult and outrage every single one of his servants until they left, but Hattie somehow remained impervious to his temper tantrums and, as a consequence, had become the one reliable soul in young Melinda's life. She thought fondly of the many hours spent with Hattie in the kitchen, of how that good woman had served as a substitute mother in many ways, advising and guiding when it came to certain matters of which her father neither knew nor cared. Whatever would she have done without Hattie for the first fifteen years of her life? It did not bear thinking about.

"I see you gained a few more inches then in all directions," Sir Ludlow barked. "I trust they taught you better manners while you were eating all that food. 'Ow to act ladylike, and whatnot."

She untied her bonnet and took off her gloves. "What happened to your foot, father?"

"Bloody gout. Hurts like a bugger."

The bandage, she noted, was slightly singed about the heel, suggesting he had fallen asleep too close to the fire on occasion.

"By the deuce, my girl, you look crumpled as an ol' dish rag. Anyone would think you walked here."

"I might as well have, father. The stagecoach was crowded and driven by a madman." Parts of her felt as if they still bounced and rattled along that endless road. "But at least I'm here now."

"*Stagecoach?*" her father bellowed. "You were meant to come in a private carriage. Lindley wrote that he would send you home in his new friend's barouche. It were all planned, girl. Why the devil did you take the stagecoach?"

She stared blankly, her head aching. "I'm sorry, father, Lindley sent no word to me about any friend's barouche." Melinda hadn't heard from her brother in a few weeks, and the last time he visited the shop it was merely to order a hat for one of his paramours— on credit— and see if she had any spare coin he could "borrow".

"But it were all planned," Sir Ludlow repeated, thumping his bandaged foot against the fender and cursing wildly. "Now you've gone and made a pig's ear of it all, as usual."

Of course it was *her* fault, despite the fact that Lindley very seldom lived up to his wild promises and she had known nothing about this one.

"At least my son knows how to make advantageous connections," her father grumbled. "When Lindley goes to London, he gets himself rich friends. When you go, you come back looking like something the cat dragged in."

"Yes, Lindley makes a lot of friends. If only he could keep them longer."

"And you return with no bloody 'usband, I see."

"Indeed, father. No husband, bloody or otherwise. There seems to be a shortage."

"Shortage, my arse! You need to look about you and keep an eye for a chance. I heard that friend o' yourn— the newspaper man's daughter— caught 'erself a knight o' the realm. Why couldn't you take a leaf from 'er book? She didn't waste any time."

"Yes, my friend Georgiana Hathaway married Commander Sir Henry Thrasher. She is very fortunate and very much in love."

"*In love?*" He snorted. "Who cares about that nonsense? No, I daresay it's the money she were after and why not? Fellow's been a recluse for years and stocked up a good fortune from his days in the navy, I shouldn't wonder. Love don't come into it if you're a bright girl and not a gormless ninny." He changed his voice to a petulant squeaky croak, evidently meant to mimic his daughter. "*Love*, she says. *She's in lorrrrve.* Saints preserve us! Is that twaddle what they filled yer daft 'ead with for the past half a dozen years? I were expectin' you to come 'ome again with some sense at least. I 'ope you ain't bein' too particular when it comes to suitors."

"Goodness gracious, no. How can a girl like me afford to be particular?"

Busy petting his dogs, he briefly squinted up at her. "Aye. Well don't stand there like a spare chapel hat peg, girl. Go and find us some supper. I'm right hungry, and you may as well make yourself useful in some capacity, now that you've returned."

A sudden spark of mischief, revived in spite of her exhaustive journey and gloomy welcome, tempted Melinda to confess that she'd rejected three proposals on her unescorted journey home. But none of them were for marriage.

And one of them was from a deliciously wicked highwayman who lived only in her head.

* * * *

Before they ate, Melinda steered the animals outside, cleared the rotting food away and washed the table down with soap and water from the pump in the yard. There was much more cleaning to be done, but she was far too tired and hungry to manage anything else just then. The needs of her stomach came first.

Fortunately, it could not have been too long since Hattie Rimple left the house, for a large veal and ham pie — not yet turned moldy or nibbled upon by mice—still sat on a shelf in the larder, beside a cheese wrapped in cloth. Having discovered these treasures, Melinda quickly carried them out to the great hall, along with a tall jug of ale. She would have pushed her father's chair up to the table for him, but he insisted on wheeling himself, bandaged foot stuck out before him. He kept a pair of crutches across his lap, for "emergencies", but Melinda sensed he enjoyed having wheels with which to run over people's feet. And crutches took far more effort.

"This is the best you can do, is it?" he grumbled, surveying the food with funereal gloom.

"I fear so for tonight, father. The hens will lay tomorrow, and in the daylight I shall dig about in the garden to see what else I can find." She would also seek out Hattie and try to persuade her back again, but she decided against mentioning that to her father. Sir Ludlow was always best advised of a plan after it was already in motion, once he knew there was no chance that he would actually be asked to contribute anything to the scheme.

Whatever he had said to offend Hattie, Melinda would have to make amends for it and coax the lady back again. In all likelihood the cook had gone to stay with her brother, who owned a smithy and an inn just a mile west down a foot-worn path— a walkway somewhat grandly referred to locally as "The Lane", suggesting it was the only one in existence.

"Damnable woman never could cook. I kept her on out o' charity and a promise made to your mother. But the ol' trout were never grateful." Sir Ludlow gingerly poked a knife at his slice of pie. "I can taste 'er bitter resentment in every bite. Pastry turns to sawdust in my mouth. I shouldn't be surprised if it's poisoned. Aye, she'd like to see me in my grave, no doubt. Dratted women! But no sooner do I get rid o' one than another comes back again. A daughter who can't even do the one damned thing she's made for."

Melinda poured herself a tankard of ale and drained it with unladylike haste.

"I don't know why you couldn't manage to find one daft feller to take you off my hands," her father grumbled. "All that money wasted. Thirty guineas a year, plus new gowns and stockings every Christmas. Now 'ere you are, back on my doorstep, a great, galumphing beast, eating my food and supping my ale." He sighed so gustily, the candles were almost extinguished. "I always knew it were a mistake to 'ave a daughter. Sons are what a man needs. Daughters are nothin' but a bloody expense, especially when they can't be traded in."

"At least you have Lindley, father, " she replied drily. "All is not lost."

"Aye, thankfully! Lindley's a good boy. Cares for 'is father and does as he's told."

But clearly he didn't care enough to visit and see the state of their father's house. Even if he did, it was highly unlikely that Lindley would do anything to help. Money drained through his fingers as easily as it did through their father's, but while Sir Ludlow was stuck in one place and could not escape the crumbling walls of Kingsthorpe Park— the material evidence of his downfall— Lindley was free to move about the country, unfettered by responsibility.

Her brother had abandoned university during his second year at Oxford, preferring instead some grand business scheme he planned to start with an acquaintance. But that had gone the way of all his projects and now he simply trundled through life seeking entertainment in one form or another, incurring debts in one place and then starting elsewhere in another. When he made the effort, his charm and good looks— Melinda had heard them described as such, although she did not see it herself— were enough to make other folk believe anything he told them. For a while at least.

Considering her father's supposed abhorrence for Hattie Rimple's cooking, he shoveled food into his mouth now with great vigor. "My son shall make me proud one day."

"Keep saying so, father, and perhaps it will come true." She knew that feeling herself.

"He doesn't stand about waiting for things to 'appen. He goes out and gets what he wants, does our Lindley."

Although she knew it was futile, Melinda could not resist another comment. "I wonder why he has not married yet either, father. After all, he is six years my senior. Do you not feel the same urgency for Lindley to marry?"

"Plenty o' time for that," he snapped in reply, hunched over his food. "Every young man needs to time to make his mark in the world, before he looks to keeping a wife. Lindley has many irons in the fire." As he spoke, crumbs flew from his mouth, keeping the dogs poised in a state of anticipation by his side. "He's a busy fellow and does not need the burden of a wife until he's thirty."

Melinda rolled her eyes and set down her knife, her appetite waning as a knot formed in her stomach.

"Speaking of making one's mark, father... in London I have begun to make one of my own."

He stuffed more pie into his mouth and stared at the fire.

"If it is successful," she added, "I should be able to manage without requiring a husband. Then you will no longer be troubled by my dearth of future prospects."

He choked into his tankard and eyed her as if she'd just announced an intention to join the navy. "You *what*?"

"Lady Bramley thinks—"

"*Who*?" he growled.

"Lady Bramley. If you recall, father, she took me under her wing when my four years at school were complete. I have been staying at her house in Mayfair."

He stared blankly. If she were not already accustomed to her father's disinterest in anything other than the one path he had chosen for her, she might have been disheartened to see that he'd quite forgotten where she was living in London or with whom.

"Lady Bramley has much advice to give. On many different subjects."

She paused, expecting more questions, but her father set down his tankard, tossed a scrap of meat to his dogs and continued his supper.

Bravely she went on, "She leased a little millinery shop. A boutique, as the French call it. And I've been...managing the place for her these past eight months. The idea is that I should, eventually, take the business over completely."

"You've been *what?*"

Melinda licked her lips. "I am told I have some talent for decorating bonnets... in a different way. Indeed, it may be my only talent." She smiled, thinking suddenly of the gentleman who once planted the idea of *Desperate Bonnets* into her mind after he saved her in mid-air. "But as Lady Bramley says, genteel women in my circumstances, unwed and with no other prospects for income, have been known to own and manage small shops. She says there is no shame in making an honest living. Better that than to let pride get in the way and end one's life in sadness and debt. She says women ought to learn to stand on their own, because good men are in rare supply and what *is* freely available can be distinctly lacking in either ornament or usefulness."

He coughed and wheezed, eyes popping.

"If I could ask you, father," she forged ahead quickly, taking advantage of his inability to speak, "for my five hundred pounds. The money mama left me. And the pearls that—"

He brought his fist down upon the table, shaking the candles and making the dogs ears, which had previously been flat to their heads in begging mode, stand upright. "I know what's to be done with you, better than that old Lady Baggage with all her advice. A willow switch to your behind is what's required! You're not too old for it, missy."

"Father, I had hoped, by now, that you would see the futility—"

"What I *shall* see, is you traipsin' up the aisle on those clumsy feet o' yourn to be wed. And that's an end to it. That's why I brought you home. I could see you weren't getting the job done yerself. We'll find somebody. Anybody." He pushed his tankard across the table. "Fill it."

Melinda blew out a frustrated sigh and then lifted the ale jug to pour again. His reaction was no more and no less than expected, but she was so tired after her journey that the cruel cudgel of his disdain did not bounce off as it usually would.

Now she had lost her appetite completely and probably ought to retire. Who knew what state she would find her old room in, or what wildlife she would have to chase out before she could lay her head down?

But a sudden clamor at the door, followed by loud laughter, curses, and demands for help, announced a new arrival. A moment later her father forgot their conversation— for the time being, at least.

"Lindley, my boy, is that you come at last?"

"Indeed, it is I, father!" Her brother stumbled into the light, snatching off his hat and complaining, "Where the devil are all the servants? Surely I'm not expected to manage my own trunk!"

Just when she thought the day's event could not be any more dire. Even Melinda would have trouble laughing at the awfulness of it.

Chapter Eight

"Go to your brother, girl. Make use of yerself. Don't sit there gawpin' and idle."

Melinda set down the ale jug and went to help. As she approached the door, she saw that her brother had a guest in tow— a fashionably attired gentleman, in a tall hat, set slightly askew, and a wide-collared coat of rich burgundy. Although her brother had put both his hands to the purpose of dragging a trunk across the threshold, this well-clad gent offered only one hand for the task. The other hand flourished a walking cane that could not, apparently, be set down. Since both men staggered and tilted like bowling pins— worse for wear on brandy, according to the fumes— Melinda suspected that fancifully decorated cane was needed to keep the other gentleman upright.

As she closed the heavy door to keep out the draft, the stranger bowed to her and swept off his hat.

"Won't you introduce me to this exquisitely beautiful creature, Goodheart? This delightful goddess I see before me?"

She glanced back over her shoulder to be sure there was no one else present to whom he might be referring. The light, of course, was dim at that end of the great hall— she could barely see *his* features either— but once she realized that he did indeed mean this remark for her, she hastened to assure him, "No need to sing for your supper in this house, sir, we will still feed you without it."

The gentleman drew back, hat clutched to his chest, the frothy layers of his silk cravat puffing out like the plumage of a preening cockatoo.

"Or if you must flatter, sir, save your compliments for my father's dogs," she added, "There it will be appreciated and serve you better. Their favor is more valuable than mine."

"This is merely my sister," Lindley mumbled belatedly, wafting a hand in her direction as he stumbled against the wall. "The day-dreaming hat-seller I told you about."

What little she could see of the stranger's features in that wavering light was favorable— and now injured. He clutched the walking cane to his chest and eyed her cautiously.

"I did not mean to be sharp, sir, but I have had a long day and flattery tends to have the same effect upon me as stinging nettles. I react accordingly. Forgive me and welcome to Kingsthorpe Park." Melinda had bad memories of other "friends" her brother had brought home in the past— loud, arrogant schoolboys, who thought they could bully her, and then drunken, lecherous university students who liked nothing better than to torment Lindley's plump and unsophisticated little sister.

This fellow, however, seemed genuinely perturbed that he might have upset her. His face softened and he beamed at her in a warmly apologetic way. "Will Rochfort at your service, Miss Goodheart. My friends call me Rocky, because I am craggy, dry, witless and dull as stone. Also quite as ungainly. Often I put my foot in my mouth and irritate weary young ladies who are far too clever and sensible to be impressed by my gauche ramblings." His grin stretched onward, until he smartly curbed it to assure her with sudden and unconvincing gravity, "But you may call me whatever you wish. I can see already that you are not to be trifled with and will not mask your feelings to save mine, so I daresay you will soon have some name for me that ought never be repeated in polite company."

"No need to make a fuss of her," Lindley drawled. "The effort is quite wasted on Melinda. Like trying to pet a guard dog."

"Why, Goodheart, what a cad you are to your own sweet sister!"

"Melinda is a tomboy, my dear fellow, and proud of it."

"My brother is quite right, sir. I have mastered very few feminine arts, but he knows I am invaluable in a game of cricket and reliable for bagging a brace of game birds, while he cannot take straight or sober aim at a single one." She looked at her brother, who sneered and turned away.

"Ah." The stranger's eyes twinkled. "I had better not get on your bad side then, madam!" He gripped her hand and dragged it to his lips. "I shall henceforth take your warning about stinging nettles into account and not speak another word of admiration for your beauty or the grace of your figure, Miss Goodheart. I shall keep those thoughts to myself."

She looked askance. "I would prefer it, sir, for if you speak them aloud too often somebody here might think you addled and cart you off to Bedlam."

"Lindley, my boy," their father bellowed from the table, "come here by the fire and eat. You must be cold and famished, eh? This ain't much of a feast, as you see, but this is all your sister could manage. We must fend for ourselves as best we can it seems, if we mean not to starve."

"Where the devil is that Rimple woman, father?"

"Ingrate upped and left, my boy. 'Tis just as well your sister's home and can make use of 'erself."

Lindley chuckled dourly. "I suppose, in a pinch, any woman in the house is better than none. Even Melinda." Leaving the luggage where he'd dropped it, he steered his friend off to be introduced to Sir Ludlow. Looking back over his shoulder, he muttered, "Do make certain the best guest room is ready for Rocky, will you? Get a fire lit and warm the bed. Mine too while you're about it. I sent Rocky's man to the kitchen, so he'll need a bite of something too— once you've seen to the horses, of course."

"Mr. Rochfort has no coachman or groom to tend his horses?"

"No, we left Town in haste and he had some disagreement with his driver, so his man, Moone, was required to drive the beasts instead. A skill for which he is ill prepared. Consequently the fellow is not in the best of tempers, but that should improve once you've fed him."

"And where is this man— Moone— to sleep?"

"Oh, a couch by the kitchen fire will do him, I daresay."

She put her hand on her brother's arm, stopping him mid-step. "I much appreciated the carriage ride, brother."

He scowled. "What?"

"Father said that you promised to bring me home in your friend's private barouche."

Eyes half closed in a slothful way, he laughed

languidly. "Ah, yes, we would have brought you, but it simply wasn't convenient. We started off from London two whole days sooner than planned due to some...circumstances that arose. And we couldn't possibly fit another trunk on the carriage."

"Never mind. It is the thought that counts, as they say."

"And you still got here. Besides, I expected old Lady Bramley to provide you with transportation. Are you so hopeless that you cannot even get anything out of that old lady, except for the lease on a tired hat shop? I'll have to give you some lessons on tapping the barrel."

"I did not want to bother Lady Bramley. I came on the stagecoach."

"So it all worked out in the end. You survived on your own."

"Yes. As I always do."

"Well, then there's an end to it." He walked away, calling out, "Good Lord, I have the thirst of a thousand sailors! What is there to drink?"

There had been no word on how long Lindley and his friend expected to stay. In his usual inconsiderate style, her brother had shown up at his own pace, depending upon *his* whim and comfort, and he would, doubtless, leave in the same way.

"Miss Goodheart," their guest called out, standing from his bench suddenly, "I do apologize for putting the lady of the house to all this nuisance."

Nobody had ever called her 'Lady of the House' before. She was accustomed to being the insignificant girl they all talked over and laughed at.

"Do not worry another moment about a bed for

me," he added. "I am quite capable of napping wherever I lay my head and a bale of straw in a quiet corner will do. I feel wretched to disrupt your supper. Do please come here and sit again."

The picture of that fashionable fellow taking to a bale of straw for his rest was highly entertaining.

"I told you not to fuss, Rocky," her brother muttered. "It's only my sister."

"That may be so for you, Lindley, but she is not *my* sister." The gentleman smiled at her again, rather naughtily this time, like a little boy eyeing the plum pudding on the sideboard at Christmas. Firelight fluttered over his face, highlighting all the handsome angles. "A circumstance for which I am grateful, as it leaves me free to think of her as I choose. With the amiable lady's permission, of course." His gaze warmed her face across the distance. "In the clandestine seclusion of my own mind."

Not quite sure how to respond to Mr. Rochfort's odd remark— surely a bold one in her father's presence— Melinda simply assured him that it was no trouble at all to make up another bed.

She dearly hoped their guest didn't turn out to be the prattling, poetry-reciting sort who would make her seek out the comforting darkness of the nearest cupboard, or priest's hole, just to escape his company. After all, she was considerably larger now and it would be far more difficult to hide silently and painlessly in so small a space.

"Don't stand there chattering away," Sir Ludlow yelled. "Go and fetch the good wine from the scullery, girl. This gnat's pee ale won't do for Lindley and his guest. Bring up my good apricot wine and the

104

gooseberry. And that blackberry. Aye, bring 'em all up. Make haste, girl, your brother's fair parched after his long journey!"

And what of her, far worse, less comfortable journey?

It was Mr. Rochfort who bounced up from his bench again, took a candle in its holder, and insisted upon helping her carry the wine. Grateful for the extra hands, she accepted his assistance.

On their way to the scullery they passed through the kitchen, where Mr. Rochfort's "man" smoked a long, clay pipe and warmed the seat of his breeches, with one shoulder propped against the wall. He was a tall, lean fellow, with a deeply-lined forehead, a mottled, fleshy nose, and bristling grey whiskers. As he watched the two of them descend the stone steps to the cool scullery, he must have heard their conversation and his master's voice, yet he remained in that lounging pose, calmly puffing on his pipe, and making no attempt to help.

Mr. Rochfort said nothing to the man, too busy telling Melinda about the acquisition of his walking cane, which was, it turned out, not needed due to any infirmity.

"It is the fashion, Miss Goodheart."

"Yes. I've always thought it looked odd to see young, able-bodied gentlemen carrying a cane. Like teats on a bull, as my father would say." At least hats and bonnets served a purpose, she thought. They kept off rain and sun, hid impossible hair after a fight with the curling papers and, depending upon the style and color chosen, they declared the wearer's purpose without a word being said. "But I suppose once men no longer carried swords they needed something to keep their hands out of trouble."

Barely paying heed to her, the gentleman continued extolling the virtues of his marvelous walking stick.

"It is Malacca wood with a handle of ivory and silver-pique work." He held it up for her inspection. "Carved, as you see, in the shape of a bulldog's head. It is very clever, Miss Goodheart. I know you will be amazed— but see— the jaws of the dog open to hold my gloves, when I am at the opera. I do not know how I ever managed without it."

She muttered wryly, "Indeed, a grave problem solved."

"Hmm?"

"I've never been to the opera," she said hastily.

"I do not care for it myself— all that wailing and warbling— but one must go from time to time, to see and be seen. I keep a box at the theatre. One of the better boxes, of course."

"Yet you take no pleasure in it?"

"Really, Miss Goodheart, I do not know anybody who does. But one must keep up appearances."

"I suppose you might lend your box to those who would like to see the opera, but cannot afford to go."

He laughed loudly. "That would be a jolly good lark, would it not? Fill my box with flower-sellers, fishmongers, and wool-packers one evening and watch the outraged faces of my friends."

"Well, actually, I meant it would be a kindness to those without means of such entertainment, sir."

He blinked, looked confused, the laughter

106

petering out. "Oh, they wouldn't understand the opera. It would be quite beyond them to enjoy it."

"But you just said that you do not enjoy it either."

With a condescending tilt of his head, he explained carefully, "I *could* enjoy it if I cared to. That is the point. It would be entirely wasted on the poor and uneducated."

"Surely everybody can appreciate good music."

"Not if they cannot afford a seat." He cast his gaze over the many wine bottles that she had loaded into a two-handled wicker basket. "Fashion is for the wealthy. It would not be fashion if everybody could afford it."

"But who decides what is fashionable? Who tells you?" She'd always felt as if she was the last to know anything of that sort, although trying to fit in with everybody else had, luckily, never been a desire of hers. Melinda knew what she liked and what she didn't— often she felt very strongly about it— and the idea of waiting to be told what she *should* like seemed illogical. She enjoyed pretty things, but she did not want to look like everybody else. When she created her bonnets, she made each one as original as possible, and her customers appreciated knowing that their purchase was unique, designed for them alone.

"The answer is simple, Miss Goodheart!" He beamed down at her. "If something is expensive and can only be afforded by a few, one knows it is fashionable."

"Oh."

Having seen how she struggled under the weight of the bottles, he said, "Allow me to help."

Grateful, she held out the basket.

Then he took one of the bottles from the top and tucked it under his arm, along with his beloved cane. "I'll carry the candle and light the way, shall I?"

He soon began another subject, but Melinda, straining along behind him with the basket of wine bottles, was still trying to make sense of the last. "Mr. Rochfort, have you ever heard the tale of 'The Emperor's New Clothes'?" she squeezed out breathlessly.

"Is it one of Lord Byron's?"

"Er...no. I think not."

"Oh, my dear Miss Goodheart," he shook his head, "one does not talk of anything these days, except Lord Byron, don't you know?"

"Do you like his work? Which is your favorite?"

"Who has the time to read these days? No, no. One *talks* of reading it. I daresay the fashion will soon be for somebody else, in which case reading it will be an utter waste of time."

It had to be a hoax, she thought. Nobody could be so insufferably vapid. Had her brother brought the fellow along as one of his wicked, practical jokes?

Surely nobody could not be so dim and irritating.

Perhaps he was a desperate criminal on the run from capture, she thought hopefully. Having taken shelter here with Lindley, he pretended to be stupid to avoid suspicion. It was all an act. It must be.

While here he would enslave the heart of a local girl who helped him escape the soldiers, only to witness him shot down on the turnpike road. After which, the devastated girl would never be parted again from the only sad thing she had left of her bold lover— a scarlet silk handkerchief. The one he had worn for a mask.

As usual, Melinda preferred her fantasy to the reality, and amused herself with this one for a while. The escape helped her tolerate his company.

But when it came to helping her carry the bottles, she would have been better off managing by herself. As usual.

After delivering the basket of wine to the great hall, and sweeping up the broken pieces from the bottle Mr. Rochfort managed to drop, she said a weary "good evening" and left her father to this jolly celebration of Lindley's homecoming.

Chapter Nine

The proud announcement of a very loud cockerel, directly below his dormer window, woke Heath Caulfield from a deep sleep— a state he must have finally achieved approximately two hours before. Most of the night he'd been kept awake by his thoughts, an aching head, and the varying noises of the countryside, which seemed always to come when least expected.

Having lived above a London tavern for the past few years, he thought he was accustomed to sleeping through all manner of ruckus, but that was a constant flow of noise and one became used to it. In the country, there were long, uneven stretches of eerie quiet before a barn owl or a fox suddenly made their presence known, and those silent pauses made that cry all the louder, all the more heart-stopping when it came.

But now the day awoke and so must he.

As he opened one eye against the bright glare slanting in through the small window, it took Heath a moment to remember exactly where he was and how he came to be there. Glancing downward, he saw one bare foot sticking out of the blanket, toes warming in the sun. Ah yes, that felt better. Near the bed sat his boots, which were probably still damp from yesterday. Didn't relish the idea of putting them back on today. He stretched his toes and let them enjoy the sun's caress a while longer.

Suddenly a deep male voice, boomed out in song, "*Fill every glass, for wine inspires us, and fires us with courage, love, and joy."*

Now fully and irreversibly awake, Heath stumbled out of bed and went to the window. Directly below, in the farmyard, a drift of young pigs snuffled around in the mud left by yesterday's rain, their curled tails all a-quiver with excitement and ears twitching. Their overseer—a stout gentleman in a leather apron— serenaded the beasts with this song as he leaned upon a gate, tankard in hand and bucket of scraps in the other.

"Women and wine should life employ. Is there ought else on earth desirous! Fill every glass..."

Was this entertainment, he mused, included in the shilling a night fee?

The singer paused only to sip from his tankard and then he chanced to glance upward and spied Heath. "A fine good morn' to thee, sir. Sausages are cookin'."

And burning too, from the smoky odor rising up through the floorboards.

"Get thee down for a bite and I'll pour thee a pint o' my best cider."

Heath nodded and the fellow, having filled his lungs and puffed out his chest, resumed his song.

This country inn was a good distance off the London road, and Heath appeared to be the only guest— in fact, the place functioned more as a home than a business, with only two spare bedchambers under the thatched roof and a very small parlor below, where food and beverages were served by the landlord while his children and an ever-growing number of dogs ran about in merry disarray. There was a blacksmith's forge attached to the building and

111

a farmyard, all of which suggested the function of an inn happened by chance rather than design. Perhaps lost and weary travelers — like him—had stumbled upon the place so often that the family who lived there eventually decided to put up a sign. In any case, last night, after a wretched few days of travel, Heath Caulfield had been relieved to discover the inn and take refuge there. The stew on offer was hearty and well-seasoned and the bed extremely firm and devoid of fleas. What more could he want?

But having so little sleep did not put him in the best of tempers today. Soon after waking, his thoughts returned again— not to the criminal he pursued there— but to the appearance of that redhead yesterday in the stagecoach. He had recognized her at once as the determined young miss who, four years ago, chased a cutpurse through the streets of Mayfair with muffin crumbs on her face. The same woman who had, only a few days ago, brought him to his knees in a hat shop.

The woman who had also, apparently, taken it upon herself to call upon his sister and deliver a bonnet. Clara had thought it all very "sweet" that a stranger should take such trouble to fulfill the task he had been unable to complete. And while smiling coyly, she had signed to him that the "hat lady" had thought him handsome.

"Don't be ridiculous," he had replied, signing crossly and probably not very well, "she didn't even look at me."

But there she was again yesterday, on the stagecoach, and this time she had stared hard at him.

The last thing Heath wanted, while here in

112

pursuit of a villain, was to be known by anybody as an officer of the law, and, if she remembered where she had seen him before, she could expose his purpose there.

Although she had not seemed to recognize Heath yesterday, he couldn't be sure. Her manner of speaking to a stranger was disturbingly informal and suspiciously lively, as he had noted during previous encounters. If he saw her again, he would proceed with great caution. In the meantime, he would merely dismiss her reappearance as a strange jest of fate.

How odd that she would take it upon herself to bring a hat to his sister. Why would she do such a thing?

It had left Clara with a certain disturbing gleam in her eye and himself with an uncomfortable flutter in his chest.

Well, there was little point wondering at the tomfoolery of such a reckless, eccentric, and outspoken young woman as that redhead with the loose stitches. She must not distract him from the task at hand. She *would* not.

After washing and shaving with water from the basin in his room, Heath dressed and descended the narrow, creaking stairs to the parlor. He suddenly felt his appetite awakening as it rarely did these days. Food would surely revive him. At least he knew what was in the sausages and the cider here. In London one could not always be certain.

He went to the open door of the house, ducked his head under the low lintel and squinted out into the sunny yard.

An apple tree squatted there, thick, twisted

branches hanging heavy with an abundance of fruit. The mob of unruly children who had last night run circles around the parlor, today attempted to knock apples from the tree, using several sticks and a rake. One of the boys had climbed the trunk and crawled along a branch which clearly would not hold his weight. The abbreviated length of the child's trousers and their tightness around the waist suggested a recent growth spurt had taken everybody by surprise. It was more than likely that, having travelled that branch many times before without incident, the boy thought he could still do the same.

Heath strode up to the tree. "Best come down from there before you fall, young man," he said firmly.

Within seconds of his warning, the branch gave way with a crack and the boy tumbled. Fortunately Heath was close enough and quick enough to catch the child before he hit the ground. It reminded him of a certain troubling young lady taking a similar fall many years ago, directly into his arms.

Thus the redhead was back again after being dismissed from his thoughts once already that morning.

It was not like Heath to be distracted, but she kept turning up in his path and, whoever she was, she had an uncanny ability to leave this usually unruffled man quite despairingly...ruffled.

Was that what his sister found amusing? He thought he'd kept his expression as nonchalant as possible in Mrs. Oliver's parlor during the bonnet discussion. Although no expert at light conversation, he had obediently drunk his too-sweet tea, replied to

Mrs. Oliver's polite inquiries, and maintained an air of only mild interest in the beribboned creation Clara kept taking out of its box to show him. But his sister, of course, did not have the problem of noise to divert and confuse her qualities of observation.

"You naughty boy! What have you been up to now?"

Heath turned, startled out of his thoughts.

"How many times have I told you not to climb this tree, Samuel?" The singing swine-herd hurried across the yard, having witnessed the rescue. He thanked Heath warmly for the swift intervention. "The boy's a proper monkey. Good thing you were there, sir! We might have had a broken arm or worse! Do come and have some breakfast now, won't you?"

Heath followed the man back inside, and the children, their quest for apples forgotten, trailed after them both.

"I hope you slept well, sir."

"I did, " he lied, "thank you." His mind was still caught up on the redhead and her loose stitches.

"Travelled far, have you?"

He forced himself to pay attention. "From London."

"London?" The landlord's eyes widened. "We don't get many *from* London, although we see a fair few leaving to go that way in hopes of making their fortune, like Dick Whittington." He laughed. "And is your journey for pleasure or business?"

"Business."

"What sort o' business would that be?"

Ah, he should not have said business! *Her* fault again for distracting him. Heath thought quickly,

glancing back out toward the sun-lit yard. "Fruit."
Yes, what could be safer than fruit? "I study the
production of fruit for the government's committee
on agriculture." Sometimes he surprised himself by
how smoothly the lies came out.

"For the government, eh? You must be a very
important fellow."

"I am just a civil servant, quite at the bottom of
the pile, I assure you. Sent hither and thither..." He
had begun to lower his backside into a chair, but the
landlord stopped him.

"Just a minute, sir." With a grand flourish, the
fellow swiped at the wooden seat with a greasy,
stained rag and an excessive degree of violence. Then
he bowed, with one leg stretched out, as if he was Sir
Walter Raleigh setting his cloak over a puddle for
Good Queen Bess, and gestured for Heath to be
seated.

"Er...Thank you."

The children's eyes had widened while they
observed their father's actions and then they looked
with curiosity at the man who prompted such peculiar
courtesy.

"Best table in the place, sir. Through the window
there you have a lovely view of my apple trees."

"Yes. Quite."

The landlord tipped his head to one side on that
stout neck, and his dark eyes gleamed thoughtfully.
"Well, you sit there and I'll fetch breakfast, sir. And
you children don't bother this important gentleman
from London or I'll tan your hides." But this threat
was made with a ruddy-cheeked grin and one wagging
finger that clearly had never been raised to punish

116

child or beast. As soon as the man returned to the kitchen his children gathered around Heath's table, the smallest attempting to climb up his leg. In rapt curiosity they stared at this apparent rarity of an "important gentleman from London."

Seldom uneasy in the presence of hardened criminals, Heath found this battalion of freckled, damp, gaping faces fairly intimidating.

"Are you a prince?" one of the girls demanded.

"I am not."

"Are you really from London, mister?" The boy he had rescued from the apple tree wanted to know.

"I am."

"Are you rich?"

"No."

"Where's your 'orse?"

"I came on the stagecoach."

"You've got big feet, mister."

"They keep me upright."

"What you doin' 'ere then?"

"Seeking peace and tranquility," he muttered. "To no apparent avail."

After puzzling over this for a moment, the boy demanded, "Do you know the king?"

"Not personally."

"But you live in London and you talk proper lordly like, with big words."

Heath gave a little smile. "Even so, His Majesty and I don't travel in the same circles."

"Where's your wife, mister?"

"My wife? What makes you think I have a wife?"

"Miss Melinda says that every old man has a wife, just to do the laundry. She says, if it weren't for the dirty washin' he's too lazy to do fer 'imself, no man would ever marry. So what did you do with your Mrs.? Is she in London?"

"Not as far as I know." He'd never thought about finding a wife. Had too much else on his mind and, as he'd often tried explaining to his sister, the deliberate acquisition of another expense in his life would be highly illogical.

"Did you lose her? Our father lost our mother."

"Did he?"

"Aye. She were 'ere one day and gorn the next. Now Aunt Hattie does the laundry."

"I see."

"Our mother ain't lost like a hair ribbon," one of the girls explained, resting her forearms on the table to peer, unblinking and solemn, into his face. "She ain't missin'. We know where she is."

"Oh?"

"The G'lord took her," she rolled her eyes dramatically upward to the low beams that crossed the ceiling. "Took her to Heaven to be an angel. Miss Melinda says that's where our mother does the laundry now."

Shifting uncomfortably on his seat, he tried in vain to remove his leg from the custody of the smallest child who had fastened himself there like a limpet. "Hmm...well...I suppose even the good lord needs clean shirts."

"Did you lose your wife like a hair ribbon, or were she took up to Heaven, mister?"

Heath twisted around, looking for the landlord. *Where the devil was that breakfast?* "P'raps 'e done 'er in, 'imself," one of the other children speculated, leaning

118

against the table so that its three legs shifted an inch, scraping across the flagged floor and making Heath's teeth hurt. "Feller looks guilty enough. Miss Melinda says 'usbands sometimes do that when they don't want a wife no more, or they want a new one."

"Aye," said Samuel, the tree climber, "They squeeze their necks like so." He put his grimy hands around his own throat and stuck out his tongue. "Or else, she says, they throw 'em off a cliff into the sea in an old sack o' chains," he added, with a matter-of-fact shrug. "Sometimes they cut 'em up and put 'em in sausages. Big, fat, juicy sausages."

The other children shrieked merrily at this gruesome suggestion. Samuel, looking pleased with himself, seemed likely to come up with even more colorful suggestions of ways to be rid of a wife, but fortunately, their father returned at that moment with a large plate of plump, burnt... sausages.

Heath glanced at his plate and then saw the children exchanging darkly meaningful looks, before they returned their wide gazes to his face, waiting for him to sample this delicacy.

Hmm. Perhaps one *didn't* always know what was in the sausages here, he mused.

Beside the plate, his landlord set down a tankard of foamy cider and a large, clay jug of the same, while proudly announcing, "This is made from my own apples. Tom Rimple is the name, sir. Although most folks call me Tipsy. I'm well known in these parts for my cider and mead. You won't find better in the county."

"I'm sure." Realizing the other man waited for him to drink, he took a quick sip.

"Why, you must take a bigger gulp than that, sir. You won't get the full effect if you peck at it."

So he took another drink, just to appease the fellow and all those watching faces. He definitely felt the "full effect" this time. The cider was strong, with a kick of searing heat that singed the back of his throat, causing a thin wheeze to escape like steam from a kettle. "Very....very good indeed."

"Better than the cider you get in London, eh?"

"It is indeed unique."

"And superior to the brackish stuff they serve at *The Willful Goat* in the village."

"I doubt it not."

The fellow looked pleased, rocking back on his heels, sticking both thumbs under the straps of his apron. "I thought you must be a discerning gentleman, as soon as I saw you, sir. A man of honest tastes, but nothing too fancy."

Heath managed a hoarse, "You must be very busy here, raising so many children all alone."

"Aye. Keeps me from growing idle, to be sure. But I do have help around the place."

"Ah. that would be a...Miss Melinda?"

"Oh, no, sir! Since my wife died, my sister, Hattie, lends a hand when she can. She works up at the Park, but looks in on me and helps with the young 'uns." He leaned closer and whispered, "Likes to think she keeps me in line. Always knows best. But I daresay, you're acquainted with nagging females. There must be a vast supply in a place like London."

"Indeed. A surfeit." Heath cut into the first sausage, still under the expectant, challenging gaze of the Rimple family. "You said your sister works up at

120

the Park, sir?"

"Aye."

"Could that be Kingsthorpe Park? It is the name of an ancient manor house nearby, I think."

"That's right, sir. You know of the place?"

"I have heard of it. I believe the Goodheart family are residents there, are they not?"

"Aye. Been there since the year thirteen hundred or thereabouts, so 'tis reckoned." The landlord shooed his children outside and once they had disappeared into the sunlight, he continued in a conspiratory tone, "That rotten old curmudgeon Sir Ludlow Goodheart lets his bull run about in other men's fields and never pays for the damage. That about sums him up in one sentence."

"Ah."

"*His* father were a good, honest man, but too generous in many ways. Gullible, you might say. My grandfather, when he were alive, always spoke well of Sir Lachlan Goodheart and his wife Ethelreda. They were good folk, respectful to others. Never thought themselves above anybody." He sighed and scratched his armpit. "But such times are long gone; went to the grave with their generation. Sir Ludlow keeps to 'imself and doesn't bother much with the rest of us. We're too lowly for 'im, despite the fact that the old vulture hasn't got a pot left to pee in."

"And does Sir Ludlow have any sons?"

Rimple gave a low chuckle. "Aye, a son, who's as much use as the father. Except for Miss Melinda, they're a bunch o' no good—"

He stopped abruptly as a woman appeared in the open doorway, puffing loudly, carrying a large bucket

121

of milk. "I thought I'd find you chatting away with this poor guest," she exclaimed. "Any excuse to forget what you're meant to be doing. Gossiping like an old woman and letting the sausages burn again."

"I were just having a word with this important gentleman from London, Hattie. He saved young Samuel from a bad fall this morning, when the lad tumbled out of yon apple tree."

"Again? How many times must that boy be told? You aren't stern enough, Tipsy." She passed the heavy bucket to him and wiped her hands on a stained apron, while quickly assessing Heath with lively eyes. "'Ow do, sir? I did not see you come in last night."

"No, there was another lady here when I arrived."

"That would be little Mo, my cousin from round the way like," she said, jerking her head to one side, as if he should know where that was, "I hope she looked after you. She's young and all bones but eager, and doesn't turn up her nose at a bit of hard work. And what might be your name, sir?"

He put down his tankard, wiped his lips on a handkerchief and stood for a bow. "Caulfield, madam."

She looked surprised and pleased, hands clasped together. "Well, I must say, there is no need to bow to me, sir. I'm just Hattie."

"I do not reserve good manners for a privileged few, madam." He smiled stiffly and sat to continue his breakfast.

"Staying only the night on your way through, were you?" She hedged closer, one hand fussing with the back of her hair, her round cheeks touched with pink.

"I must stay a few days. I have some business in the county."

"What sort of business might that be?"

From the kitchen her brother yelled, "Fruit!"

"Fruit?" She frowned at Heath, fingers stilled.

"Nothing of any great significance, madam. I believe it would bore you to hear of it. Certainly it would bore me to tell it."

"Ah." She chuckled. "You don't mean to tell and I shan't press. There's some folks around here that are nosy, but not me. I know when to mind my own business."

Heath said nothing, but while he continued his breakfast, the lady hovered by his chair, just as her brother had done before.

"We don't get many visitors from London," she added. "We're too far off the toll road generally and the stage coach doesn't even stop until it gets to Kingsthorpe village. Most folk miss us completely, but there's just the odd one or two that gets lost."

Ah, yes, the village. He had hoped to find it last night, not realizing that he got out of the coach too soon. Distracted by the talkative redhead he had followed her out of the carriage without thinking to ask where he was. An unusual lapse for him.

"The village is not too far, is it?"

"Just under three miles down the lane. You won't find much in the way of lively society there, just a church, a haberdasher, a butcher, and a rowdy tavern called *The Willful Goat*— which, I should warn you, is most often full of farm-workers. A merry lot on a good day, but wretched unruly with a few jars of ale inside 'em." She propped both hands on her waist and sighed. "The militia used to be encamped not far off, but they've gone now. So that's all there is for entertainment."

"The peace and quiet will be a pleasant respite for me, madam." He raised his tankard. "And I find Mr. Rimple's cider sufficient refreshment, so I doubt I'll be frequenting the village tavern."

"Well, as I said, I'm Hattie. We're simple folk and don't stand on much ceremony. You can call me plain ol' Hattie and I shan't object."

"Thank you. That's most kind." He looked down at his plate and said casually, "Your brother was telling me that you work at Kingsthorpe Park."

"For more than twenty years. Not that my loyalty is ever appreciated by the old—"

Yet again the conversation was halted prematurely by the arrival of a figure in the doorway— this one panting as if she'd run across several fields to get there. Poised in a frame of bright sunlight, she exclaimed breathlessly, "Hattie! There you are! You simply must come back. We cannot do without you."

At first, with the light behind her, she was merely a dark, flat silhouette, the features of her face lost in shadow. But when she stepped into the room, slim shafts of drowsy autumn gold filtered through the leaded window and touched her gently, filling in the colors and curves, turning that outline into a vibrant, shapely young woman.

Damn.

Chapter Ten

His throat went dry and the flutter in his chest seemed to fall to his stomach, then back up again. He reached for his tankard so hastily that his fingertips almost knocked it from the edge of the small table.

Thankfully, she was on business too urgent to grant him more than the briefest of dismissive glances. Leaving muddy footprints across the flagged floor, she marched quickly up to Hattie Rimple and declared, "Whatever my father's done now, I shall make recompense. Do come back, I beg you! Do not desert me, dear Hattie. Tell me what must be done to make things right again. I shall move heaven and earth if need be."

She was just as intense in her plea for help, as she was in her pursuit of the purse robber four years ago. Clearly not a woman who did anything half-heartedly, and felt everything deeply.

As he had known from their first encounter.

Today she was autumn in living form, a blur of copper and gold, moving so fast that she spared no thought for dignity or her appearance. Her straw bonnet, knocked off the back of her head, had been left to dangle behind, the ribbons clinging around her neck. Several crisp yellow leaves drifted in her wake, as if they were caught on her hair and clothes at some point during the journey, only becoming dislodged when she skidded to a halt.

Two minutes later and he would have finished his breakfast, but she had caught him before he could get away and she was the only person there who knew what he was. If she remembered his face.

This could ruin any chance he had of taking the "Cuckoo" by surprise. Hopefully his plain, forgettable features would work in his favor again, as they usually did.

Meanwhile, Hattie Rimple embraced the young woman with warmth. "My dear Miss Melinda, you needn't have run all the way here just to see me. Look at the state of your petticoat! The lane is a mess of mud after yesterday's rain, I'm sure."

Her name, at last he knew, was Melinda. Ah. Then *she* was responsible for the wicked ideas put into young Rimple minds about murderous husbands and wives subjected to endless laundry.

An unwelcome, unexpected smile itched at his mouth. Quickly he lifted that tankard of cider again and drained it.

"What do I care about mud? I would scale a mountain and swim an ocean to bring you back to Kingsthorpe, Hattie. Although, I daresay I would sink half way across. At least my death would be for a good cause."

"My dear girl, nobody said anything to me about you coming home just yet."

"No." The young woman sighed gustily. "I don't suppose they would. It is never a very exciting event for my father, even when he summons me. My return pales in importance to that of my brother."

"And if I had known you were coming— curse Sir Ludlow for not telling me he'd sent for you— I would have made your favorite rhubarb pie."

So she was Sir Ludlow Goodheart's daughter, and sister of the disreputable Lindley. He might have known. The first time he met her he'd suspected it would not be the last— that she would, inevitably, cross his path again. She was the sort of woman bound to find chaos, whether or not she caused it herself.

Neither his sister nor Mrs. Oliver had mentioned her name and he had not asked, too confused by why she had taken it upon herself to go there and, wary of his sister's smug expression, not wanting to give the event too much of his attention. If only they had volunteered her name and then he would have been warned.

As he had thought grimly to himself yesterday— of all the stagecoaches traveling the country he had to wave down one with her in it.

With a strangely unsteady hand, he poured a second tankard of cider from the clay jug, drank it down thirstily and felt his head begin to spin.

* * * *

Melinda ignored the stitch in her side, as well as the fellow eating his breakfast. When she was on a mission there was no time to consider anything else.

Clasping the housekeeper's hands, she implored, "Hattie, you will come back to us, won't you?"

"My dear girl, I half expected you never to return to Kingsthorpe. I thought you'd find something better for yourself by now. I hoped you would."

"I have. But, as you know, my idea of something better is not the same as my father's." And that was all she would say on the subject, for when she took a second glance at the stranger, she found his solemn brown eyes watching her over the rim of his tankard.

He looked away at once, but she knew he'd been listening.

"This is a gentleman from London," said Hattie, following her glance. "Mr. Caulfield, this is Miss Goodheart from up at Kingsthorpe Park." She turned back to Melinda and added, "He was just asking me about your father's house, my dear, and here you are."

"Oh?" She looked again at the man, and this time realized it was Mr. Highly Improbable, whom she last saw at the crossroads yesterday at sunset. So this is where he ended up. Today, shaven and less dusty, there was something even more familiar about his features. "You have an interest in Kingsthorpe Park, sir?"

He stood for a stiff bow, his heels clipped briskly together, arms at his sides. "I had just learned from the landlord here that the Park is not far away, Miss Goodheart. It is a name I heard mentioned before, although I know not where."

The frustrating memory flickered in and out, like a slender flame in a draft. She waited for him to mention having seen her yesterday on the stagecoach, but he did not. Instead he leaned slightly to one side and from the sudden, uneasy expression on his face, she guessed that Tipsy Rimple's cider was doing its work. The potency of that cloudy beverage often took gentlemen of the Town by uncomfortable surprise.

Should she say anything? His demeanor did not encourage friendly chatter today any more than it had yesterday, and Melinda had tried then, only to have his cold, stony shoulder turned to her. So an awkward silence descended until, having looked at everything except her face, he finally wheezed, "Would you excuse me? I must be getting on with my day," before walking outside in his shirt sleeves, abandoning his hat and his coat, which he left hung over the back of a chair.

Both women wandered to the window, through which they could watch his progress across the yard.

"He's an odd fellow," Hattie whispered. "Didn't want to tell me what he's doing here."

"Not that you would be nosy enough to ask," Melinda replied wryly.

"Of course not." The lady feigned outrage, hands on her waist. "You know me. I mind my own business."

"Surprising how you always manage to find time for other people's too."

"And you do not, young lady? Your grandmother used to say you had more curiosity than a cat in all its nine lives, although you'd rather make up a story than know the truth."

There was no arguing with that. They both fell silent then, watching as he strode along under the apple trees, tripping over the hens and children when they got in his way. The youngest Rimple, a boy who was still a babe in arms when Melinda defied tradition to attend his mother's funeral two years ago, caught the gentleman around one boot. There he clung fast with all four limbs, causing Mr. Caulfield an uneven hobble for the remainder of his route to the gate.

"As if he could fool a woman with as many years in the world as me," Hattie muttered smugly. "Fruit, indeed!"

"Fruit?"

"That's the reason he gave for being here, but

even about that he was guarded. Who has cause to be secretive about fruit, I ask you? Nobody in their right mind."

Melinda thought of how he had jealously gripped his books yesterday, not wanted the coachman to touch his trunk, and tried to keep his face hidden under the brim of his hat, all while avoiding conversation. "I suspect he is a secretive fellow in general, Hattie."

They now observed as the gentleman swiped a persistent wasp away with his gloved hands. He twisted about frantically, with the small child still attached to his leg and the other Rimple siblings joyfully mimicking his awkward dance.

She could not shake off this idea of having met him before.

"I can guess why he's come away from London," Hattie continued, her voice still hushed— more for dramatic effect now rather than discretion, since the fellow was far enough away not to hear above the children's laughter. "Woman trouble," she said gravely, shaking her head. "Poor, sad young man."

Melinda exclaimed, "Woman trouble? What on earth brings you to that conclusion?"

"He's polite, shy, and soft-spoken. That's the type that gets their heart broken."

"*Shy?*"

"You saw how quickly he made himself absent just now. He could barely look you in the eye! Mo says he was the same to her last night when he arrived— said nothing but, *have you got a spare room?*"

She arched an eyebrow. "What else should he say to little Mo? I love her dearly, but she's hardly a fount

130

of witty conversation. Besides, London folk are often less friendly than we are in the country."

"But further," Hattie continued in a hushed tone, "he wouldn't let her touch his books and Mo says he's only got one other little trunk with him, barely big enough for a change of clothes. I'd say that means he left in haste and without plans. What do you make of it? You usually have some good ideas. Not that I should encourage them."

"He doesn't look very shy to me. Just annoyed and rather surly. I cannot say that I have any idea about him. He's just too..." she yawned, "dull."

"You've already decided that, have you?"

"It's his face, Hattie. I do not care for it. And you know I have an instinct for these things." In truth she could not say what it was about his face that bothered her. But it did.

The subject of their discussion still tried to remove the child from his leg, while becoming steadily hotter in the bright morning sun. It was an unusually warm day for September, and sweat gleamed on his brow already. Then, in his struggle with the clinging Rimple, he bent over, presenting an all too appealing target for the goat, who came trotting over to nudge him in the buttocks. The first impact was a mere tap compared to the second, which, as he scrambled in surprise to get away, almost tipped him head over heels.

He must have heard Melinda laughing, for when he turned toward the window his face finally had some expression. And a deep scarlet color.

She jumped when Tom Rimple came up behind them to exclaim, "I know why yon fellow came here, and it was naught to do with females."

His sister glared over her shoulder. "What do you know about it?"

He puffed out his chest. "He's an inspector for the National Cider and Ale Competition. 'Tis plain. My cider were the first thing he asked for this morning. And he sucked down *two* tankards! Nearly emptied the jug. I can tell a man who knows his scrumpy."

"Don't be daft! You and that wretched competition! I shall be glad when it's over."

"I'm telling you, Hattie, he's an inspector come to taste my cider."

"You said the same about the fellow that stayed last week."

"No, no, this is the one! That last guest were just a ruse. I expect they try to confuse us by sending out all sorts to muddy the waters." He ducked his head, looking from side to side, wriggling the stout fingers of both hands in the air by his ears. "They mean to catch us unawares." He sniffed and nodded. "But he's the real one, I'd stake my life upon it. Fruit, he said. Fruit! He tries not to be noticed, and that's how I know."

"*Muddy you?* It doesn't take much to muddy your waters, Tipsy Rimple. And why would anybody go to such lengths for a silly competition? The world does not begin and end with your blessed cider, for goodness sake. There's much more to life than that." She leaned over and said to Melinda, "I reckon he's drunk so much of it himself, he's pickled his brain."

"When that prize money comes to me, you'll sing a different tune, woman. When all His Majesty's accolades rain down on my cider and I get the Royal warrant for my barrels, then you'll think of my efforts with a kinder opinion."

Outside, by the gate, their guest had finally succeeded in removing the child from his leg, and the goat from his breeches, then quickly slipped through to freedom in the lane beyond. The gate secured, he took one last look over toward the window, brushed himself down briskly, and marched off with a very business-like stride, one clawed hand sweeping back through his rumpled hair.

Whatever his purpose there, Melinda decided firmly that the plain, unsociable fellow was not of much interest to her. She had far more pressing matters on her mind, problems of her own to solve.

"Hattie, you will come back to us, won't you? I can manage much of the housework myself, but it's the cooking that quite undoes me."

The other woman looked vexed and hot. Fanning herself with her apron, she walked away from the sunny window. "Your father is an impossible man, and I had quite made up my mind never to go back..." she sank to the chair vacated by Mr. Highly Improbable, "but now you are there, my dear, I cannot leave you alone to suffer, can I? My conscience won't allow it."

Relief swept Melinda across the room to throw her arms around Hattie's shoulders. "Thank heavens! My brother brought home a guest, and I have had a sleepless night wondering what I shall do to manage things. They'll have to be fed, of course."

"I suppose men are best not left to manage the cooking," said Hattie, glaring at her brother as she patted Melinda's arm in reassurance. "They're likely to burn the house down if left to their own devices."

"Hush, woman. I don't know what our fine guest from London must have thought to hear you berating me like a common scold. When I'm called up to the palace, I shan't take you, if you can't behave yerself."

"Oh, go back to your sausages!"

"The only woman trouble our guest has got is *you*, and your romantic fancies. I tell you, he's an inspector for the Great National Cider and Ale Competition, and when he's drunk his fill around the county, he'll see mine is the best. That's when Thomas Arthur Rimple will finally get the recognition he deserves and folk around these parts will show 'im proper respect."

"Just look at that smoke, you fool!" Hattie shouted. "The sausages will be burned to a cinder! And I know when a gentleman has been ill-used by love. I know that Mr. Caulfield has woman troubles, and I'd stake my life on it."

Grumbling under his breath and swiping his apron at the smoke, Tipsy went back to the kitchen.

Suddenly Hattie gripped her hands. "So Master Lindley is home too, is he? Oh, dear. I feared as much."

"Yes, he is his usual insufferable self. Came with a fancy new friend in a private barouche. Now there are four tired horses to take care of too in the stables and no groom left to do it. The gentleman my brother brought with him travels only with a valet called Moone," she chuckled, "who is the least obliging servant I've ever seen. He will not tend the horses himself as he says it is not *'what he signed up for.'* You

134

would be extremely diverted by Moone."

Hattie tipped her head to one side, her shrewd eyes searching Melinda's face, ferreting out the details she had skimmed over. "Your brother brought home another gentleman with a manservant, did he? And what's the gentleman like then?"

"Akin to most men, if one doesn't actually listen to him or need him for anything important, I suppose he's tolerable in small doses."

"You like *his* face then, do you?" Hattie winked. "If he's tolerable he must be handsome at least."

"Mr. Rochfort's face has a certain...appeal." If only the same could be said of his mind.

As for the other newcomer, she still had no particular opinion about the awkward Mr. Caulfield from London, and could venture no suggestion of her own as to why he was there. Yesterday, when she was certain that carriage held the last remnants of the human race, she had briefly considered him for a husband, but no wonder, considering the poor competition he had at the time.

Chapter Eleven

Having secured Hattie's promise to return to Kingsthorpe Park, Melinda started back along the muddy lane at a much more leisurely pace than she came down it earlier. She felt no great haste to get home, and it was such a pleasant day for September that it would surely be a travesty not to enjoy a good walk. She'd been up since the first dew-laden daisy opened its petals. There were fires to light, floors to sweep, and the kitchen to scrub, and with her mind full of so many thoughts last night, there had been no room for sleep in any case. Now the fresh air and birdsong lifted her spirits back where they should be.

Cheered by the success of her mission that morning, she reflected upon the goodness of Hattie Rimple, who had not only sent her back to Kingsthorpe Park with a basket full of provisions, but had promised to return in time to cook dinner that evening. Now with her most immediate problem solved, Melinda could get her thoughts in order and prepare to confront her father again today.

Her basket was so heavy that she was forced to stop a few times and set it down, resting by the hedge to enjoy the view across the fields. Some distance ahead from where she stood, the lane took a deep bend and started steeply downhill with little warning. When they were children, and snow was thick upon the ground, she and Lindley used to slide down that part of the lane on tin trays and platters from the kitchen, taking turns to give each other the necessary push from the top of the slope and keeping a look out through the trees at this spot for any soul coming in the other direction.

Unfortunately, if there was somebody coming, the watcher could only shout a warning and hope it was heard— not actually stop the person flying along on the tray— and nine times out of ten Lindley didn't even bother to shout for her when it was his turn to be the "look-out".

Reminded of this childhood game, and out of habit as much as sentiment, Melinda stopped and looked through the bushes. Yes, she could see the winding lane where it dropped quite steeply down the hill. There was the old stump against which she once cut her knee. There too was the lovely silver birch where she banged her head and, for a few moments, lost consciousness— the only time she ever saw her father show genuine concern for her, and the only time her brother was ever punished.

Good thing she had a strong skull.

That is not what people mean when they call you headstrong, Miss Goodheart," her old headmistress used to point out scornfully.

Well, Melinda preferred to interpret the meaning differently.

Lindley, of course, had always given his sister's tray an extra hard shove down the hill. He said it was because she was too small and light to go fast unless he really pushed her. That would hardly be a problem now, of course.

As she stood there watching the lane ahead and reminiscing, Melinda spied two white shirt sleeves through the greenery. It was a man walking along without a coat. In the next moment he fully appeared through a gap in the hedge and she saw it was Mr. Caulfield. What was he still doing in her lane? He had left Tipsy Rimple's parlor half an hour before she did, and the last time she saw him he was walking along at a brisk pace. Yet there he was on the path ahead of her, moving like a man with no particular destination.

She decided to let him get farther ahead before she started down the slope. The fellow clearly sought solitude, and she would not want to intrude.

But he had stopped by a five-barred gate, to stare down across the top field toward her father's house.

If he did not soon continue his course, Melinda would be forced to meet up with him in the lane and she was not much in the mood for another attempt at conversation with the stiff, unfriendly stranger. Yesterday, in the coach, he had closed his eyes to escape her, but he could not do that now.

Frustrated, she set down her basket and waited again, counting to twenty. When she looked through the trees once more, he was still there, staring down at her father's house, forearms resting on the gate. He wiped his brow with a folded handkerchief and smoothed back his hair.

She knew him. And not just from the stagecoach yesterday. But from where else?

Melinda squinted, trying to remember where she might have seen him before.

Caulfield? The name meant nothing, and he had assured her that he didn't know her.

But there was something about that fellow....

She took a deep breath, picked up her basket, and quickened her own pace, resolved to find out what he was up to.

Since her feet traveled much faster on the downward slope and he did not move from that point at the curve, but stood there surveying the distant, ragged shape of Kingsthorpe Park, she was soon upon him. Much quicker, in fact, than she'd anticipated due to the wet mud and her clumsy feet.

"Miss Good—"

She slipped and tumbled forward, dropping her basket and all the contents. The gentleman, fortunately, had speedy instincts and saved himself from being bowled over the gate by grabbing her around the arms.

"Oops," she exclaimed, her heart's rhythm scattered like pins, and any attempt to restore it further disrupted by the sudden heat and heaviness of his hands upon her.

"Miss Goodheart!" He was very slightly flushed, his brows drawn together in a cross scowl as he set her back on her feet. "Do have a care, madam."

She realized at once that her sleeve felt loose. The seam had torn again. And thus she remembered where she'd seen him before. It came to her with a jolt and the snap of her stitches.

I am an officer of Bow Street, madam, entrusted by the magistrate to keep the peace and apprehend criminals. I must explain to you, the peril that can befall a member of the fairer sex, especially when she is left untended and happens to be of a venturesome, foolhardy spirit.

"This lane is steep and in a treacherous condition," he lectured her today, "you should take this path with more caution, madam, or you could suffer injury."

"Sir, I know this lane as well as I know the back

of my hand. I could run the distance with my eyes closed."

"I wouldn't recommend it, but if you must, kindly wait until I am not in your path. Or anywhere within five miles. I'd prefer to remain upright and—"

"And I know who you are," she exclaimed, breathless.

Mr. Caulfield belatedly removed his hands from her person and now held the left one, fingers spread wide, against the front of his waistcoat. "I...have an interest in history and architecture. Kingsthorpe Park is Plantagenet era, is it not?" he said, as if she had not spoken.

"You lied to me in the stagecoach, sir!"

"I beg your pardon?"

"You're an agent of the Bow Street Magistrate. At first I did not recall where I'd seen you before, but now I remember."

"You must be confused, Miss Goodheart."

"Indeed I am not. We have met before, and you knew it yesterday on that coach. Why did you not say when I asked? Instead you lied and said it was *highly improbable* that I knew you."

He looked away from her, a bead of sweat trickling down his temple. "I wonder, Miss Goodheart, if I might prevail upon you to keep the information you have about me to yourself. At least while I am here. It will not be for long."

"Why?" He was suddenly slightly more interesting. "Are you here on official business?" she demanded eagerly. Since he still looked away over the fields, she stepped closer and tugged on his shirt sleeve. "If there is anything amiss going on, we ought to be informed. My father is the Justice of the Peace in this county, so any such matter should be brought to his attention. Are you on the trail of a despicable criminal who has left a dozen victims in his wake? If so, I could be of help to you."

He looked down at her fingers. "No."

"Oh." She released his sleeve, and her shoulders sank slightly. "Why are you here then?"

He ground his jaw, dabbed that bead of sweat from his forehead with the folded handkerchief again, and replied, "I came into the country for my health. The physician thought it would be beneficial."

Melinda studied him thoughtfully for a moment. "I know illness and the incapacitated male, sir, for we've had a few in our family. And you are not one." He felt solid when she ran into him. Certainly, his grip was firm enough to tear her clothes. Again. And she'd seen him scale the side of a stagecoach as if it were nothing. "You are much too... robust. Which suggests you're lying to me again."

He said nothing, his expression utterly blank.

Blood from a stone, she thought grimly.

"I will not be the only curious soul, sir. Strangers are a rarity in Kingsthorpe, and there is bound to be speculation about your purpose here. You'll need a better excuse than fruit."

Still no reply, just a soft, measured sigh and an almost imperceptible narrowing of his eyes.

"You want me to keep your profession a secret and yet you give me no reason why I should." With an arch of her eyebrow, she added, "Your smug face annoys me immensely, and you've already lied to me at least once."

Finally his lips parted. "I see I expect too much of you, when I ask for prudence and discretion. I cannot expect such consideration from an irrational creature. It is probably not in your nature, being a young, silly thing who likes to talk. So you must do as you wish with the information you possess about me. As for my face, Miss Goodheart, I have never been fond of it myself, but it is adequate for my purposes, and anything finer would probably have been a hindrance. It would, most certainly, have been wasted on me."

Well, when he *did* speak he certainly had plenty to say.

"If one wants a favor," she said pertly, "one ought to be pleasant to the person who can grant it, don't you think? And not imply that she is an absurd chatterbox."

"Since you had no qualm in telling me, with blunt candor, what you thought of my face, it would seem neither of us give compliments for the sake of it."

Melinda watched him tucking that folded handkerchief away into a small pocket in his waistcoat, his movements very precise and tidy. Clearly he would tell her nothing more about his reason for being in Kingsthorpe. Perhaps he chased *her*, she mused. What had she done now?

"So you will not tell me your purpose here."

"I'll let you speculate, madam. I suspect that would be more entertaining for you than the plain, unexciting truth." He knew that about her already, she mused. It was rather infuriating to be read so easily, while he kept his own pages tightly shut.

"How funny it is that we keep running into each

other, sir."

"Funny is not the adjective I would choose."

She laughed. "Vexing then."

"With that I can agree." Suddenly he hunkered down and began to put all the fallen items back in her basket. He still wore leather gloves, which looked odd beside bared forearms and rolled up shirt sleeves.

Melinda let her gaze travel over his strong arms and wide shoulders. "If you *were* on the trail of a dangerous highwayman, I might have been of use to you in apprehending the villain. I am quite without fear. You have, after all, seen me in action."

"Indeed," he huffed. "Thrice."

"*Thrice?* How so?"

He looked up at her, his eyes half shut against the sun. "That was me in your hat shop three days ago. The man you crushed to the floor, and who was then beaten severely by an angry lady wielding a parasol."

Now she was even further amused. *That* was him too? The lovelorn fellow? No wonder she had sensed a familiarity with his...aura, she supposed one could call it...when he entered her shop. A recognition from some sense deeper than the customary five.

"Hattie was right then, after all. You *are* crossed in love."

"I beg your pardon?"

"Lady Clara Beauspur. The young lady for whom you came into my shop. You left her portrait and her address behind when you departed in haste, so I delivered a bonnet to her on your behalf. Did she not tell you?"

"Ah." His hands paused in the process of

143

refilling the basket. His shoulders went rigid.

"I hope you are not offended."

He squinted up at her. "Too late now if I am, is it not? Like meddling in other folk's business, do you?"

"I object to the term *meddling*, sir. You wanted a bonnet for your young lady, and I delivered it."

"My young lady? What exactly did she tell you?"

"You needn't be so wary. She told me how hard you work, how you never rest, and how much she adores you."

"She did?" His expression was dismayed.

"Lady Clara worries about you and waits patiently for your visits. She agreed with me that love should conquer all and nothing should stand in its path." Melinda wanted to pat his shoulder to comfort, but perhaps that would be too forward. Then he moved again, in any case, and continued repacking her basket.

"Lady Clara," he muttered, "enjoys her mischief."

"Well, I wanted only to help your state of affairs."

"My state of affairs? Do tell me what that is? I am quite at a loss."

"It's obvious. She is a titled lady— an aristocrat's daughter— and I suppose her family does not approve of a match with an officer of the police. Worry not, these problems can be resolved, if one is determined."

Melinda heard a low groan and, for a long moment, feared she might have gone too far in her eagerness to do a good deed. But when he looked up at her he seemed to be mulling something over. At last, in a calmer voice, he said, "I wondered where I'd

144

misplaced the miniature."

Relieved, she exclaimed, "Lady Clara is delightful. I liked her very much."

"Did you?"

"I saw no mischief in her. Indeed, she was very well behaved and proper." She smiled. "Nothing like me at all."

"I would hope not." He finished reloading the basket and stood.

"If you confide in me, I might be able to advise you."

He looked doubtful. "Your expertise reaches beyond bonnets, does it?"

"I do know a man in love when I see one."

His narrowed gaze moved slowly over her upturned face. "Do you?"

"You must love her dearly to go to all that trouble. A ladies' bonnet shop is clearly not your province."

But his expression gave nothing away. It remained a closed box, inscrutable.

"Evidently," she said firmly, "you need my help."

"Miss Goodheart, all I require from you is the assurance that you will keep my profession to yourself while I am here."

Melinda gave a heavy sigh and reached for her basket, but he held it away from her.

"Well, madam?"

She put her hands behind her back. "It would quite enliven things, if you *were* here on business. It would even make you interesting. Slightly."

"Miss Goodheart, I hate to disappoint you, but I am a very ordinary, *uninteresting*, humdrum fellow."

Tucking her basket under one arm, he added, "I can, however, promise you that whatever else I may or may not be, I am a gentleman. While I am here, I will allow no harm to befall you."

"Oh, lord." She rolled her eyes. "Just as I feared."

"You would rather be in harm's way, madam?" He looked puzzled.

She shook her head. "A hint of danger would not go amiss. No woman wants to be assured that nothing exciting will ever happen to her."

"I don't follow, Miss Goodheart. I begin to think we are having two separate conversations. On two different planets."

"For example— oh, do pay attention— if only you were a little more daring, you might have won Lady Clara's heart already and swept her off her feet, away from the clutches of her haughty family, but instead you keep her waiting in that little cottage. Alas, you thought only of sending her a *practical* bonnet." She clasped her hands together imploringly. "A lady sometimes wants adventure. Something *im*practical in her life. Life without risk is no life at all."

His mouth opened, closed, and opened again. "Miss Goodheart, can I depend upon your discretion, or not?"

"Oh, very well," she exclaimed.

He gave a terse nod, but when she reached again for her basket, he kept it. "I'll carry it for you, since we are walking the same lane, madam." He cocked an eyebrow. "If I can be trusted to carry it. Even with my face being so smug and irritating." There was almost a smile. Transient and ethereal as a mischievous ghost in a graveyard mist, it passed before she could be sure of it. "Lead on, Miss Goodheart."

So she did, head high and arms swinging.

Of all the people to meet again...

She laughed.

"Something amuses, madam?"

Now she knew why his face was so grim. "You do have some very bad luck, don't you?"

"Uniquely so, it seems," he muttered, "when in *your* vicinity."

Chapter Twelve

He had to lie to her, of course. There was nothing to assure him that she could be trusted with the truth. All he knew of the woman was that she could run very fast, had no apparent fear of injury, and threw herself whole-heartedly— and bodily— into her endeavors, however ill-advised.

Heath never took anybody into his confidence. He was a man who preferred to work alone, just as he lived, risking only his own self. He simply could not risk this reckless young woman knowing anything about his purpose there. The lie, therefore, regrettable though it might be, was necessary.

He wished there was some way he could warn her about Lindley Goodheart's travelling companion, but there was no chance of it for now. At least, if there was trouble, he would be there to make certain she was safe. He could watch over her. It didn't seem as if anybody else had taken that task upon themselves, and she did not welcome assistance. Seemed almost to resent it.

As she trotted along at that jaunty pace, a reddish brown curl bounced against the back of her neck. Her straw bonnet still had not been replaced upon her head, but was left to dangle by its ribbons. The heels of her walking boots were thick with mud— and worse— like the hem of her gown.

He shook his head.

"I feel you disapproving of me, Mr. Caulfield," she shouted, her tone amused.

How the devil did she know that?

Then she laughed over her shoulder. "I have eyes in the back of my—"

Wherever her eyes were, they were not presently employed in looking where she stepped. Her foot slipped in a soft, wet cowpat. She would have tumbled onto her behind, but Heath caught her mid-fall. Again. Of course, he had to use his right hand, since the left was holding her basket.

"Once again, it appears a very good thing that I am here to rescue you, Miss Goodheart," he muttered with feeling. Who was responsible for catching her when he was not passing? Or did she generally land on her posterior?

Before she was fully upright, she slipped again and pulled the glove half off his right hand. Her gaze went at once to those two wooden fingers and the leather strap that kept them in place.

Heath instantly let go of her, set the basket down and retrieved his glove from her hand.

"Oh," she murmured. "I am sorry."

He felt the fiery heat of mortification in his face. Rather than look at her pitying expression, he focused on replacing the glove, angrily pulling it back up his right hand, covering the sight that was, to him, heinous.

"I'd better carry my own basket," she said softly, further feeding the flame of his fury.

"No. I can manage." He snatched her basket by the handle with his left hand again and gestured with a terse nod. "Let us continue, Miss Goodheart."

"But I—"

"Continue, madam!"

To his shock, she had reached out toward his

maimed hand, as if she meant to....do what? He had no idea. Confusion, embarrassment, and frustration wove through his blood and up into his throat where it made a tight knot of rope. A garrote.

"If you please," he choked out crossly.

So she turned and walked on, with greater care this time, looking down at her feet.

After a while he was recovered enough to mutter, "So now you know all my secrets, Miss Goodheart. You'll have much to gossip about me now."

To which this chit of a girl replied, without looking over her shoulder this time, "I'm quite certain I don't know *all* your secrets, Mr. Caulfield. Nobody, not even you, could be so *humdrum* as to have only two."

His humiliation dissipated, replaced by surprise and annoyance. For a moment he could not even shut his lips.

"But rest assured," she promised airily, "I'm not in the least curious to know what else you're hiding, so you needn't be so alarmed. I really don't care whether you have eight fingers or twenty. You think you're the only one with problems, but I have plenty of my own. Problems, which, by the way, could make your dull hair curl if you knew the half of it."

His pulse struggled to recover its steady rhythm, as if he was the one who had slipped and been rescued. He felt both relieved and irritated. Even more confusing, there was an underlying pinch of sweetly awkward gratitude, because he sensed she tried to put him at his ease in the only way she knew how— with humor. And he was not accustomed to anybody making that effort for him.

150

"Now you're disapproving of me again," she shouted in a sing-song voice, marching on ahead.

No, he was not. In fact he was feeling...otherwise.

But to keep up with her, Heath was forced to quicken his own pace. He felt certain this was her way of trying to get him as muddy and disorderly as herself.

* * * *

"Won't you come in, sir? I can give you a tour and introduce you to my father, who is always glad to talk about the Goodheart family history, although I suspect he makes much of it up. Not, perhaps, as much as I do." When he said nothing, she added wryly, "If history and architecture are truly one of your interests, there is much of it here to be observed. One thing we have plenty of is moldy old stone."

But at the door of the manor house Mr. Caulfield made his stilted excuses, handed her the basket and took his leave. "You must let me know the cost of the bonnet," he said, "and I'll settle the bill."

"That is not necessary. After your beating from Lady Bramley—"

"I insist, madam."

He was going to be all proud and say he did not accept charity, of course. His dark brown eyes simmered with annoyance, although she had no idea what she'd done now to upset the fellow.

"Perhaps you will come back later," she suggested, wishing there was some way to make his face less sad and weary. Surely it was not permanently like that. "Hattie Rimple will cook dinner, and you are welcome to join us. She's an excellent cook."

Mr. Caulfield made no response to her offer. He asked her only for directions to the village, so she pointed.

"Do you see there, the needle point of a tall spire where it pricks a hole in the cerulean velvet sky? Follow that puffy trail of white cotton stuffing where it spills out. Below that, a filigree border of rusty tree-tops marks one side of the village common."

"Walk toward the church, in plainer words, then," he muttered.

"Suit yourself. I tried to make it more interesting for you."

He shot her one last, curious glance, bowed, and then was off, not looking back.

Probably just as well, she mused, for the house was not at its best and in daylight all the ceiling stains, sagging walls, woodworm, spider webs and moth holes were more visible. Even she had a hard time imagining them away. He would, undoubtedly, look about the place with that same stern, critical eye as he looked at her.

What a strange man he was and how embarrassed he had been about his hand. But men were like that; they tried to hide anything they saw as a weakness. To her such a wound was a mark of bravery and more meaningful than a shiny medal. A person who got through their life with everything intact had probably not made good use of themselves.

She had wanted to ask how it happened, but they were not yet friends and he was so very cautious. If he stayed a while she might succeed in breaking down his walls with her hard head. Then she could advise him on his courtship of Lady Clara. Because everything about the poor fellow was practically screaming out for her help and advice.

During their walk, whenever she thought he was becoming easier in her company he had put that wall up again, or lowered the portcullis and pulled up the drawbridge—whatever it was, it kept her at a distance. Almost as if he was afraid of her. Or of what she might do to him.

He had asked her about *Desperate Bonnets* and how she came to manage the shop. So she told him about Lady Bramley encouraging the young ladies to make their own way in life and not to be discouraged by obstacles.

"She especially encouraged me," Melinda had explained, "because I have little chance of finding a husband. "

"We *must make the best of things*," Lady Bramley often said. And although it was customary for folk to give the blithe reassurance that where one door closes another will open, the kindly patroness would say, "*Where one door closes one must open it again. That is the very function of a door. There would be no such invention as a hinge if that were not the case.*"

Having absorbed this lesson with great optimism, Melinda was determined to open her own doors and not wait for a man to open them for her.

But having said all this to Mr. Caulfield she found him looking at her as if she might bite. Thus he closed his own door again and shut her out. With a complicated series of bolts. She could almost hear them clanging shut.

Peculiar fellow. Lady Clara certainly had her

work cut out for her.

Melinda watched until he had disappeared from view, then she turned to go inside and walked right into the door, which she could have sworn she'd opened already.

* * * *

Naturally she couldn't give him simple, straightforward directions, but much to Heath's surprise he did find the village of Kingsthorpe by following the trail of white cloud as she suggested.

He stepped over a stile, passed through a gap in the trees, and there was the village common, upon which a set of stocks stood empty, waiting for a miscreant to be seated in them. There was, as Hattie Rimple had warned him, not much else to the place, but a few thatched cottages, a butcher, a carpenter, a tavern and a shop that seemed to sell a little of everything, while also serving as a post office. That was where he went first, needing a few items for himself and with a letter to post to his sister.

A few casual enquiries later and he had learned that while most of the villagers held little respect for Sir Ludlow or his son, they had great fondness for the daughter. She had spent most of her childhood taking care of her father and brother, receiving no reward for it, and then being sent off to a ladies' academy in London, where she was expected to catch herself a husband.

He also learned that Master Lindley Goodheart, like his father, owed money to almost every tradesman in the county, and that a barouche and four, bearing him and a gentleman by the name of

Rochfort, had stopped in the village yesterday on its way to the manor house.

"A handsome enough fellow," Rochfort was described by the shopkeeper's wife, "and seemed generous with his coin too. He'll be good for custom while he's here."

"Good for custom, madam?"

"All the young girls around these parts will be in to buy material for a new frock, or ribbons and trimmings to spruce up an old one," she exclaimed, chuckling. "Mark my words, a pretty cock with good manners and coin to spend always sets the hens to clucking and fluffing their feathers."

Her husband added, "Mayhap he'll set his eye on Miss Goodheart. Her father won't object, surely, if the fellow is rich enough. Sir Ludlow can't be too fussy now. It seems the young lady came home without a single prospect on the horizon."

"That's why her father sent for her. He's given up waiting for her to find a husband, so he's going to get her one."

"'Tis about time something good came her way. She's always the first to help anybody else. Never turns her back on one in need."

Heath thought of the concern and pity on her face when she glimpsed his wooden fingers. Alas, he had reacted sternly and been sharp with her, but he had let no woman near him since he was wounded. So she was the first and he was not prepared. Even his sister had not seen his hand.

He'd taught himself to write and shoot with his left, so that no one else would ever know of his infirmity, unless he removed his glove. But Heath knew, of course. He was, every day, made aware of no longer being "whole". For a man who took pride in his physical well-being and worked hard to maintain it, the loss of his fingers and much of the use in that hand was agonizing.

Now Miss Goodheart knew. He supposed it didn't really matter. After all, he was not trying to impress her. Probably couldn't, even if he tried. His face was against him from the start.

He could hear her laughing at him again, and he shook his head.

She was just young, fanciful, romantic and giddy enough to be taken in by the "Cuckoo" and his artful charm. And if she became enamored it would be with all of herself, deeply and irrevocably. Just as she did everything.

It occurred to Heath, finally, that there was a reason why fate kept bringing himself and the redhead together. Perhaps it was not for her to get in his way, after all, but for him to be in hers.

Chapter Thirteen

Melinda's brother and his friend had finally emerged from sleep. As she entered the kitchen, they were searching for food, turning the place upside down in that ineffectual but noisy way employed by men, whenever they were obliged to do something they thought a woman ought to be doing for them. And they were especially limp and useless when suffering the effects of too much wine the night before. As she'd said to Mr. Caulfield, she was familiar with the incapacitated male.

In her absence, the fire had been left untended until it was almost out completely, none of the men giving it any thought, except for the fact that they were getting colder by the minute and wondering why it was warmer outside than in. Moone, the so-called manservant, clearly had not "signed up" for such a menial task as tending the fire, although what, exactly, his job entailed she could not comprehend. Mr. Rochfort gave him no orders and seemed simply to tolerate his presence, occasionally looking bemused at something the sullen fellow muttered.

At some point during the night, Moone had rooted himself to a bench by the wall. There he remained the following morning too, swaddled in his coat, eyes closed, arms folded and boots stretched out. Melinda was obliged to step over his feet as she entered the kitchen, for he did not move them out of her way. He might have been asleep, although with the noise made by the other two she sincerely doubted it. There was a sinister, tomb-like stillness about the fellow that made her think he listened to every word.

"There you are," Lindley exclaimed, his face grey and eyes tinged with yellow. "Where have you been? Dawdling in the sunshine while we starve?"

She set her basket down on the table with a bang, knowing how it would make his headache throb worse. "I suggest you don't try my temper today, brother dear, I enjoyed very little sleep last night and am in no mood to tolerate a whining baby. I came home to see father about some important plans for the future, so although you and I have the misfortune to be here at the same time, do not assume that I have nothing else to do but cater to your needs."

"I thought father sent for you."

She hesitated. "Yes, he did. But I had a matter to discuss with him in any case."

"Which is?"

"No business of yours, brother."

He sneered. "I see that school has made you impudent, sister. Did they teach you nothing useful? Father says you've failed to catch the interest of even one suitor. No doubt you scared them all off."

"I do my best."

"I suppose you mean to go back to London and that hat shop."

"At the first opportunity."

"But father has no intention of supporting you in— oh what did he call it last night?— *This asinine notion some meddling old sow has put into her head.*"

So they had talked about her after she retired to bed, and while they sat up drinking wine into the small hours. Even in front of their guest they had discussed her lack of prospects. Of course they had. She was an easy subject for mockery and neither Lindley nor her father cared much about discretion.

"In his eyes it's quite out of the question, of course," Lindley continued, propping his arrogant backside on the kitchen table. "I knew what he would say, the moment I saw you working there. I warned you, but you wouldn't listen to me, as usual."

"You were happy enough to use my services. I have sent three bonnets to women for you in the last few weeks alone. One of them to France. And you still have not paid the bill."

He dismissed that with a flick of his fingers. "All in good time. Dear Mimi promised to send me something in return, and then I shall be able to pay you three times over."

"Save your ludicrous promises for our father. He might still believe them, but I long since came to my senses." She slammed the jar of pickled onions onto the table.

"How typical that you take your frustration out on me. It is not my fault. While some little governess post might have been respectable for the plain, drab daughter of a baronet, you must have realized he would never agree to let you work in a shop."

She saw that Mr. Rochfort had taken himself over to the open door, where he stood looking out, tapping the brass ferrule of his cane on the flagged stone and politely pretending not to hear their debate.

"And if you came home for that five hundred pounds our mama left you, I'm afraid you'll be disappointed."

"That bequest was put aside for me. I do not see

why I cannot use it as I would choose. I believe mama would understand."

"Ah, yes. Poor mama." Lindley's sigh of sympathy was no more believable than the companionable tap to her shoulder. "When she died, we couldn't have known how difficult getting you married off was going to be. You were just a sweet little thing then and there was no sign of how insufferable you would turn out. Now we know five hundred pounds is sadly inadequate for the task it was assigned."

"Nevertheless, it was meant for me," she whispered, further embarrassed that Mr. Rochfort was obliged to begin whistling now.

"Father would sooner use it for your funeral expenses as he would to encourage your wayward ideas. A daughter dead would be less of an embarrassment than one in trade."

Their guest had walked outside, whistling louder, and Melinda was intensely grateful for it, even though she knew he must have heard most of the conversation already. At least he was kind enough to spare her some humiliation. Moone, on the other hand, remained in his corner, unmoving. A menacing potted plant.

"Of course, there are also Eccentric Ethelreda's old pearls and that box of tarnished rubble that came with it." Lindley cradled his chin thoughtfully between thumb and forefinger. "Not that you can get anything for the necklace. The pearls are only wax-filled glass— *Roman Pearls* as they are called—and much less than a hundred years old, whatever tale father likes to tell of their provenance. The crimson stone in the clasp was the only thing of any potential value."

"The stone you stole!"

"Took to be valued, sister dear," he corrected her. "I thought you'd like to know what it was worth. By the by, I did you a favor and saved you years of false hope. The stone turned out to be paste from the last century and hardly worth the cost of the stagecoach ride to London."

"So you brought it back then?"

He took a swig and winced before he answered. "Like I said, it was worth nothing. I'll replace it with another gaudy, paste stone if it means that much to you. Good lord, I do believe Old Tipsy's cider is more rancid than ever." He smacked his lips and took another gulp. "But when a man has a thirst anything will do."

She could not speak. Rather than stand there looking at his self-satisfied, spoiled face another moment, Melinda marched outside into the kitchen garden.

As she paced up and down between the tall cane rows of peas and green beans, Melinda struggled to calm her temper. After all these years with her father and brother she should have known that her plans would not go smoothly. Nothing in her life had ever been easy, but she always managed somehow. So she would find a way this time too. She must.

Giving herself this bolstering talk, Melinda had forgotten the presence of Mr. Rochfort until he stepped out in front of her.

"I am sorry, Miss Goodheart. It seems I have come upon your family at a difficult time, when there are matters to resolve."

Shaking her head, she strode to the end of the path where a little stone bench waited in the shade of a much-tentacled, long-untended rose arbor. "I do not think you could have come upon us at any *better* time, sir. There are always difficulties and unresolved matters in our family. You must take us as you find us, I fear."

When she sat, he gestured to the space beside her. "May I, Miss Goodheart?"

"Of course."

He ducked beneath the overblown roses and their torn, shattered petticoats, to join her on the little bench, both hands now resting on the carved head of his walking cane. "If I have contributed to your problems in any way, it grieves me terribly. I am, to be sure, an inconvenient guest at such a time."

"None of it is your fault, sir." She angrily tugged her skirt away from a thorny stalk. "As I said, we are always like this. I do not think this house has ever seen much peace, nor ever will while we are all under its roof together. Ouch!" A thorn had stuck in her thumb and drawn blood. "We are, each of us, extremely stubborn and selfish. This does not make for tranquil family conversation whether there are strangers present or not. I only feel sorry for you that you must be exposed to it."

Mr. Rochfort stared at her bloody finger, and the color drained from his face until it looked like the breast of a plucked goose. He clutched the ruffles at his throat and seemed about to topple backward off the stone bench.

"Are you alright, sir?" She quickly sucked the

wounded thumb and wiped it on her pinafore. "It was just a little scratch. See?"

He swallowed, a lace-edged kerchief clutched to his lips. "I'm afraid I do not manage the sight of...bl...bl...bl..."

"Blood?" She held it up to show him.

The poor fellow turned his head and wretched quietly into his kerchief.

Melinda fought her sense of mischief. Fanning him with her pinafore, she urged him to take deep breaths. "Shall I fetch a glass of brandy?"

Finally he recovered enough to open his eyes and manage a smile. As the color returned to his face, she was struck by the warm, deep blue of his eyes where sunlight, broken into a dappled pattern by the swaying cluster of roses overhead, danced and glittered across his features. She had to admit that the little vulnerability he had just revealed made him a more sympathetic character and his good looks helped tremendously. He was exceptionally pleasing to look at.

One would not require any artwork in the house if he lived in it, she thought. But he would be a nuisance to keep dusted.

Lindley came to the kitchen door at that moment, a crust of bread in one hand. "Rocky, where are you?" he yelled through a bulging, full mouth. "I want to play cards."

"I shall be in presently," the gentleman called back. "I am taking the air with Miss Goodheart."

"Well, don't take too much of it. You're not accustomed to the country air. I wouldn't want it going to your head." Lindley disappeared again, and

Mr. Rochfort made no move to get up.

"Have you known my brother long, sir?"

"A few weeks. The night we met I beat him at a game of Hazard and he accused me of playing with crooked dice. Ever since then he's been determined to win back every penny. And more. Your brother likes to wager on anything. He even wagered on what time we would get here and what there would be for supper. It is a habit that could one day bring about his ruin, as it has for so many." For just a moment he looked stern and then his smile was back. "Such a pity you and I did not meet sooner, in London, but Lindley seldom spoke of his little sister."

"No, I don't suppose he did."

"What scant information he gave naturally spurred my curiosity."

"It did? Oh, dear."

He laughed gently. "And I must tell you, Miss Goodheart, that I am not disappointed now that we have met."

Melinda sighed. "You could hardly have found me *worse* than my brother described, I'm sure. I can only imagine what he told you of me."

Mr. Rochfort seemed to find that very amusing and his answer was, she suspected, tactful. "You are most refreshing, Miss Goodheart. Artless and straightforward. But now I must remember to hold my tongue," he added, "or else it might wander off on the subject of my admiration for your pretty, autumnal hair and delightfully sincere, wide auburn eyes, Miss Goodheart. Then you will be tempted to shout at me again."

"I'm sorry I sounded cross yesterday, sir. I simply

164

assumed you were making sport of me. Most people do."

"I'm afraid that just as gambling is your brother's habit, flirting with pretty young ladies is mine." He looked at her thoughtfully. "But you must tell me about your plans for the future. You sound most determined to keep your hat shop and escape the plans your father makes for you."

"Yes. I am determined. I always am, in anything I make up my mind to do. I shall be back in London before the winter."

"You know what you desire from life, Miss Goodheart. That is an enviable quality, to be sure. I wish I had your *joie de vivre*."

She wiped her hands on her pinafore. "I do not follow blindly where I am supposed to, I'm afraid. I cannot conform to expectations. I couldn't even if I tried. I do not think I was made for it."

It seemed doubtful that he would understand, being such an avid, unquestioning follower of fashion himself, but to her surprise he smiled slowly and nodded. "I do admire a lady who knows her mind and won't be swayed."

"You do?"

"Of course. I would never hold anybody back from wanting more, wanting better. I can appreciate a strong mind, even if I am not one myself. I follow because I must. Alone I am weak, and so I follow the herd. I have never known what I want, only what I am told to want. I read my part and it is written for me. But you, Miss Goodheart— you write your own play. You are an independent soul."

She was greatly cheered by this speech. It was

exactly what she wanted to hear and, in her opinion, showed him to be more self-aware and contemplative than he had first appeared. Perhaps there was hope for him after all and she had judged him too harshly.

"You know, Mr. Rochfort," she said carefully, "you do not have to follow fashion all the time."

He looked quizzical.

"You can go your own way, sir. The world will not end if you do."

"But I have not your bravery."

Melinda laughed. "I think I am brave because I am poor. If I were rich I daresay I wouldn't have to be nearly as brave."

Again they heard Lindley calling for him.

Mr. Rochfort ducked his head and groaned somewhat dramatically. "I am in no haste to lose another hand of cards to your brother, Miss Goodheart. I swear he is out to empty my pockets. Let us slip away before he comes for me."

So she let him take her arm and tuck it under his as they slipped away, hiding behind the hedges and green bean canes until they were safely around the corner and out of Lindley's view.

"Now you must tell me... was that you I saw mounting a ladder very early this morning, Miss Goodheart? I happened to wake early, and when I glanced out of my window, there you were climbing the side of the house in your pinafore and with a rag tied, turban-like around your head! I thought my eyes must be deceiving me!"

She sighed. "I'm afraid it was me, yes. Some of the spouts are blocked with leaves and old bird's nests." Melinda pointed up at the stone gargoyle faces

166

that kept guard at the corners of the building, their gaping mouths meant to let rainwater flow from the roof. "A few are too high for me, even with a ladder."

"Gracious, Miss Goodheart! You must not attempt such repairs yourself. I shall get my man, Moone, to do it, if there are no other outside servants."

But from what she had seen of Moone he would not be at all keen. To give him menial tasks, or indeed any physical labor, would probably make him even more churlish than he was already. Melinda said nothing. She always hesitated to ask for help because men, in her experience, seldom completed a task as she would want it done. Or even at all. There were, for example, entire wings of the house that were left unfinished by various males of previous generations— men with ambition and imagination, but no lasting resolve and very little willpower.

"Has Mr. Moone been long in your employ?" she asked.

"Oh, no, just a few days."

"I see." That could explain why the post did not seem to suit the man very well.

He patted her hand where it rested on his sleeve. "You must write out a list of repairs and I shall see to it that he gets them done. He might as well put himself to some use."

"That is too kind of you, Mr. Rochfort," she muttered doubtfully.

"Not at all! You must worry about nothing, my dear lady. Leave it all in my hands. It is the least I can do. If I can, in any way, lighten your burden whilst I am here, I am at your disposal, Miss Goodheart."

He spoke very proudly and confidently. Had she not already experienced his idea of "helping", she might have believed his promise. Alas, however well-meaning his words, he was clearly more ornamental than he was practical use.

As they walked on, she heard her brother calling impatiently for his friend, but Mr. Rochfort ignored it and gave Melinda every twinkle of his dashing attention.

"Make haste, Miss Goodheart!" he whispered, tugging her closer and lengthening his stride. "I believe your spirit of rebellion has influenced me already for the better. I am feeling quite terribly willful and determined to escape."

Chapter Fourteen

"What the devil is that bitter hag doing in my kitchen?" her father demanded. "I didn't ask her to come back."

"No, but I did," Melinda replied firmly.

"Who gave you the right to meddle, girl?"

"Father, we have a guest and he must be fed. If it was only Lindley, it wouldn't matter, but we do not want Mr. Rochfort to think we Goodhearts inhospitable, do we? I'm sure he's accustomed to the finest dinners, and my cooking might accidentally poison the gentleman."

Sir Ludlow had nothing to say to that and could only content himself with a little grumble under his breath, for he had already taken a liking to his son's friend. Mr. Rochfort had proven that he could drink a vast amount of wine and still— with the help of his fashionable cane— remain partially upright. He also knew exactly what to say to placate and impress the old man, which was never an easy task. Hopefully his presence would keep her father in an even temper, for a while at least.

"Father, where is the box of jewelry left to me by Grandmother Ethelreda Goodheart? I should like to look at it again. It's been years since I last saw it."

"Lindley has it. He asked to look at it this morning."

Her heart sank. "It is not his to touch. I wish you would tell him, father." But her plea fell upon deaf ears, of course.

"Your brother knows about jewelry. He has an

eye for it."

"He has an eye for taking what is not his."

"We're going to get you married, my girl, and those beads will have to help us now."

She took a calming breath and smoothed both hands over her pinafore. "About the five hundred pounds, father."

"What about it?"

"I know it was meant for a dowry, but I——"

"You can give over whining, for I haven't got five hundred spare at present." His brows lowered like heavy rain clouds. "This house takes every penny to keep maintained."

Now her head ached. "You spent my dowry?"

With his bandaged foot stuck out before him, he rolled his chair over to the nearest window, rapidly bumping the wheels across the uneven stone floor as if he had somewhere important to go. "I needed coin, and it was all I had to hand at the time." One clawed hand proudly stroked the thick fur collar of his cloak. "There were naught else to be done. We needed to put on a good face for your brother's friend. Like I told that Rimple woman, money has to be spent to make money."

She frowned. "You spent my dowry on a new cloak?"

"Part of it. Five hundred wasn't going to get you anywhere, girl. And I have appearances to maintain, especially with your brother bringing guests of that caliber here to Kingsthorpe Park." Glancing back over his shoulder, he added, "Don't screw up yer face like a sick cat. We'll scrape together some coin for a dowry when the time comes. I'll sell that bull if I have

170

to. He's got a fine pedigree has that bull."

"Perhaps you should hold onto him then," she cried. "I daresay he's worth more than I."

"Certainly don't complain as much."

Once again she felt deflated. One of the Montgolfier brothers' hot air balloons punctured and drifting to earth.

"Stop your squawking, girl, and look about you. If you play the game right, you'll soon have more than five hundred pounds to spend. Your brother's brought this daft, rich feller to Kingsthorpe for you, so don't make a pig's ear of this opportunity, like you do all the others."

"Brought him here for me? What can you mean?"

"We knew you couldn't get one for yerself, so be grateful to Lindley. This feller is worth a very pretty penny. It was lucky he fell into our hands. Now go and polish your cheeks and put on your best frock. Get out of that ol' dust-rag pinafore and start acting like a young lady instead of a housemaid."

Really, it should not be such a surprise. Lindley had pushed her down a treacherous, snowy hill on a tray in the dark before. This was just an adult version of the same entertainment for him. She'd known her brother for twenty-one years, and he had never changed. He was heartless and utterly selfish.

As she left the hall in frustration, Mr. Rochfort met her in the passage and in his hands he carried the very box she sought. Her first panicked thought was that he might have overheard their conversation, but, even if he had, he was too gentlemanly to mention it.

"Perhaps you are looking for this, Miss

Goodheart? Your brother took it out to show me today. I thought I had better return it to you," he lowered his voice apologetically, "before any further disaster befalls the family treasures."

Relieved she took the carved box, checked it over swiftly for any signs of damage, and thanked him. "Not that we can truly call them treasures. I'm sure they're not worth much at all, but they *are* mine."

"Indeed. And you should have them."

Her heart warmed further toward the gentleman. It was not his fault that her father and brother had formed expectations without consulting her. And probably not consulting *him* either. She could only hope the gentleman was oblivious to her family's motives. They were not subtle but he was, fortunately, not the sharpest of blades.

"And there is something more you should know, Miss Goodheart. I hesitate to tell you, but the crimson stone your brother took from the clasp— whether it was genuine or not I couldn't say— but I saw him use it to pay a gambling debt quite recently. I did not know then that it belonged to you, or I would have prevented it. I foolishly believed it to be Lindley's."

She sighed. "I had suspected as much of its fate. But thank you."

It was pleasant to feel as if she had an ally in the house for once.

That afternoon, as the daylight faded, Melinda went to her room to dress for dinner. She took the box of jewelry with her and examined the remaining pieces, holding each one up to a candle. As a little girl she had thought them all magical, perhaps because she was so seldom allowed to touch them. She had expected their luster to fade in the time between, but it had not. Not for her. The gold had chipped off in places, the "pearls" themselves needed cleaning, and there was a large empty setting where that beautiful stone once sat, but in Melinda's eyes this jewelry was still precious. All the more so because it was left to her by their grandmother.

"You must look beyond what is apparent," Ethelreda would say to Melinda, patting her on the head. "Turn your eye to the unexpected, little one. That of most value often goes unnoticed."

Everybody else dismissed the old lady's ramblings, but Melinda had not forgotten her smiling green eyes, or her love of rhubarb, secrets, and extravagant wigs. A lady after her own heart.

It was Ethelreda who had told her where all the secret chambers in the house were located— "priest holes" and hiding-places, some of which even Melinda's father knew nothing about. Ethelreda had understood that sometimes a woman needed escape from the injustice and incompetence of the world that surrounded her.

She closed the box and ran a hand over the rough pattern carved across the lid. The heavy box had been made especially to hold this jewelry, so her grandmother had said, and it was crafted for this purpose by a local carpenter— another Rimple, as it happened— now long since dead. It was a well made, sturdy box, and while that rustic, somewhat primitive attempt at decoration across the lid exposed the carpenter's lack of skill in delicate artistry, it also revealed his desire to please and make something pretty for the lady who commissioned the work. He was probably more at ease making simple coffins, cupboards and stools. But her grandmother would have paid handsomely for the work and no doubt she wanted to give the task to a local man. That was the sort of lady she was.

Dear Grandmother Ethelreda. Her beloved jewelry— over which such care had been taken to preserve it for future generations— did not deserve the indignity of Lindley poking it apart to see how much coin he might get for it.

He would not put his unworthy hands upon it again. Wax-filled glass or not, she would hide it, as she should have done before.

She shook her head as she thought of her brother taking the box out to look the contents over and then showing it to his friend. What must Mr. Rochfort have thought? It was bad enough that he should hear them quarreling about her dowry, but that he should also be subjected to her father and brother thrusting her at him, like an old piece of furniture they wanted rid of, was truly shameful.

But how like Lindley to drag one of his gambling acquaintances there and expect wealth to be inducement enough for his sister, even though she had always insisted that nothing less than true love would ever lead her to the altar. He didn't listen to her any more than he'd ever listened to Grandmother Ethelreda. For Lindley and their father, marriage was a matter of business, a bargain to be struck, and Melinda was another part of the estate, property that ought to be disposed of in any way that most benefitted their pockets.

* * * *

Hattie Rimple, two of her cousins, and her young nephew Samuel, had soon brought noisy life back to the kitchen. Melinda hastened to offer her own services as soon as she was dressed that evening, but Hattie had everything in hand, as she always did.

Furthermore, she had brought other assistance, of an unexpected sort.

As Melinda stood by the fire discussing the dinner menu with Hattie, the outside door opened and Mr. Caulfield came in carrying an empty bucket. He paused to wipe his boots on the iron scraper.

"I found some treats you can give to them, like you asked, sir," Hattie called out. "Mo, show Mr. Caulfield those carrots and wind-fallen apples in the larder, will you?"

Melinda stared in surprise.

"The gentleman heard that you were in want of a groom, so he offered to lend a hand," said Hattie. "It seems he has some experience with the beasts, and he's not afraid of a little work."

She didn't know what to say. He gave her a nod and then followed Mo into the larder. Hattie added, "He was most eager to help. Such a pleasant, unfussy gentleman and— why the face, madam? He said you invited him."

"Yes, but, I invited him here to *dine*, not to tend the horses!"

The housekeeper gave an easy shrug. "He wanted to do it— volunteered as soon as he came back to the inn today— and if I were you I wouldn't protest. Somebody needs to look after the beasts."

That was true; it did solve another problem for her. However, she knew he was *not* a groom and it felt very odd to make use of him as such. He had not wanted to come in earlier and had seemed rather annoyed with Melinda, but now he put himself to work for her. What could be the meaning of it? He had already "saved" her enough times.

She looked around the kitchen and saw that Mr. Rochfort's valet still lurked in a corner of the kitchen, reading the paper and picking his teeth, both feet up on a stool. While the clatter of work went on around him he appeared impervious. In that warm corner he took his leisure while another gentleman, who had no obligation to do so, found work voluntarily.

"Mr. Moone, are you not needed to dress your master for dinner?" Melinda asked coolly.

The unpleasant fellow did not look up from his paper. "My *master*," his lip curled, "will call me when he feels like it. I don't need a chit of a girl to give me orders." He turned a page and read on, unmoved. Clearly, Mr. Rochfort had yet to pass along that list of much-needed repairs she gave to him earlier. Or else he had, and Moone's reaction was exactly as expected.

Mr. Caulfield walked by her again with a full bucket of oats and scraps for the horses.

"Thank you for coming to our rescue, sir," she called out.

Whether he heard or not above the clanging pots she could not be sure, for he bowed his head, ducked through a steam cloud, and vanished through the door to the garden.

Hattie sidled up to her and whispered, "See? Shy. Just as I said."

"Well, do not get any match-making ideas for the poor fellow while he's here."

"I'm sure the thought never passed this mind of mine."

"Harriet Rimple, I am familiar with that gleam in your eye! I have been the subject of your romantic experiments in the past. Remember the curate who was here two years ago? The one you decided was the man for me? He went grey overnight and required a three-month convalescence by the sea once you were done with him."

Hattie's entire frame shook with the vibrations of her good humor. "Oh, I've given up on you. And that unhappy Mr. Caulfield needs a good girl, not a wicked, devious miss. You'd be the worst possible choice for him. Especially if he wants to keep that lovely thick head of hair on his head, because if he had to live long with you, he'd resort to tearing it out by the handful."

Melinda realized she'd been picking a loose thread from the lace around her puffed sleeve. *Did he have good hair?* She hadn't noticed.

She could say nothing about Lady Clara, of course. He was such a guarded, private man, and it would be up to him to tell, if and when he wanted to.

Hattie thought him shy, but *she* knew he had words to say when he wanted. He simply chose them well and sometimes they pricked like daggers.

Silly, irrational girl, for instance.

Clutching a rolling pin, she followed Hattie around the table. "You make me sound quite impossible. Am I so very bad?" She always meant well, but people, it seemed, failed to take that into account.

"You are," came the brisk reply, "and I daresay it's too late now to change. But you can roll out that pastry, if you want to make a start on improvement."

Melinda barely heard. She put down the rolling pin and picked up a knife. "Well, I'm relieved to hear that I am *not* the subject of your cunning marital schemes anymore."

"You have other plans, so I hear. Bonnets, eh? There's an odd thing to wager your future upon. What does your father think about that?"

"It doesn't matter what he thinks, for I am resolved. As Mr. Rochfort agrees, a lady should know her own mind and not be swayed."

"Oh, well then, you've got it all sorted out, haven't you?"

"Yes." She glanced over at the door through which Mr. Caulfield had gone. It was good of him to help with the horses and she should thank him for it. She knew nobody else would.

"I hear your handsome Mr. Rochfort has no shortage of admirers down in the village already. My cousin said he flirted with all the girls on his way through yesterday. Not very discerning it seems. Anything in a petticoat catches his eye. I wouldn't think there is anything special or meaningful in his attention, if I were you. As my mother used to say, a stray dog will go with anybody who feeds it."

Melinda scowled at her reflection in the knife's blade and found an unruly curl that required fixing. "Poor Mr. Rochfort. He told me himself that flirting is a habit of his. He cannot help being so amiable and charming. So open about his faults and accepting of other folk's."

"Is that so? Got you eating out of his hand already, has he? Aye. With that handsome face he can be forgiven much."

"Is he handsome? I'm sure I barely noticed." Giving up on that stubborn curl of hair, she used the knife to spear an apple from the pile that stood ready to make a pie. "He is genial company. An uncomplicated sort of man."

"Simple-headed in other words. I suppose you think you could pull the fleece over his eyes, but he'd be the one pulling it over yours. There's none so clever as those who act stupid."

"Mr. Rochfort is a very pleasant gentleman and I like him."

"Why's that then? I know you're not impressed by wealth, so it must be that he agreed with one of your ideas and told you that you're in the right, eh?"

She bit her tongue. "No." When Hattie merely looked at her in that knowing way, she added crossly, "And I have nothing more to say on the subject of Mr. Rochfort."

"Fellow reminds me of my Uncle Walter," Hattie muttered from the side of her mouth. "He were a sly fellow and could change his manners to suit the person he wanted to please. He was the *charming* sort too. Of course it did him no favors when my aunt caught him with one of his fancy strumpets. He didn't know who to please then and got a slapping from all sides."

Once again Melinda looked over at the door through which Mr. Caulfield had gone with his bucket of scraps. "There is nothing amiss with being friendly and sociable. Some men, on the other hand, are the naturally *unfriendly*, complicated, unsociable sort, and one can only guess what they are thinking, because they give out no clues whatsoever. And guessing is not good when one has a vivid imagination."

Ouch! She'd cut her finger while pulling the apple from the knife point.

Hattie reached over and took the large blade from Melinda's hand, tut-tutting as she did so. "Let's not have any bloodshed while we have guests in the house, eh? Not all over your best frock. I'd better peel the apples myself."

Chapter Fifteen

Washing horses in the stable yard, Heath was thoroughly absorbed in the task when he heard the clang of an iron gate and footsteps. He looked up to see who it was, and the distant shape emerging from the garden wall was immediately recognizable. In haste he fumbled for his leather gloves where he'd set them aside on a hay bale to keep dry. Covering his wooden fingers was the first consideration, then he scrambled for his shirt, where he'd hung it over the door of a loose box. Alarmed to be caught in a state of undress, he jerked it over his head, aware that the linen would now become wet and soiled, but having no choice in the matter.

"Miss Goodheart, I thought you would all be at dinner," he exclaimed, breathless. It was colder that evening and darker now. He worked by the glow of a brazier and several rush torches placed in iron sconces along the stable wall. But even by this dim, changeable light he saw at once the heightened color in her face and knew she had observed more of his bared form than a young, unmarried lady should. "Forgive me," he muttered, "I did not expect—"

"It's quite all right, Mr. Caulfield," she interrupted in a high rush of chatter. "I told you once before that I am not a fading lily. The sight of a naked male chest, while terrifying and scandalous for a girl of weaker constitution, leaves me quite..." he heard her pause to bite into an apple, "quite indifferent."

They stood for a moment, saying nothing. Chewing on her apple, she had halted a few steps away from him, a gentle breeze blowing the hem of her dark blue gown against her ankles, and toying with the fringe of a light shawl that she wore around her shoulders. A cluster of coppery ringlets danced against her cheeks, catching the flickering darts of fire light from the brazier.

"Should you eat that before dinner?" he muttered. "It could spoil your appetite."

"Not mine. My old headmistress used to say I have the appetite, as well as the grace, of a carthorse. And she was quite right."

Something about her was different tonight, he realized. Ah, yes, her stitches were all in their place— so far— there was no mud, no impatient dashing about, and her hair was arranged in tidy curls. Miss Goodheart looked like a "normal" young lady this evening. If there could be such a thing.

He was still not deceived into believing her harmless, however. Her eyes held a pert, mischievous challenge and her lips were lopsided just enough that even in repose they appeared ready to laugh or throw out a flippant comment.

Miss Goodheart lacked the usual meekness and gentility expected in a young lady, for she was boldly unpredictable— even brazen. There were, indeed, many reasons to regard her with suspicion, not the least of which was the fact that she stood before him eating an apple. It suddenly struck Heath as quite indecent for a young lady to stand in public chewing an apple. Could it be the similarity to Eve that caused the act to seem so improper?

Perhaps sensing his unease, the mare at his side gave a low whinny and shook its mane. Grateful of the excuse to put his hands to work, he gently patted the animal's neck and offered a carrot from the bucket.

"So you possess an affinity with horses, sir," she said at last. "And experience as a groom, Hattie tells me."

"Just as well, is it not, when some gentlemen never bother to visit the stables, and ride around with four good beasts they know and care nothing about?"

"I —"

"Four good beasts they drive almost into the ground in their desire to travel at reckless speed," he added. Ah, he had not meant for that to come out. Too late, it had. Those who abused their horses happened to hit one of his sore points. "And some men serve in the cavalry, as I did, where they must learn to tend the animal themselves, to keep it in good health and spirits. Vital for their own safety as well as the horse's."

"I was about to say, sir, that I quite agree. I too am fond of horses. So we have found something to concur upon, at least."

He relaxed his shoulders. "Ah."

Like him, horses were often nothing more to most people than beasts of burden, something seldom thought about until they defied the whip and leapt a fence they shouldn't. But he didn't want to find her *too* agreeable or like-minded, so he sought a change of subject. He cleared his throat.

"I see Mr. Rochfort's man is of little use about the place."

"To put it lightly. He causes more work than he relieves."

183

"And he reads the newspaper. It is rare to find servants who read. They are usually discouraged from an education of that kind, are they not?"

"My father never wanted a house servant who might be capable of reading his correspondence and knowing all his business." She paused, put her chin up. "But Mr. Rochfort is a pleasant gentleman, who would never hold anybody back from bettering themselves."

The tone of admiration in her voice was evident.

"He says people should stand to their guns, even women," she added. "Mr. Rochfort agrees with me that women ought to be given more freedom to do as they please."

"Mr. Rochfort sounds entertaining. And loquacious. Hardly seems to have had time to say all that. In just a day."

"He is a friendly gentleman. The sort with which one can be at ease very quickly. Consequently, I feel as if I've known him longer already."

A typical rake and charlatan, in other words, ingratiating himself with the lady of the house. But Heath said nothing.

A sudden memory of this woman dangling from a drainpipe returned to remind him of her reckless and impulsive nature. He shook his head and continued brushing the horse's mane.

After a pause, she said, "It is very good of you to help, sir. My father's groom left some time ago, along with the last of the farm horses." She walked over to where he stood and rubbed the horse's muzzle with a gentle hand. "I remember when these stables were full of magnificent hunters and darling, sweet-natured

Shires, but of course they are all gone now, sold off one by one."

He watched her plant a soft kiss on the mare's muzzle and felt a sudden, burning heaviness in his chest. He took a quick breath. Back to business. "Sir Ludlow no longer farms his land?"

"A few acres have been sold off, and he leases the rest to a local farmer in exchange for a portion of the harvest profit. He won't sell it all because he still expects to leave Kingsthorpe to my brother one day." She sighed. "Not that Lindley cares. He has no interest in this place and would rather travel. Doubtless he will sell it all one day, or wager it away, without a thought for our proud ancestry. Still, my father maintains a fantasy of Lindley taking his rightful place as the next master of Kingsthorpe. And we all have one of those, do we not?"

"One what?"

"A fantasy."

Heath was amused. "I do not."

In the flickering light of the brazier her face took on an unlikely tint of angelic gold, as if she had just stepped out of a medieval fresco. She raised her eyebrows. "Why not?"

"Real life takes up too much of my time."

"That sounds very dull."

He scratched the side of his nose. "Yes, I think we've already established what you think of me."

She laughed at that, even though he had not meant it to be funny.

"And what does Sir Ludlow plan for his only daughter?"

"A drowning, in all probability," she quipped.

When he raised his eyebrows, she added reluctantly, "He desires that I should marry, preferably a rich, elderly man who is not in possession of his full wits."

"And what do you want?" Again he saw her clinging to that drainpipe, worrying about the fate of her best slippers. "What is *your* fantasy, madam?"

Her eyes brightened even more, swirling with those errant fireflies. "A life of daring adventure. A legion of handsome young lovers. And a little hat shop." She took another bite of her apple, loud and crisp.

Heath quickly looked down and away, rubbing a hand over his mouth.

"Pardon, sir?" she demanded crisply.

"I said, I wish you the best of fortune with those ideas."

She fussed with her shawl. "You will stay to dine, I hope? Since you are here."

"I only came for the horses." He gestured at his loose, damp, stained shirt. "I am not dressed for dinner, Miss Goodheart."

"Then tuck in your shirt, button your waistcoat and don your dusty coat. I can assure you, nobody is very particular at our table and that will be more than sufficient."

He considered it. Rochfort would be at dinner too, of course. A perfect opportunity to meet the scoundrel, face to face.

"You must be in need of sustenance," she continued. "After all your hard work here with the horses, dinner is the least we could offer in return."

"I was not expecting payment, madam. I came for the horses."

"Oh, don't be such a stick-in-the-mud," she exclaimed merrily. "Just come to dinner."

"Why would you want me there?"

"To interrogate you, of course, and find out all your secrets. The great mystery of Mr. Caulfield... and his *fruit*."

He glared.

"I hope you have studied the subject, because you might be tested."

"You test me already, Miss Goodheart," he muttered, turning and tipping a bucket of dirty water away over the cobbles.

"I don't suppose I'll ever know why you are really here."

"I suppose not."

"Good lord, sir, you are the most taciturn and guarded of creatures!"

"And you are the most unguarded."

For a woman who claimed to have enough problems and concerns to make his "dull hair curl", she was remarkably light-hearted and enthusiastic about life. The sort of person around whom he usually beat a wide path. Although he supposed that could be said of most folk he encountered.

"Hold still, sir," she exclaimed suddenly. At the same moment she reached up toward his face and, not knowing what she meant to do, he disobeyed her command, somehow resulting in a collision of her fingers with his lips. She was not wearing gloves. He tasted apple. And a hint of blood. Surely a warning if ever there was one.

But she had only reached for a stray horsehair that was stuck to his cheek.

"Well, really," she chuckled, "I did not intend to hurt you."

"I didn't know that, did I? My history with you lends itself to another conclusion."

"Mr. Caulfield, I can assure you that when I mean to land a punch or poke you in the eye you will be made fully aware of my intentions several moments before I raise a hand. I am not a person who intentionally disguises their thoughts or their feelings. I give my opponent fair warning."

"Hmm. I notice you said *when* not *if* you mean to poke me in the eye."

"See," she replied with an arch grin, "now you have even greater forewarning."

Another pain seized his chest, but quickly dulled to an ache this time. A yearning. He turned away, and discreetly let the tip of his tongue sweep over his lower lip.

"You said you were a cavalry man," she continued in a more serious tone. "Is that how you were wounded?"

"Yes."

"I am sorry."

"Are you?"

There was a pause and then she exclaimed, "You needn't be afraid to talk of it to me. I am not squeamish in the least. When one has had so many scrapes as I, one cannot afford to be."

"There is not much to tell, Miss Goodheart. It was a battle. I was shot in the hand. I subsequently lost two of my fingers. Many men lost more than that."

She nodded. "You manage very well despite the

loss."

"I find ways to compensate."

"And you prefer other people not to know of it."

"Yes."

"You don't like people to know much at all, do you?"

"Makes life easier."

"Easier?"

"Folk pass quickly in and out of my life. It is not necessary that they become acquainted with the minutia. It would waste their time and mine."

Her eyes opened wide, two somber pools of deep, rich toffee. "Mr. Caulfield, you must be the oddest person I've ever met."

"Likewise."

As she reached to pat the horse again, her shawl casually dropped from one arm to reveal that her evening dress showed much more flesh than her day gowns. The dancing torchlight caressed her exposed skin with a soft, teasing touch, a blush of color that drew his gaze. He could see every breath she took, even imagine the gentle pulse at the side of her neck. When he made the nervous mistake of licking his lips again, a very light wisp of her perfume, left there by the accidental brush of her fingers, greeted the tip of his tongue. The effect was not unlike the kick of Tom Rimple's cider.

Too much skin was displayed. She ought to be wearing gloves. And a lace tuck for modesty.

"I believe I just heard your stomach complaining, Mr. Caulfield," she said, looking up at him with warm concern, "so I have my proof that you're hungry."

A lady, of course, would not have mentioned it,

but she did. Could not even pretend that she hadn't heard the growling.

"I daresay, burnt sausages are the only thing you've had all day."

True. But he'd lasted for days on less before.

The deciding factor was not his hunger. No, it was Rochfort. That villain would have the unhindered pleasure of admiring Miss Goodheart's attributes tonight, if Heath was not there to spoil his entertainment in some way. So what choice did he have? The practiced seducer would have no luck while Heath was at hand to cause an obstruction.

This woman needed rescue and, as he had told her before, it was his duty to aid a female in distress. Good thing he didn't need to be asked, because he knew she never would.

* * * *

"Since you insist, and I cannot otherwise be rid of you it seems, I will come to dinner."

"Excellent!" Melinda felt pleased with herself for persuading him; clearly that was no easy mission. She gathered up the fallen end of her shawl, because as he turned away again, taking his stern gaze from her, she felt a chilly breeze across her shoulders. The temperature had certainly dropped this evening. "Fancy thinking you could simply tend the horses and leave again, without allowing me to show my appreciation, Mr. Caulfield."

"Show your... appreciation," he grumbled, shaking his head.

"What could you have been thinking to assume I'd let you tend my guest's horses and then send you on your way? We may be country folk, but we still have manners and some social graces. What would your young lady think of us if we did not invite you to dine, sir, but let you go hungry?"

His head snapped around. "My young lady?" He stared, his eyes dark between the fluttering shadows.

"Lady Clara, of course!"

"Oh. Yes." He looked down at his stained shirt.

"I am glad Lady Clara does not pass in and out of your life like everybody else," Melinda continued with a smile. "She must be special indeed, since only she is allowed to remain."

He sniffed, unrolling his shirt sleeves.

"Does *she* know all your secrets, I wonder?"

"More than most," he muttered, still no smile in response to hers.

Melinda felt a sudden twinge of envy, but banked it quickly. She swallowed. "We eat promptly at seven, and my father is very disagreeable if he has to wait."

He nodded, shrugging into his waistcoat.

She had started to turn away, but she stopped and looked at him again. "You will come in, won't you? You won't run away?"

"Why, exactly, would I run away?"

She considered thoughtfully. "I do not know. There is something of a wounded, wild animal about you. A fear of being brought indoors and domesticated."

He stared. The mare turned her head to give him a nudge, as if to say, "*Why have you stopped petting me?*"

Afraid to keep looking at him and noticing his fine head of hair, Melinda hurried back to the gate in the garden wall, her pulse beating with a strange sort of excitement.

Hattie would probably try to make something significant out of her wish to invite Mr. Caulfield to dinner, she thought, but it was nothing more than civil gratitude for his help, and a desire to show him that, even if he thought he didn't need one, he had a friend. He and Lady Clara would have her assistance and her loyalty. It was decided. There were few things she enjoyed better than solving other people's problems, especially if they were fighting against society's rules. And fighting for love was the noblest of causes.

She opened the gate and looked back, once more, to watch him pet the dappled mare again. His gloved hands ran smoothly over its mane as he whispered to the animal. Ears pricked, it let out a soft whinny, head nodding.

Yes, he had a way with the horses.

Another cool breeze brushed Melinda's skin, and even tickled in some peculiar places beneath her corset. It was very fortunate that this timid, secretive suitor had Lady Clara waiting so patiently for him, or else a certain vivid imagination might have been tempted...

But no, as Hattie had said, the man would not have a moment's peace with a woman like her. He was much better off with the quiet, elegant, and accomplished Lady Clara.

He gently stroked the mare's silver mane again.

Hugging her shawl tighter across her bosom, hoping she wasn't due to catch a chill, Melinda continued on her way.

Chapter Sixteen

"This is Mr. Caulfield, who once caught me when I fell from a drainpipe," was her idea of an introduction.

And nobody seemed surprised by it.

Her brother chortled. "If the fellow caught you, why didn't he bloody keep you?"

At the far end of the table, her father was a shrunken figure with black hair that hung long and lank to his shoulders, and was surprisingly devoid of grey. Framed by the amber glow of the great fireplace and clad in a long, burgundy robe with a fur collar, he seemed, like his house, to belong to another time. "What's this one want from us then?" he muttered, staring with hard, gleaming eyes.

"Not everybody wants something from us, father. Mr. Caulfield came to help us with Mr. Rochfort's horses. He has a fondness for the animals and experience in grooming. Since he declines payment for his services, I invited him to dine with us."

The others were already seated around the table. Although all heads turned in his direction, Miss Goodheart was the only one who stood to welcome Heath. Candlelight shimmered over her curls as she smiled and gestured for him to take the seat opposite.

Her brother was clearly already drunk and had difficulty focusing on anything for very long. "A groom?" he slurred into his wine glass. "A groom at our table, how very *earthy* we have become. Is this some form of fashionable charity? I heard something about that ladies' academy turning out revolutionaries and now I see the proof."

"Mr. Caulfield is not a groom." She hesitated, and Heath suspected she was not certain what to call him. In the end she settled for, "He is a gentleman. And even if he were a groom by profession, there would be nothing amiss with feeding him at our table."

"Oh, indeed! Bring them all in...the Rimple woman and her tribe of slack-jawed nieces, cousins, and stray what-nots from the kitchens too. Why the devil not?"

"Please do sit, Mr. Caulfield," she said, "and I will let Hattie know we're ready for the soup." He admired the way she ignored Lindley. It must take considerable restraint not to slap the back of the slovenly cad's head as he bent over his glass. Or else she had put up with it for so long that she no longer noticed.

Once the bell had been rung, she proceeded with the other introductions.

"This is my father, of course, Sir Ludlow Goodheart. And this is Mr. Rochfort, a friend of my brother's."

To Heath it felt as if time slowed so that everything moved through thick treacle. For a while he heard nothing, his head filled with an echoing ring.

So here before him at last was "John Croft", the fellow who had seduced his sister, persuaded her to run away with him to London, and then, when he discovered that their father would never condone a marriage to him, even under the most necessary circumstances— that no dowry would ever be granted—had abandoned her utterly.

John Croft was exactly what he had expected. Exactly as Clara had described. A primped, pretty, fashionable fellow with affected manners. Heath could now add a sly countenance to that description.

Anger stabbed at him, a white-hot knife plunging through his gut and twisting.

Had his sister been so lost and lonely at home, so neglected and unloved, that she turned to the first man who crept in and showed her attention? This dandy? He knew the answer to that, of course. The lack of familial affection at Beauspur Rising was undeniable. While it had rendered Heath wary of anybody's affection, it had led his younger sister in the opposite direction— to cling desperately where she found any little sign of it.

But he took a deep breath, forced the fury down. Remembered what he was there to do— catch the "Cuckoo" in the act, before he got away again and disappeared into another identity.

The sound at last returned to his ears, and time quickened to its normal pace.

Sir Ludlow continued boring holes into Heath's face with those strangely intense eyes. "You're a visitor to the county, sir?" he snapped out.

"I am."

"Mr. Caulfield has taken lodgings at Tipsy Rimple's smithy," said Miss Goodheart. "Imagine my surprise when I saw him there today and remembered that we met before." She shot him a little smile, eyes simmering beneath her lashes. "Many years ago, while I was in mid-air."

"Indeed?" Rochfort looked at him, the foolish

grin sliding off his face.

"And oddly enough he rescued me on another occasion too, when my purse was stolen in the street. He gallantly retrieved it for me, because I am, of course, a helpless woman, in need of a firm hand to protect me."

"I shouldn't think there was anything in your purse anyway," Lindley muttered. "Nothing of value."

"If there were, you would have taken it already, is that not so, brother dear?"

The sloth-like fellow merely turned up his lip and burped.

"But the fact that I had so little in my purse makes Mr. Caulfield even more gallant for coming to my rescue," she continued. "Someone like you, Lindley, wouldn't think it worth his while, but Mr. Caulfield considers it his gentlemanly duty to save ladies in distress. Even if there is no reward in it for him and even if they can save themselves."

"Damn fellow has his work cut out for him if he means to run around saving you," Lindley mumbled.

"I have advised him not to make a habit of it." She smiled again at Heath, and he felt that odd twinge in his stomach again. But the knife had gone and some soothing elixir went about the business of healing his wound.

How easily she smiled at a stranger, even one who discouraged her.

Suddenly he awoke to the fact that Rochfort was squinting hard at him, clearly very curious. Dangerously so. Heath quickly picked up his spoon for the soup.

"Miss Goodheart was telling me today, Sir

Ludlow, that your family has owned this land for centuries."

"Aye. Since Hubert de Bon Coeur fought alongside Edward 'Longshanks' against the Scots. When he took a fancy to a highborn wench at court, her family only agreed to the match if he changed his name to Goodheart and so he did."

"A peculiar lot apparently," grumbled his son, "to prefer the oh-so plain and pedestrian *Goodheart* to the flare and luster of *de Bon Coeur*. What man would change his name just to claim a woman, in any case? He must have been an idiot. I'm thinking of reverting to the original."

"Of course," his sister remarked, "it's all about the surface with you. Why not try living up to the name for once, instead of worrying how it sounds?"

Rochfort intervened, turning to her with a smile, "Ah, and so the dynasty was built on love, Miss Goodheart."

Her father grunted, "Love? Pah! They say she were a mute with a large dowry and good birthing hips. That's three reasons to like the wench, but I doubt love came into it. Only women as thick as my useless daughter believe in that."

For a moment they all ate in silence.

"Let's toast to mute wenches," Lindley slurred, raising his wine glass. "The best kind of woman. Pity parliament cannot pass a law to render them all silent."

Heath thought of his sister and looked up to find Miss Goodheart watching him with sympathy and concern. He almost jumped out of his seat when she chirped anxiously, "Mr. Caulfield has an interest in history and architecture."

It was a clumsy diversion, of course, but with the best of intentions. To save his feelings. Again, something to which he was unaccustomed.

Her brother snorted. "So you're a scholar, in addition to your love of grooming horses?"

"I do not find the two interests mutually exclusive," Heath replied carefully. "At least, not in my case."

"See, brother dear, some men are capable of doing two things at once and caring about something other than themselves."

Rochfort set down his glass, looking from Miss Goodheart to Heath. "History and architecture?"

"Yes. The countryside hereabouts is very beautiful with many ancient sites, I understand."

The villain dripped with more smiles. They blossomed, fell off him and blossomed again as easily as sweat from the forehead of a guilty man. "I see why you were lured here, sir. So much wild abundance and natural beauty."

Heath did not return the smiles. "Yes. I look forward to my explorations."

"And how long do you mean to stay?"

He shrugged. "As long as need be. And you, sir?"

Rochfort's jaw sharpened, and he glanced across at Lindley Goodheart. "I know not. It depends."

For a short while there was nothing other than the sound of spoons against bowls. Apparently they were all hungry.

Then Rochfort spoke up again. "You met Miss Goodheart when she was in London at the ladies' academy, sir?" The casual tone did not fool Heath.

The fellow was evidently perturbed to find another gentleman guest at that table. One *she* had invited.

"I did."

"I was rescuing a hat," she interjected proudly.

Her father frowned, and Lindley burped again. That was, it seemed, the sum total of their interest in her adventures.

"And you were in mid-air?" Rochfort pressed, looking concerned. But as an actor might portray the emotion, turning in his chair and over-reaching as if his expression must be seen from the farthest seat.

"Of course," she replied with a chuckle. "Where else would I be?"

Heath sipped his wine and glanced across the table at her again. Miss Goodheart's hair seemed more vibrant than ever tonight, that lush cornucopia of colors brighter than the fire itself. He felt hot just looking at her. "It was, apparently, a *desperate* situation. *Desperate situations require extreme measures.*"

Her gaze met his, and his blood warmed another degree. "How clever of you to remember that from so long ago!"

"Only a fool would forget the warning." In truth he had never been able to. She hung about his mind like curls of wood smoke from a blocked chimney. Fortunately he liked the smell of wood smoke. Or he was beginning to. He'd never thought about it before.

She looked confused for a moment, then regarded her plate crossly, releasing him from her gaze. Meanwhile, Rochfort grew restless, fidgeting in his seat, a cool glint of annoyance in his stare now as he reached for more wine.

"I would not blame you, sir, if you came to

Kingsthorpe, not to admire the history and architecture, but to cast your gaze upon the delightful Miss Goodheart again." It was a clumsy accusation, badly disguised as teasing humor.

"Oh good lord," she exclaimed, sounding amused, "Mr. Caulfield didn't come here for me. He thinks me the most awful, giddy, and silly young thing. Which I am, of course."

"And that's why you can't get yourself a husband," her father shouted. "Can't make a damned effort, can you? All that money wasted on that blasted school."

"I told you it was throwing good money after bad," his son drawled.

"I were promised a daughter transformed into a lady. I've a mind to get my money back."

"Indeed, father. The only thing they did was feed her."

"And put ideas in her head. As if she hadn't enough o' them already."

"It's quite appalling, father. That ladies' academy misrepresented itself in all those advertisements. You ought to sue. We'll never be rid of her now, and she'll cost more to keep than the sow."

The coarse informality of this conversation about a lady, and before strangers, was astonishing, but only Heath seemed to have any reaction. The others continued their dinner unabated. Miss Goodheart's cheeks darkened, but she hid her embarrassment well, and since Heath was the only one who looked at her, he was, in all likelihood, the only one who noticed that she spilled her soup.

Suddenly he was forced to remember how it had

been at his own family's dining table when the awkward conversation either missed him out completely or was focused on belittling him in some way. Nobody spoke unless his father led the conversation, and if anyone had ever been pleasant toward Heath, or given praise for anything he did, he supposed he would not have known how to react. He might have thought he sat at the wrong family's table.

"Yes, I am an awful drain on you all," she exclaimed, beaming. "I'm sure you'll be glad when I am back with my Desperate Bonnets and you need never think of me again."

So that surely explained the quirk of her lip, ever ready to smile, jest and make light. That was how she defended herself from their rancor— with cheerful, irrepressible optimism. She was bolder than his sister who would have crumpled under their cruel remarks.

Heath felt the need to speak up on her behalf.

"I've heard of very few ladies' academies in London that are capable of providing a sound education. Indeed, many have a reputation for doing the very opposite."

"Education, my arse!" the old man cried. "She weren't there for an education. She were there to learn how to get 'erself a husband and make connections. Failed on both counts. Just two friends she made there, and one of them a foundling charity case at the school— no money and no prospects— the other a newspaperman's daughter who at least had the sense to get herself a knighted naval commander. But what does my daughter do? Goes to work in a bloody hat shop."

Another uncomfortable pause began, broken

201

only by the arrival of the next course. Heath, feeling responsible for the silence, looked around for another subject. "Do you have a library, Sir Ludlow? Your family must have gathered a fine collection over the years."

The old man glared as if Heath had just said something highly offensive, and his daughter hurriedly intervened, "Mr. Caulfield is very fond of books, father. In fact, he carries some around with him wherever he goes."

"Oh aye?" He sniffed. "I suppose he reads alone too. A singular pastime."

"My father does not believe in too much reading," she explained. "He thinks it leads to a warped mind."

"Why should I believe what some gormless feller I don't know, and never will know, scribbles down in some book?" Sir Ludlow yelled. "Bloody monks and trouble-makers, that's who writes books. Never met a monk who wasn't a lyin' cheat and a whoremonger."

"But we could talk about books," she exclaimed eagerly. "That would be a change of topic for our table. Something new. And Mr. Rochfort is a devotee of Lord Byron. Are you not, Mr. Rochfort?"

The fellow mumbled something indistinct, Lindley snorted with amusement and then there was silence again, until Heath said softly, "I do enjoy books, Miss Goodheart. I read for pleasure as well as educating myself."

Sir Ludlow sneered. "And you read alone, no doubt. Silent and in your 'ead. That's how they get you! That's how they get into your brain and plant their wretched ideas."

202

"Most often I read alone, sir, because I am...alone." He stopped then, feeling flushed. Everybody had paused to stare at him, and he was not accustomed to talking about himself. Usually he avoided it. "But I prefer the solitude." He fumbled for his wine glass. "And I do not care for the sound of my own voice so I would rather not read aloud."

He needn't have worried, for he soon realized Sir Ludlow and his son were not that interested in him. His words were lost beneath the cacophony of dogs fighting over scraps thrown to them, and Lindley bellowing for another jug of wine.

But through all the noise, Miss Goodheart studied him thoughtfully, which only deepened the heat in his face.

"You are not at all what I thought you were when we first met," she said finally, adding with a wry little smirk, "You may be very tightly wrapped, but I am unwrapping you slowly, piece by piece."

"May you not be disappointed, madam, by what you find in the end."

"Well, I do know that I was right when I said you must have many more secrets than only two."

He frowned across at her. At least, he thought he frowned, but it did not stop her smile. For a moment, at least.

Then, once again, the fireflies that danced in her eyes dimmed their lights. She seemed puzzled, annoyed with herself. She lifted her wine and took a sip.

For just a moment, Heath had forgotten there was anybody else at the table. He raised a hand to his neck-cloth and loosened it just enough to let the air cool his overheated skin.

She was distracting him again from his purpose there. This was very bad indeed. He only intended to protect her from Rochfort's dangerous clutches, and then capture the villain. It should not become personal. He should not care beyond what was proper and a gentleman's duty.

Yet her eyes drew him ever closer in. Her lilting smile made Heath forget what he was there to do.

The odd thing was, he knew she didn't mean to do it. Melinda Goodheart was not the sort of girl to flirt. She chattered too much and playfully, but she spoke with honesty even if the truth was not pretty. Disguise of any kind would be beyond her. He knew all that already.

She had no interest in him, thought him already spoken for— yes, her little mistake in regard to Clara was amusing, and now he knew what his sister had found so droll about the entire incident. He would probably never live it down.

But if he corrected her misunderstanding it could lead to questions about his sister and with Rochfort in the vicinity he could not risk it. Better avoid the subject altogether.

And then he heard the villain's sharp cough, and Heath realized that he'd allowed his gaze, once again, to settle with too much appreciation upon Miss Goodheart.

Chapter Seventeen

He really must learn to look at life with a little more joy, Melinda thought, studying his grim face through the candlelight, or else he would never win his lady love. He was far too serious about everything. He must learn to unclench that deathly grip on his chords and let the tension ease. As she had said to him today, no woman wants to think that her life will be completely without misadventure.

Poor fellow. It was a good thing she had run into him again, although he did not see it as fortunate, of course.

Sometimes, when he looked at her in that solemn manner, she felt her heart quicken to an excitable beat, which confused her. The only other time she experienced such a sensation was when she saw a freshly baked rhubarb pie, or had the chance to hold a warm and squirming puppy.

She thought of Lady Clara and the gentle, reassuring squeeze of her soft hands in that sunny parlor. The dear lady had the kindest, most hopeful smile. How terrible it must be not to hear, and to rely upon another to communicate accurately for you. For Melinda, accustomed to saying whatever she thought, as soon as she thought it, to live in a world of silence would be intolerable.

Lindley's callous toast to "mute wenches" had brought color to Mr. Caulfield's face and a spark of anger to his eyes, but she was only one who noticed— and, of course, the only one present who knew about Lady Clara. Desperately ashamed of her brother's rude, unfeeling nature, she had almost expired on the spot. Really, she mused darkly, Lindley had been responsible for a great many of her near-death experiences. And even if she had caused him a few in return, at least Melinda's attempts on his life were only in her imagination.

Mr. Rochfort suddenly tapped her arm. "Oh, Miss Goodheart, perhaps you and I might take a ride tomorrow. I should like to go up that little hill you told me about and visit the spring."

"I wouldn't suggest riding your horses tomorrow," Mr. Caulfield interjected. "They need rest after their hard journey. If you don't mind me saying so, sir."

This remark, although uttered without any hint of recrimination, seemed to upset Mr. Rochfort. His voice had a definite edge to it when he replied, "Is that so? Well, I'm sure fresh horses can be found hereabouts."

Across the table, Caulfield speared a slice of roasted pheasant on his fork and said in a quiet voice, "It's harvest time and in the country most beasts are employed in the fields, sir. Not standing idle to be ridden for leisure, I think you'll find."

"I thank you for your advice, sir. But if Miss Goodheart wants to ride, it will be my pleasure to take her out. Horses are meant to be ridden. Miss Goodheart's enjoyment is my first consideration."

"Fortunately you've got two feet to trot along under your own power. You're not incapacitated, and no one has yet whipped you to a state of near exhaustion. Sir."

Melinda felt a slight prick of ice in the formerly

warm air of her father's hall. Mr. Caulfield's face was free of expression as usual, but there was a resolute squaring of his shoulders and a firmness in the way he set down his words. It made her feel as if nothing bad or wrong could ever happen in his presence. Because he would not allow it. She knew now why the horses liked him and why the dappled mare had pushed her muzzle into his hand.

Why Lady Clara waited so patiently.

But it wouldn't do for *her*. No, indeed. To know one sailed on calm waters all the time would surely be wretched. Without the ups and downs of life, it would all be very flat and uninspiring. She would soon be bored with nothing to challenge her mind, nothing to quicken her pulse, and then she might become, like Mr. Rochfort, a fashionable ornament, afraid to move without being told which direction she should take. A life of idle nothingness.

"A walk would suit me, Mr. Rochfort," she hastily assured the man at her side, suddenly breathless. "I prefer it to riding, truth be told."

The debate, she sensed, was merely paused. Both men were like dogs with hackles raised, snarling over the same bone. She wondered why they had taken a disliking to each other so quickly.

Men. Would she ever understand them?

"Mr. Caulfield has some business here," she blurted anxiously. "With fruit."

"What's that? *Fruit?*" Her father scowled down the table.

The gentleman across the table cleared his throat. "I am here to study fruit yield. For the government."

Nobody seemed to know what to say about that.

Lindley groaned, reaching for more wine and pushing his plate of food away. Mr. Rochfort grumbled under his breath about a wine stain on his neck cloth, and her father stared, aghast, as Mr. Caulfield began a long and tedious speech about the importance of a healthy bee population.

And as he spoke, he looked at her as if he suspected she raised that subject with deliberate mischief. It seemed as if he thought that of most things she did, but this was not an uncommon mistake. There were, of course, the features of her face which, even in repose, had caught the sharp tail end of Mrs. Lightbody's wrath, whenever that lady was looking for a culprit.

For a man who did not like the sound of his own voice he certainly spoke at length on the subject of pollination and a healthy bee habitat. His sentences droned on for one of those half hours that feels like half a day. But since nobody else at the table even made a pretense of listening, Melinda occasionally exclaimed, "Goodness," "you don't say?" and "how fascinating" whenever she could squeeze one in.

Finally, having received a hard kick under the table from Lindley she stayed quiet, giving Mr. Caulfield no further encouragement.

* * * *

After dinner, Heath walked with Hattie Rimple, her cousins, and her nephew back to the inn. He had insisted on taking a lantern, which was a very good thing, for although the harvest moon was high and full, lighting their way along the lane quite effectively, every so often there was a shadowy dip or a sharp corner where that glow could not reach. Then the extra light was useful and Hattie continually praised him for thinking to bring it. As if it was, quite possibly, the greatest notion since somebody thought to harness a plow to oxen.

Heath had much to think about that evening, but the good lady liked to talk and so he had little chance of concentrating.

"Miss Melinda tells me I'm not to come up with any match-making schemes for you, sir."

He winced. "Does she?"

"You must know, sir, that any healthy young gentleman who stays a while in Kingsthorpe is bound to become the subject of speculation. Every mother from here to Castlebridge will be throwing her unwed daughters at you, if you're not already taken."

"Me?" The lantern swayed as he helped her around a puddle. "I am not the sort of man likely to become a figure of romantic fancies, surely."

She looked up at him, her face glowing like the moon itself. "You're a man. You're alive. And you're polite, a proper gent. We don't get many like that around here, but we have got a large number of young women desperate enough to take any man with working parts."

Yes, he had noticed an excess of giggling girls in the village that day, clustered wherever he looked, like gangs of loitering, beribboned ruffians. Their overly-sweet fragrance was enough to fog a man's senses at fifty paces. Perhaps, bearing this in mind, he ought to go along with Miss Goodheart's mistaken assumption about Clara. So he said, "Miss Goodheart knows I have a young lady already," and hoped that would be the end of it.

It was not. Naturally.

Hattie was staring at his face. "Well, that is a pity. You may not be rich, but I always say that with the right match a couple can be just as happy without money as they can with it. In most cases, happier." She heaved a deep sigh. "All she's got in front of her now is that preening cock her brother brought home with him."

"You refer to Miss Goodheart and...Mr. Rochfort."

"Of course."

"You do not like the fellow?"

"Handsome as the very devil. A man like that has an eye that wanders, a tongue that lies, and hands that never get dirty. Strutting about the place in his fine clothes, turning his nose up at my pie pastry."

"Ah. That would be *no* then."

She lowered her voice suddenly. "But I've noticed a very odd thing about that fellow."

"Hmm?"

"He doesn't say a word to his valet. Not a single thing. Moone just does as he pleases. Sits by the fire all day and goes off to *The Willful Goat* in the evening."

Heath frowned. "Ah."

"What do you reckon o' that then? Most rich gents I've known don't travel without a handful of servants, but this one doesn't even have a coachman to drive his horses, and gives no orders to his valet."

He considered for a moment. "What do you infer from that, Miss Rimple?"

"*Hattie*, for pity's sake! Nobody has called me

210

Miss Rimple since I were sixteen and Clem Finney went off to Castlebridge and never came back."

"Clem Finney?" He was trying to follow.

"We were meant to be married, but he got other ideas in his head and went off to make his fortune. Aimed for London, but got no further than Castlebridge, so I heard. I've been Hattie ever since. Don't know why really, but that's the way it is. I didn't care to be Miss Rimple anymore, and that's about the size of it."

"Ah."

"But what do you think then?" She nudged. "About Rochfort?"

"I think he is...like most other gentlemen of his class and upbringing."

"A shiftless rogue then."

He smiled, his lips feeling too soft this evening, particularly whenever he thought of Melinda Goodheart's eyes in candlelight. How they had reached for him with warmth, curiosity and concern. "Why not ask Miss Goodheart what she thinks. Doubtless she will come up with some solution more exciting than the one I can offer." She liked her mysteries, as he knew already. And Heath could not show any suspicion of Rochfort just yet. "I am simply a civil servant here to study fruit yield."

When they arrived at the inn, Tom 'Tipsy' Rimple was waiting with a tankard of cider for him. Since it would be rude to go directly to bed, Heath sat up a while with the fellow and played dominos. It was years since he'd played a game of any sort, but he found it oddly restful that night. Tipsy's company was easy and pleasant. One did not need to speak much, for Tipsy always had plenty to talk about. A steady, honest fellow, he worked from morning till night, managing the smithy and forge, tending his orchards, singing "The Beggar's Opera" to his pigs, and worrying over his gaggle of motherless children. Yet he never seemed tired or unhappy. Even when chiding one of his offspring he barely even altered his voice above a merry sing-song timbre.

"'Tis a good life, this is," he said at the end of the evening, as Heath, his eyelids drooping, staggered up the stairs to his room above the parlor. It was a statement he was to repeat every evening and Heath found himself agreeing.

As his head finally dropped to the pillow, Miss Goodheart's smile still dominated his thoughts and, eventually, his dreams.

It soon became a nightly tradition.

Chapter Eighteen

The next morning Mr. Rochfort sought her out after breakfast and held her to the promise of showing him the spring where, according to family legend, the waters had the power to extend one's life indefinitely.

"Considering all the Goodhearts who have drunk it and now lie entombed in the Kingsthorpe churchyard, it seems a doubtful claim," she told him with a smile. "Besides, who would want to live forever? How dreadful."

He looked surprised. "You would not, madam?"

"Goodness, no! We would have little incentive to enjoy life to the fullest if we knew it was forever. We wouldn't bother to make the best of everything, if we thought it could never be taken away from us. We would never apologize to anybody, or try to make anything right. If time was never running out for any of us, there would be no sense of urgency, no desire for improvement. Just...greed...and boredom...and hopelessness."

"I would never have imagined that anybody could make immortality sound so wretched, Miss Goodheart."

"I'm sorry," she muttered, chagrinned. "But that is what I believe. We go in the ground at the end of all this, sir, and we had better have made the most of it while we could."

He threw up his hands. "This conversation has become much too somber. Now...let us talk about bonnets again and your splendid little shop. Tell me how you create your designs."

"Well, I consider the customer's features, coloring, and character, Mr. Rochfort. I consider their purpose for the hat or bonnet, and I—"

But she sensed he was not listening at all. He had stooped into the long grass and plucked some wildflowers, which he began poking, one by one, into her hair.

Then he said suddenly, "I suspect, Miss Goodheart, that your brother brought me here with certain intentions."

Her heart sank. There was no point pretending. "It had occurred to me too," she replied flatly. "He's hardly subtle."

"I am meant to put you off this idea of yours. This hat shop."

"Very likely. But I must tell you, sir, that I have no intention of marrying unless I am in love. I hope you don't think that I had any hand in bringing you here. There are no expectations on my part."

"Yes. I see that you are very decided in your opinions. All of them."

"You may rest assured, sir, that whatever my brother told you, I am not desperate for a husband. And, as you know, I have no dowry with which to encourage anybody in their right mind."

"You are delightfully and refreshingly honest, Miss Goodheart." He gave a rather sad smile. "I may be in love with you already."

She didn't believe that for a moment, but before anything more could be said, a figure appeared with a great amount of rustling and crackling, striding through the trees very near to where they stood and

214

stomping over the grass. It was Mr. Caulfield with his coat over one shoulder, making more noise than he usually made, which suggested it was deliberate.

They all stopped in surprise— or two of them, at least, were startled. She did not know how long he'd been there in the trees, close enough to hear their voices. He didn't look very happy, but then he never did.

"Good morning," Melinda called out, stepping away from Rochfort, smoothing both hands over her dress. "Where are you going, sir?"

"To your father's stables, Miss Goodheart."

She saw then that Sam Rimple was running to keep up with him. "Good morning, young Master Rimple."

"Good day, Miss Melinda. I'm 'elpin' mend the ol' place," the boy replied proudly.

"Won't you stay and taste the spring water, Mr. Caulfield? It could give you eternal life."

"I'd rather not outstay my welcome." He gave another of his abrupt bows, looked askance at the flowers liberally sprinkled through her hair and said, "Excuse me. I have enough to do in this life."

Thus, man and boy marched onward down the slope.

"What an odd fellow that Caulfield is," Rochfort exclaimed, moving closer to her. "So very taciturn and solemn."

"Yes, he is." She sighed, plucking one of the blooms from behind her ear, because it had begun to itch.

"He certainly does not follow your concept of living life to the fullest. There is a distinct lack of fun about his demeanor."

"I suppose he has much on his mind."

"*Fruit,* you mean?" he sneered. "Does he never laugh?"

"He believes laughter is for people with a nervous complaint."

"Good lord. I confess I found him tiresome at dinner. That common way of pushing himself into the conversation. And then he had nothing to talk about except bees."

"I do not think he is very comfortable in society."

"But he is a gentleman, you say, not a servant? He seemed somewhat out of place at dinner yesterday. I wonder if he truly belonged there, although, of course, I would not doubt your judgment, Miss Goodheart. It shows a generosity of spirit to feed the fellow at your table. Even if he was not thankful and had so little of interest to contribute to the conversation. I suppose that is what you meant when you suggested I open my opera box to milkmaids and blacksmiths."

"I did not invite him to dinner to be charitable, but to thank him. In all honesty, I am not sure what to make of Mr. Caulfield, but he is... helpful."

"And enormously tedious. I almost died of ennui while he talked. I did not think he would stop."

Mr. Rochfort liked to exaggerate, evidently. Caulfield had been the quietest person at the table.

She looked after the vanishing figures. "We should go back to the house. I have left everybody to do the work." She felt guilty not working alongside him to put the house back together. It was her place

216

to do so, rather than his.

More than that, she wanted to go with him. She wanted to walk at his side, like young Samuel. There was, she must admit, something comforting about his solemn strength. Once in a while. Not all the time, of course. That would allow no room for adventure. Besides, she was too clumsy and would bump into him. Too ungainly and impatient to play the damsel in distress, she had learned, early in life, to look after herself.

"...whatever else I may or may not be, I am a gentleman. While I am here, I will allow no harm to befall you."

Allowing a man to guard her suddenly, after managing so many years by herself, could only feel awkward and unwarranted. Worst of all, it brought focus upon all her terribly unfeminine traits and despite what her brother said, she was not proud of them.

Rochfort gripped her hand and turned it over to examine her palm, which, to her shame, was currently an unladylike degree of moist. "The lady of the house is not meant to *work*, Miss Goodheart. She is meant to look pretty and entertain her guest. For all your charmingly rebellious ways, I cannot have you acquiring rough palms and housemaid's knee now, can I?"

She felt another flower falling loose from her hair, as if the petals were shriveled by Mr. Caulfield's disdain. "Alas, I suspect the life of a lady of leisure is not for me." Melinda was much too restless to sit around while other people got things done, whether that meant rescuing a bonnet from a roof or her purse from a robber. "I should go back to the house," she said, retrieving her hand.

"Surely you would not leave me to run after that surly groom?"

"No, of course not," she murmured. "I was merely thinking of the work to be done."

Rochfort caught her hand again. "Moone tells me that Caulfield has a young lady. Apparently it was talked of this morning in the kitchen before breakfast. There was much speculation."

So he must have told someone. That news would quickly spread. "Oh." At least now she needn't worry about the possibility of letting it slip herself.

"Difficult to believe in light of his temperament," Rochfort continued. "The fellow lacks charm, looks *and* fashion. The poor woman, whoever she is, must be desperate." He crossly brushed down his sleeve, for some stray petals had landed there and apparently offended his highly-tuned sartorial taste. "How were you introduced to Caulfield again? I was rather confused by the story last night. The one about rescuing a bonnet."

"Oh, it doesn't matter. It was a very long time ago. We were never really properly introduced."

"Well, I must say, whether engaged to another woman or not, he gave *you* rather an indecent amount of attention at dinner. I almost called the fellow out."

Melinda drew back in astonishment, not only at what he said, but at the fact that he thought he had the right to make such a threat.

"Indeed," he added somberly, "I would not be surprised if his business here is nothing to do with fruit at all, and that he came to pursue you. His very aspect at dinner yesterday was of a possessive nature.

Do we know this young lady of his even exists?"

"You are mistaken, sir. Mr. Caulfield has no interest in me. And I know the lady in question. At least, I have met her, so I can assure you that she exists." Melinda raised a hand to her ribs where she felt a sharp pain, as if she was winded.

"Oh? Do tell what she is like. I cannot picture her at all. What woman would tie herself to such a dour fellow?"

"She is very elegant and gracious, but not in the least haughty. I was quite delighted by her when we met."

"You are merely being polite, the way ladies are obliged to be when discussing their peers," he remarked airily. "I have seldom heard one young lady say, in company, that another is anything other than elegant and delightful. Even when the subject of her discourse is the most dreadful prig with an unsightly shoulder hunch and pimples."

"Mr. Rochfort, I can assure you I speak truthfully when I describe the lady. She is, in fact, everything I wish I could be." No sooner had she said this than Melinda remembered the impediments Lady Clara was forced to overcome all her life. How the poor girl lived in a world of silence. It was wicked to envy the woman.

"I heard that sigh, madam! What could it mean?"

"Nothing at all," she replied hurriedly. "Only that we all have our difficulties and nobody's life is perfection. The path of true love never does run smoothly, as they say."

"Now I am most curious."

She shook her head. "It is nothing, sir." But the

pity must have been clear to read in her expression.

"What would be this lady's name?"

"I could not say, sir. It is a private matter."

"Tell me," he pressed.

"No, sir, I cannot. Please put Mr. Caulfield and his friend out of your mind. We should not discuss the matter. It is none of our business." Melinda would have a stern word with Hattie about gossiping in the kitchen.

To her horror, Mr. Rochfort added, "I shall tease Caulfield about this lady and see if I can finally get some other expression out of that severe, disapproving face."

"Oh, please do not speak of it to him! It is not the sort of thing to tease anybody about, and he does not like to talk of personal matters."

"But I do love a riddle. Aha! Perhaps that heavy sigh was envy of the mysterious lady," his eyes narrowed, "because you are in love with him yourself. As I suspected there is some history between you and not just the rescuing of a bonnet or a purse. I should be on my guard then against this rival."

"Nonsense, sir!" Her face felt hot. "That is not what I meant at all. I am not in love with anybody."

"Then you refer to *their* love when you speak of its path not being smooth? There is a difficulty that keeps them apart? Hmm." He pressed a finger to his lips. "I wonder what it might be."

Melinda fervently wished Mr. Rochfort could go back to being self-absorbed. So she said lightly, "Let us walk on up the hill. There is a lovely view of the house from there."

He looked at her for a moment and then he

laughed. "Quite right, Miss Goodheart! *I* am supposed to be making love to you, am I not?"

"I really do not think that is necessary."

"Your brother will expect it."

"My brother expects a lot of things," she muttered. "I blame it on the clothes he had as a child."

Mr. Rochfort looked curious.

She explained, "It was a frugal measure— probably one instituted by Hattie Rimple— but his clothes were all made too large so that, as he grew, they would last him longer. As a result he spent much of his time trying to see over his collars and waiting to fill his breeches. Always waiting. It must have contributed to his tremendous sense of entitlement, don't you think?"

He laughed at that. "Perhaps you are right, Miss Goodheart. But he has brought me here to pay court to you. It would be impolite of me not to do so." Walking backward up the hill, he tugged her along with him. "Come. Let us ramble on together, so that they all wonder where we have gone. Let us be absent so long they think we have run off together to Gretna Green."

"But it looks like rain." Which sounded feeble even to her ears, since rain had never stopped her in her life.

"Then we shall take cozy shelter together until it passes. Our pleasures are fleeting, Miss Goodheart, and if, as you say, we must only live once and for a brief time, we had better make the most of it."

"But I don't—"

"If you want me to put Caulfield's lady love out

of my mind and not tease the fellow about his interest in you, Miss Goodheart, you had better distract me with other entertainments." Bringing her hand to his lips, he planted a lingering kiss upon it.

Alas, what choice did she have? She could not let him torment Mr. Caulfield about Lady Clara.

Besides, just a half hour's ramble would hardly matter. Rochfort seemed to think people would notice they were gone, but Melinda knew differently. After all, she'd once hidden for almost a whole day and been entirely forgotten about by anybody in the house.

* * * *

Two hours and thirty-nine minutes later— he checked his fob watch— Heath spied the two drenched ramblers stumbling through the kitchen garden, bedraggled as drowned rats. He was fixing a broken window latch in the kitchen when he first heard them, then he saw the couple emerge from under the overgrown rose arbor.

With skirts and petticoats lifted, Melinda ran ahead of her companion. Rochfort looked exhausted and, taking more caution with his steps, struggled to keep up with her. They laughed like fools, as if there might be anything remotely fun about getting caught in the rain. He twisted the window latch angrily. Did they have no inkling of how worried everyone had become?

Well...how worried he and Hattie had become. Lindley was merely cross because he had wanted Rochfort for a game of cards, but nobody had shown concern for Melinda's reputation or safety.

As soon as he saw her, Heath's anxiety turned to relief, followed quickly by anger when he took greater note of the state she was in. It was rare for him to lose his temper, but today it bubbled and brewed with considerable power, barely contained beneath his calm exterior. It had not come suddenly, but began when he first saw them standing together as he walked through the trees.

When he watched Rochfort threading flowers through her hair.

From then on it had built like a teetering stack of bricks, unsteady as her old ladder in the hat shop.

A young woman's reputation could never be too well guarded, and men who were careless of that fact roused his fury as few things did. Rochfort clearly had no concern for anything but his own immediate pleasure. And he seemed far more stupid a fellow than Heath had expected. Where was the stealth and cunning? The "Cuckoo" must be very good at hiding his intelligence— a master at the art, for there was scant evidence of it.

Some flowers still remained in Miss Goodheart's hair now, although they were defeated by wind and rain, flattened among her tumbled locks. Her bonnet was lost. When she saw Heath holding the door open for her, she blushed, although that might have been the result of her hurried pace more than any shame in being gone so long, unchaperoned, with a gentleman who was not a relative.

With no apology or explanation offered, Rochfort immediately ordered a bath in his room— although who he expected to carry buckets of hot water up that narrow, treacherously winding staircase for him was not clear. Moone certainly wouldn't. The valet was nowhere in sight. His orders given to a kitchen full of disgusted or bemused people, he strode off to his room, without the slightest concern for Melinda, who stood in the kitchen, dripping all over the floor and shivering, but still smiling brightly.

"Good heavens, you all look very grim. What is the matter?"

"Where do you think you've been all this time?" Hattie exclaimed, banging her pots around with fervor. "With a strange gentleman too! Is that what they taught you in London?"

"Mr. Rochfort is not strange."

Heath needed to do something to quell his temper and stop himself from going after Rochfort, so without a word, he took his coat and put it around her wet shoulders, concentrating on the one thing he could do at that moment.

Hattie continued, "He should not have kept you out in the rain, young lady. It was inconsiderate! What if you catch cold?"

"If I catch one it is highly unlikely to be the end of me. I have the unromantic and unladylike constitution of an ox, as you well know, Hattie." She sneezed and Heath, having tucked his coat more securely around her, took out his handkerchief and pressed it into her hand. "It was only a little fun," she sputtered. "No need to make a fuss."

"Fun, indeed! When I was a young lass, if I went off for so long with a single man, just the two of us, my father would have got out the blunderbuss from under his bed and there would have been a wedding in three Sundays."

"That was the old days, dear Hattie. These are modern times." She wilted where she stood, blowing her nose into Heath's handkerchief and trying her hardest to keep that careless smile pinned to her face.

Hattie pointed to the window where gusts of rain could be seen and heard attacking the house from all angles like a frenzy of arrowheads in a siege. "And when it started to rain, this modern gentleman didn't think to bring you straight home?"

She put her chin up and said airily, "We decided we weren't ready to come in, and Mr. Rochfort kept saying the rain would stop." Heath had seen that expression on her face before, when she knew she was wrong and didn't want to admit it. Or she was hiding something. For some reason she could not look Heath in the eye.

"So we must all suffer— worrying and fretting," Hattie exclaimed. "Now look at you! Dripping all over my newly scrubbed floor. Clumps of mud on your feet—and where's he gone? Where's his explanation for keeping you out?"

"Mr. Rochfort can answer for himself. As for me, I am certainly too old to be chided in this fashion. I am the lady of the house. If I want to go walking with a gentleman I shall, for pity's sake."

"And that is exactly why you'll get yourself into trouble, young lady. You're too headstrong and always have been!"

"Yes, I do have a strong head and I am glad of it!"

"It's one thing to have a head, but it's quite another to make use of what's in it."

"Harriet Rimple, you forget your place, and I

begin to see why my father dismissed you. If you do not hold your tongue, I shall—"

Heath swept the quarrelling miscreant into his arms before any further damage was done and carried her across to the fire, setting her down on a bench beside it and promptly crouching to remove her filthy walking boots.

She was clearly too startled to make a protest and, as her backside bumped down onto the wooden bench, was temporarily rendered silent. Or else she was too exhausted by her adventures and the subsequent shouting match. Even Hattie said nothing, merely stared in amazement. Her frail little cousin— Bo or Flo, or whatever her damned name was— exhaled a gasp, almost dropping the ham she carried across the kitchen and stubbing her toe on the table leg at the same time.

Heath concentrated on the little buttons of the wanderer's half boots. Clearly they weren't made for a man's fingers to tackle.

"Mr. Rochfort thought it would be a jolly good lark to be out in the rain, and I agreed," she explained sulkily. "It was nobody's fault. You're all over-reacting."

Finally managing the buttons, Heath tugged the first boot off by the heel and dropped it.

"Mr. Rochfort wanted to walk up the hill and admire the scenery. He thought there would be no harm in it."

He winced as he bit the inside of his cheek.

"Mr. Rochfort thought—"

"And what did you think?" he muttered tightly as he pulled off her second boot and set them both to

226

dry on the hearthstones. "Or did you not think at all?"

Not waiting for her reply, he turned his attention to throwing more logs on the fire, making a vast deal of clattering noise. Jabbing hard into the flames with an iron poker was also good exercise at that moment. Satisfying.

"Well, really!" she exhaled in a rush, "who gave you permission to throw me around like a sack of coal? Such a lot of fuss about nothing. I've been in far worse scrapes."

He had no doubt of it. The difference this time being that he was around.

Rochfort was evidently gaining her trust, making her think she had an ally in mischief. Encouraging that wayward streak in her. That was the way he worked. Not so stupid, after all.

Heath moved a three-legged stool to where she sat and propped her feet up on it so that her stockings would dry faster.

"Are you supposed to be touching my ankles?" she demanded, querulous, clutching his wadded handkerchief and drawing his coat tighter around her body.

"No." *But certainly no one else will— not while I'm here to stop them.* His thoughts turned violent when he imagined the scrawny neck of Master Rochfort at the mercy of his very strong, well-exercised left hand.

"I hope you do not throw Lady Clara about in this fashion."

"*She* knows how to behave herself."

"Ha! Perhaps she does not object to being ordered about. But I do not know who put you in charge of *me*," she exclaimed.

227

"Is there anybody in charge? There doesn't appear to be, madam."

"Oh yes, I had forgotten how women are helpless and cannot be trusted to look after themselves."

He looked at her and carefully ran a thumb over his left eyebrow before turning away.

"Speak up, do!" she cried. "I know you have something to say."

Heath moved her boots closer to the fire. "I don't believe you want to hear it."

"But I do. I cannot abide a man who holds everything inside and lets it fester. Lord, you are so tiresome with your long, doom-laden silences."

"Very well then." He straightened up. "I may have formed an opinion that is unjust. It sometimes happens that first impressions are later proven false, as you pointed out yesterday evening, madam, at dinner. But so far in our acquaintance you've done nothing to disprove mine. Of you."

Her lips parted and then snapped shut.

He had not meant to take his anger out on her, but thoughts of his sister's mistreatment and abandonment— even seven years later— were still raw wounds, not yet healed it seemed. The intensity of his feelings took him by surprise.

Hattie, however, approved. "Ooh, that told you, didn't it? You asked and he told, Miss Headstrong and Proud Of It."

"Why have you taken such a dislike to Mr. Rochfort?" she demanded of Heath. "I suppose that must remain a mystery too, not considered a matter worth discussing with me."

"I dislike him, madam, because he treats his horses ill. He is indolent, selfish, and thoughtless. Is that enough reason or do you want more?" He gathered a breath and the shreds of his temper. "If you were my sister, I would not have brought him here."

Melinda blew her nose loudly into his handkerchief and he could tell she struggled to hold her own thoughts inside for once. But he was not about to ask her for them. That had been *her* mistake. It would not be his.

Sensing the danger of looking at her much longer that day, he walked out of the kitchen and into the cool passage, where he met Moone standing by the wall, filling a long pipe with tobacco. How long he'd been there in the shadows behind the door was not apparent, but his hair was damp, there was fresh mud on his boots and a hint of high color on his whiskered cheeks, suggesting he'd not long come in out of the cold rain.

He jerked his head at Heath in sullen greeting, his eyes two watchful, colorless slits.

"Mr. Moone."

"Mr. *Caulfield.*"

Heath walked on, a new uneasiness settling over him.

Chapter Nineteen

He walked to Kingsthorpe Park every day, carrying baskets and crates for Hattie, using the excuse of fixing any hole or leak he found while he was there. Slipping casually into the general, day-to-day workings of the house, he had soon become a sight that was expected and commonplace enough not to be remarked upon.

Whenever he encountered Lindley Goodheart around the house or grounds, the fellow treated him like a servant, which was to say he gave him no notice at all. Rochfort, on the other hand, did not seem to know what to make of him and, to be safe— and perhaps to stay on Melinda's good side— continued his sickly, condescending smiles and comments.

"You do work hard, sir," Hattie exclaimed when she found him up a ladder one day. "I'm sure nobody has ever bothered so with this old house."

But he felt great satisfaction in putting the place back together, even one small step at a time. "I don't like to see a magnificent piece of history left to the elements," he said simply.

Understanding the bones of the old place, appreciating the hardships through which it had lived, he knew how to tend Kingsthorpe Park just as he groomed the horses.

"You'll wear yourself out," Hattie chided him. "What demons you must have chasing you! Sit a while and have a bit of bread and cheese. You need fattening up! Those gargoyle spouts can wait. Let my cousin get you a cup of ale, you must be thirsty."

Demons, yes. She had no idea.

After putting Melinda "in her place", Heath could do no wrong in the eyes of the cook. She was intent on feeding and watering him at every opportunity and even between those opportunities sometimes, sending her meek little cousin to him with a pasty or some other treat he could enjoy while he worked.

"Miss Melinda is not a wicked girl, you know, sir, but I see that gentleman Rochfort leading her astray. She's not accustomed to that sort of attention from gentlemen. It was good of you to tell her straight. Her brother doesn't care, and her father is off in his own world."

Heath nodded and ate. And ate.

His waist expanded. If he stayed much longer in the country, he'd have to order new clothes.

Whenever she set a plate of food before him, the strangely unhelpful but never-too-far-away "Moone" lurched into view sooner or later, demanding the same for himself, although what he actually did to earn replenishment was not clear. He took orders from nobody, or so it seemed. If any were even given to the fellow it must have been by coded signal, he mused.

"Have you been long in your master's service?" Heath asked him one day.

"Long enough," was the sharp reply.

"Travelled a great deal?" He'd seen the state of those horses and the luggage, of course.

The manservant glared. "We get about."

"And you'll stay a while, I suppose. Your master seems fond of the place."

231

"He's never fond of any place for long."

"Is that so? Must be hard work for you."

Moone gave a half-hearted shrug and sucked on his pipe. "We'll leave before the month is out, as soon as we have what we came for."

"And what might that be?" Heath kept his expression nonchalant, barely interested.

Moone wheezed and choked out a cloud of smoke. "I don't ask. I just go along. T'aint for me to question."

He'd learned from Hattie's gossip that Moone spent his evenings at *The Willful Goat,* playing dice and any other game that was going. Although he did not boast openly about his master's great wealth, he showed it in many sly ways— keeping his snuff in a silver box, smoking expensive tobacco, wagering high and mentioning the many sights he'd seen on travels abroad.

Well, if the "Cuckoo" and his servant expected a quick getaway this time, Heath had put paid to that. On the second morning he had moved those four stolen horses to the warm stables by Tipsy Rimple's forge.

"The blacksmith says they all need new shoes," he informed Moone. "And a tooth filing."

He already knew that the man knew almost nothing about horses.

So when Moone replied, "That shouldn't take long, eh?" Heath assured him that it shouldn't.

But it would. He had no intention of returning the horses and, just to be sure, he had Hastings' coach up on blocks too. If Rochfort and his manservant wanted to leave in haste they'd have to go on foot.

For now, the villain seemed to be in no particular hurry and content to hang about Melinda Goodheart. Perhaps she distracted *him* too. She had a habit of it with her streams of chatter and ever-changing expressions that made it just as challenging for one's mind to keep up with her as it was for one's feet.

Despite a few sneezes and snuffles she had recovered quickly from her drenching, just as she'd said she would. It was Rochfort who suffered the worst cold, but that only worked in the villain's favor, for it made him a figure of sympathy in her eyes. Being a woman who lived up to her family's name, she was, unfortunately, too kind, her heart strings easily played upon by the scoundrel. For a day or two Rochfort was confined to bed and she nursed him with broths and jellies, tripping up and down those treacherous stairs all day long in answer to the tinkle of his demanding bell.

Although Heath expected her to bear a grudge over their quarrel and avoid him, as most women he knew would, she came to find him the day after it happened.

"I have apologized to Hattie for the way I spoke to her after I was caught in the rain," she said, as she joined him walking across the courtyard, both of them on their way to the water pump. "It was wrong of me to shout at her, when she's always been good to me. Now I must apologize to you."

He was pleased, but not really knowing why it mattered to him that much.

"I will launder your handkerchief on washday and return it to you."

Knowing how little she looked forward to

laundry, he smirked. "That's alright, Miss Goodheart. You can keep it."

"But I couldn't. I believe Lady Bramley would say it is not proper."

"I'm amused and yet bewildered, madam, by the ephemeral quality of your propriety. It comes and goes like rheumatism."

"I am trying to apologize to you, sir. There is no occasion to be rude."

Finally he shook his head. "It's a handkerchief, not a love letter. Do as you will with it."

She kept it. And he was pleased again, without knowing why.

Thus he was apparently forgiven for speaking so harshly to her on the day of the rainstorm and they never mentioned it again.

But Heath was unable to forget what had happened and how swiftly the anger had come upon him. Nor could he forget how relieved he had been to see her safe. How he had taken her in his arms because he had to hold her, even if it was just for a moment. It was not like him to be impulsive, or to let his emotions run away with rationality, and it troubled him. He knew he'd had no right to address her that way. He had aimed his anger at her, when it was Rochfort who had truly deserved it.

But his feelings for Melinda Goodheart had grown into something other than mild horror, confusion and disbelief that any young woman would be left to her own devices so frequently. His anxieties had developed beyond mere gentlemanly concern for her reputation and physical safety.

"You are here so often, Mr. Caulfield, I begin to

think Hattie goes out of her way to make jobs for you," she teased, holding her water jug under the pump while he filled it. "Or else you are spying on us."

He studied her smug face. "Why? What crimes have you committed? Sounds as if you have a guilty conscience, madam."

"I'd hardly be likely to confess to you, would I?" she scoffed.

He gave a lazy shrug. Thought about not answering, but then heard himself say, "You have no inkling of the methods I would employ to draw out your confession."

"Ha! I, sir, would go to the gallows unrepentant. Do what you like to me, I would never confess. You would get nothing out of me."

Heath felt a smile curving his mouth. It physically hurt to deny it.

"I see you are amused, sir. Finally. Gracious, what has brought that about?"

"Just my thoughts."

"About what, pray tell?"

How I could make you sing like a lark if I had you to myself. But he must get that thought out of his head at once. "Nothing in particular."

"Another secret for the solitary mind not to be shared with a silly young thing?"

"If you like."

She groaned.

"You already told me that you are an open book, madam. You could keep nothing from me."

She gave him an arch look. "Do you dare me to try?"

"No. I do not dare young ladies to misbehave and lie to me. That would be a very irrational, impractical thing to do." There, now he was back in control. "And Hattie is not the one who finds me work to do. I found this discarded on the floor by the fire." Heath took from his waistcoat pocket a small, crumpled list of household chores.

"Oh, but this was meant for Mr. Moone," she exclaimed.

"Hmm. Seems he found other things to do. Mostly at *The Willful Goat* of an evening."

She put her head on one side, hands on her waist. "Do you apply yourself so diligently to these tedious errands to avoid trouble? My former headmistress claimed one should fill one's day with uninspiring tasks to avoid temptation. You must be a student of the same philosophy."

"I must be."

"But all work and no play makes Mr. Caulfield a very dull boy. Even Lady Clara said as much to me, that you never have time to visit her. And Rocky calls you tedious and somber."

"Now it's *Rocky*?"

"It is what his friends call him, and I am a friend."

"Most men only need one name," he replied gruffly.

The distant sound of a clattering bell intruded, and she glanced upward at the window to Rochfort's chamber.

"Why not let Moone manage his master's needs?" Heath growled, pumping harder, water splashing over the rim of her jug. "He seems to have little else to do."

"But I feel it is my fault," she replied. "If I had not agreed to stay out in the rain that day, Mr. Rochfort would not be ill now. I should have known. I daresay he was pampered by nursery-maids and nannies, and he does not have my sturdy constitution."

"Perhaps that is so," he told her, amused, "but Mr. Rochfort is now well beyond the age when he might reasonably deny responsibility for his own actions. He must pay for his mistakes. And his crimes."

"So should I, but you still carried me like a kitten and looked after me."

"It's time somebody did."

"I'm not the sort of girl who needs to be treated like porcelain. I've been dropped on my head more times than I can count, and I am remarkably resilient, as Lindley says."

"My hands will never let you fall."

He felt her gaze studying his face, saw her fingers fidgeting with her apron. Something had shocked her.

Abruptly, he realized he'd spoken the dreadful words aloud, when he thought that they — along with other troubling thoughts and ideas about Melinda Goodheart—were only in his head.

Alarmed, he resumed pumping, until she put her hand on his and softly advised him that her jug was full.

Heath tried to maintain a practical frame of mind. Not to feel so...strangely glad... when he had her company to himself. Or felt her hand on his. "Besides," He straightened up and smoothed his hair back. "Rochfort should take the responsibility for making *you* stay out in the damned rain." He'd never said *damn* in a lady's presence before. What had got into him?

Melinda didn't bat an eyelid. "It was my choice too. I am just as much to blame."

"That is different."

"How so, sir?"

"I told you before. You're a woman."

She chuckled. "So I need take no responsibility for my actions? How naughty I could be." The chuckled turned devious. "I am free to do anything and get away with it then."

Uh oh. "Nothing is free. A bill will always be due. Eventually. Somebody has to pay it."

"As long as it's worth the price. One should enjoy life. I do not care what I must pay in the end, or what punishment I'm due. I'd rather have no regrets and be content in the knowledge that I did the best I could, loved all that I could and lived life to the fullest." She paused, chewing on her lower lip. "As it is surely meant to be lived." Then she smiled. "Life without risk is no life at all."

Damn, again. He'd pumped water all over his boots and soaked them.

Now she was staring at him, her lips slightly parted, her cheeks flushed. "You're clumsy today, Mr. Caulfield."

His gaze went to her mouth.

Was it too much to ask, just to have one thing he wanted for once? To not deny himself a little pleasure? It was as if she'd woken him from a deep sleep, during which he'd seen and done much, but felt, heard and tasted nothing. For years he had not had a moment to stop and feel.

"I'm going fishing," he said abruptly. "Come with me."

"Oh." Her eyes widened.

"I promised to take Sam Rimple out on the lake. He can be our chaperone." He smiled. Just a little. His heartbeat was too fast.

She looked down at the cobbles and his wet boots. "I feel too sorry for the fish. Here comes a juicy worm, a fleeting moment of joy— followed by a grim, ignoble end. Victims of a dastardly trick. The sad fish have scant excitement in their life as it is. They must swim round and round in circles in those calm waters and never get anywhere new. It is all very sad."

"Perhaps they are content with their life the way it is, without excitement, their territory always familiar."

"But they must long for their freedom. They must dream of a life in the wild, open sea."

"Not if they're freshwater fish. Most cannot survive in saltwater."

"You're a dreadfully practical, know-it-all sort of person, aren't you?"

"I find it keeps me alive and sane."

"Oh," she laughed, "poor Lady Clara."

Suddenly there was a rattling, a great rusty groan, and a clank as Mr. Rochfort's bedchamber window struggled open above them, followed by another loud, churlish ring of the brass bell he kept by his bed. "Miss Goodheart! Miss Goodheart!"

She dampened those soft lips with a quick flick

of her tongue. "The patient!"

Taking the filled water jug under one arm, she hurried indoors to see what the whining babe needed.

Heath looked up at that open window. Very well, if that was the way Rochfort meant to play, that was the only damn hinge in the house that he would not oil. And he'd find somewhere to shove that blasted bell.

A satisfying thought indeed.

Chapter Twenty

"Miss Goodheart, I hope I did not call you away from anything important."

"Of course not." She hurried into the room and poured the jug of water into a bowl beside the fire to warm it. "I will make a mustard plaster for your congestion." Feeling a draft, she looked across the room and saw that the window was still open. "Now that won't do, will it?"

"The wind blew it open," he muttered, "and I was too weak to close it."

But she knew that was highly unlikely for the latch was stiff and would not be moved without considerable strife. He must have got out of bed himself and opened it, although he now feigned a frailty in all his limbs.

As she moved to close the squeaky latch, she saw Caulfield still standing in the yard, talking now to young Sam Rimple. He smiled as the boy talked. Even more shocking, he laughed with the boy. They did not look up at her.

My hands will never let you fall.

Oh, why would he say such a thing to her, when he had Lady Clara's heart and loyalty? He did not strike her as the sort of man who would be unfaithful to his love. He was too steady, too upright. There was no weakness in *his* limbs.

Melinda realized it must be her fault then. She talked too much, was too unguarded. He had warned her of it. He deliberately did not smile at *her* because he feared encouraging her. She had been too stupid to

241

realize it and he was being kind. Too kind to hurt her feelings.

But why would he invite her to go fishing with him?

Perhaps he wanted to push her in and drown her, she thought morosely. He wouldn't be the first man to have those feelings.

"Miss Goodheart!" The patient sniffled weakly from the bed. "Might I have some of that broth again? And will you sit with me? Your company makes me feel so much improved."

She remembered what Mr. Caulfield had said. "It is really Mr. Moone who ought to sit here."

"*Moone?*" He rolled his head against the pillow and moaned. "He is no use to me."

"Your valet does seem to go his own way." She ventured, "I wonder why you hired him?"

He did not answer, but drooped miserably against his pillow.

Melinda got another blanket out of the press and spread it over his bed. "He abandoned the list of chores you had me write for him, and Mr. Caulfield found it."

"Oh, that tiresome Caulfield is still hanging about, is he?"

"Thank goodness he is. We would have no one to tend your horses without him."

"They're not my horses," the man snapped.

She frowned. "But I thought—"

"They belong to George Hastings. That tight purse. Your brother wagered that I couldn't take them from under his nose."

"You *stole* the horses?"

242

He sniffed. "I didn't steal them. I merely," he waved his hand in the air, "requisitioned them for a while. The horses and the carriage. And a box of wigs." He exhaled a peal of laughter. "It was a jolly good lark."

Melinda wondered if he was delirious with fever. But no, the more she considered the story the more she believed it. Her brother loved his wicked games, urging people to do dangerous things for his entertainment, and Mr. Rochfort was just foolish enough to go along with it.

"So that is why you had no coachman? And why my brother left London sooner than he expected?"

"I daresay we livened up that enormously dull house party. George Hastings deserved it, and everybody there should thank me."

He turned his head against the pillow when he heard Lindley's footstep approach. There was no mistaking the sound. No one else in the house made quite as much discontented noise as Lindley.

"When are you going to get up?" her brother bellowed, tilting steeply and rolling his shoulder against the doorframe. "Still malingering, Rocky? It's only a blessed cold. And I'm excessively bored."

Melinda walked around the bed. "Why do you not sit here and keep your friend company then if you lack occupation? It's not truly proper for me to be in here." It was all she could do to hold her temper and keep a partially civil tongue in her head.

"It's a woman's place to tend the sick," he grumbled.

"Funny how it is a woman's place to do anything unpleasant."

"Sick people are so tiresome. So...needy." He yawned widely. "I'd forgotten how bloody mind-numbing the country is. Moone's gone out. Father's napping. Even the damned horses have disappeared. There's nothing to do. Nothing!"

"Why not help Mr. Caulfield then?" she exclaimed. "He seems to find plenty to do."

At that he sneered, flopping into the room, grabbing the poker from the fireplace and lazily swinging it about like a drunken sword-fighter. "If you ask me, that fellow has some sort of nervous condition that keeps him moving about. I did think he had his eye on you, sister— never seen anybody look at you the way he does— but, according to the Rimple woman, he has a commitment to some trollop already?"

"Hardly a trollop," she snapped.

"Not that it matters to us. He cannot be worth more than sixpence and is therefore no use to you, sister."

Melinda pressed her lips together and straightened the blanket.

"Rochfort here is worth ten of him."

The man in the bed laughed uneasily. "Miss Goodheart is not impressed. I fear I cannot make her fall in love with me."

"That's why she has me to show her the way."

Today her brother's laughter made her feel sick.

"By the by," he said suddenly, "Moone tells me that her name is *Lady* Clara."

"Whose name?"

"Lady Clara is the paramour of that thick-necked groom. You knew that, of course, did you not, sister?

244

Rocky says you met her."

"So? I do not know why Mr. Caulfield and his affairs concern you so much."

"I don't like him hanging around my house. I don't like his face."

Melinda realized her brother sounded just like her, not so long ago.

"Moone overheard you both in the kitchen the other day," he added smoothly, "and he came to me directly with this news. *Lady* Clara. He heard you say it. Fancy that. The grubby fellow Caulfield aims above his station."

"And Mr. Moone seems to do a great deal of listening. It is the *only* thing he's done since he came here."

"But he always hears the most useful things." Her brother's lips parted slowly in a nasty grin. "Worth his weight in gold. Astounding what he's found out for me in servants' halls over the years. That's where all the gossip can be found."

Rochfort grumbled sulkily, "Your sister doesn't think we should tease Caulfield about his lady."

Lindley laughed, maintaining his lolling pose against the mantle. "Really? He is above teasing? I didn't realize you were such a friend of the mysterious and surly Mr. Caulfield, sister. I thought your acquaintance was only passing, but I see now you know him better than you let on."

Flustered, she walked around the bed and ladled another dish of broth from the pot that stood warming by the fire.

"*Lady* Clara, eh?" her brother persisted. "How very odd that a noblewoman should hitch her cart to that of a groom. Her family can't know."

"He's not a groom. As I told you, Mr. Caulfield is a gentleman."

Rochfort hitched himself up against his pillow. "I think there is something dreadfully sad about the lady, or about the circumstances of their courtship. Your sister almost gave it away, but I could not pry it out of her, try as I might. Her countenance was full of compassion and close to tears when she begged me not to joke about it. *The course of true love never did run smooth*, or some such."

Although she knew Rochfort thought he was only playing another game and teasing, Lindley's eyes sparked with dangerous interest, casting off their bored mist. "Hmm. What could be amiss with the absent Lady Clara and why will my sister not tell?" The angles of his face sharpened. "What favor does she owe Caulfield that she keeps his secrets from us? Come to think of it, my sister has not created any outrageous story about her dour handyman, which is most unlike her." He pulled on a lock of her hair as she passed within his reach. "What can be the meaning of it?"

"Go away, brother, and bother somebody else.""Oh? Shall I bother *him* then? I'll go and ask him about Lady Clara, shall I? Why he's hanging around here trying to impress you, watching you— according to Moone— with the eyes of a faithful dog, if he has a woman already? And one far above him in consequence? What can be the meaning of his behavior?"

Melinda set the bowl of broth on a tray and took it to the bed, but she really wanted to throw it at her

246

brother. "He is merely helping around the house, because that is the useful sort of man he is. Unlike some people. Kindly leave him alone."

But her brother had dug his fangs in now. Like a dog with a juicy bone, he would not give it up. And the more it bothered her, the more savage he would be.

"My sister always has stories to make up about people, Rocky," he said, watching Melinda slyly, "and yet this civil servant who supposedly came to count bees and fruit— of all things— is saved from the horrors of her imagination. What can be the truth about poor Lady Clara? Perhaps she has a glass eye and a cork leg. There must be something wrong with her if that fellow is the best she can get." Suddenly he rested his chin in the vee between thumb and forefinger, feigning thoughtfulness. "Of course, I did hear a tale once about a Lady Clara seduced by some unworthy cad, ruined by him. Her family never recovered from the scandal. I believe they disowned her, but these things can never be entirely covered up. Could this be the same couple?"

"Oh, wait!" Rochfort sat up. "I believe I heard that story. Five years ago now it must be, or something thereabouts. I think I had just purchased a very fine new cutaway with an emerald lining...yes, it was quite beautiful... and I remember my tailor mentioning it. Was it not the Earl of Waverly's daughter? Or some such—"

"I am sure there is more than one Lady Clara in England," Melinda snapped.

"I have it," Lindley cried, finger jabbed toward the ceiling. "Lady Clara *Beauspur*. That was her name.

An innocent maiden quite ruined. Her father did not approve of the fellow, but it was too late. The young lady's reputation and her heart, no doubt, were torn apart beyond repair."

"Beauspur, that's the Duke of Ormandsey's estate," said Rochfort. "Is that the family? Good lord, I thought it was all boys. Never knew there was a daughter. Or was there? Come to think of it...yes, she was an invalid of some sort, I think. Never went out of the house. Never went out into society."

"Yes, I believe Beauspur was the name. What a coincidence if it should be the same Lady Clara. And if that grim Caulfield fellow is the disreputable lover for whom she threw in her lot."

"Leave them alone," she exclaimed, her head suddenly feeling very tight. "You know nothing about them." Acting as nonchalantly as she could, she added, "Now you are the one making up stories about people, brother. I did not know you had the imagination." She tried to snatch the poker from his hand, but he swung it away from her.

"This Caulfield fellow certainly gets above himself if he thinks to rival Rocky for your attentions. I shall have him thrashed. He will not treat my sister like that other little hussy he stole from the bosom of her family."

Melinda felt her temper bubbling beyond her control. "Why not concern yourself with your own troubles, Lindley. Your debts, for instance. Mr. Caulfield has spent his time fixing this house, and all you can do is sneer at him and speculate upon matters which are not your business."

He grinned unpleasantly and looked over her

head at Rochfort. "My sister has always maintained a soft spot for the underdog, the bullied, the unsightly, the weak. She thinks she can save them all." He paused and then circled her slowly, hands behind his back. "Tell you what, sister dear, I'll give you two hundred pounds if you tell me what Caulfield is really doing here. And another three hundred if you tell me about his lady love. There's your five hundred." His eyes gleamed. "The very thing for which you came home."

She swallowed hard and gripped the bed post. "You have five hundred pounds to spare suddenly?"

"As it happens," he replied with a shrug. "I've had luck at the tables of late."

"Then why not pay off some of your debts to the local tradesmen?" she exclaimed. "Your reputation could benefit from a little generosity. Just a small sign of your willingness to pay would go a long way to improving—"

"I don't owe half the bills they claim I owe. Honestly, these country peasants and their demanding ways quite wear on one's nerves. I remember now why I stay away."

"Lindley, I would call you a pig, but that would insult the noble beasts."

He blinked and pursed his lips, as if to smother laughter. Not that he ever cared about hiding his amusement at her expense.

"At least Mr. Caulfield doesn't play mean-spirited pranks," she exclaimed. "He does not encourage people to commit crimes."

"What are you blabbering on about?"

"Horse theft for example." The words fell heavily

from her tongue. Suddenly she panicked. Is that why Caulfield was here? The horses! Of course.

Lindley looked over at his friend, who blustered, "It was only a game, Miss Goodheart. No harm done. And as your brother said, it taught Hastings a lesson, which he well deserved."

The fire crackled and wheezed behind her, but suddenly with a hint of sly menace. As if it too laughed at her.

Melinda turned to the man in the bed. "Take care, Mr. Rochfort, when you play games with my brother. You will find he has no conscience to bother him and you will be the one left to pay the consequences."

"Better have no conscience," Lindley snapped, "than bleed your heart for every sad bastard that crawls along looking for pity."

"I'd rather my heart bleed, than that it feel nothing."

"And that is precisely why you'll never get anywhere in life, sister dearest."

"Like you?"

Slowly his lip curled in the familiar sneer. "You have no inkling. You never did. You're all so damnably stupid."

Melinda was accustomed to his insults, of course. But this time there was something more sinister in the newly hardened lines of Lindley's face. It lasted no more than a few seconds, but for just a moment he looked like another man, and then his countenance returned to the usual sleepy fretfulness.

"Now I am even more wretchedly bored," he groaned, throwing his arms in the air. "I say we have a party. A ball. We'll invite all the local petticoat. That should cheer the place up."

"And who will pay for that?" she demanded.

"It needn't cost much, sister. The Rimple woman will help if *you* ask her. Just throw a few things together. The locals cannot expect much considering the dearth of entertainment hereabouts. They should be thankful for anything we put together."

"Father won't like it. You know he dislikes having villagers up at the house unless they work in the kitchen."

"Leave father to me," Lindley drawled cockily. "You deal with the common folk since they are your favorites. If I say it is a good idea and that Rocky suggested it, father will agree. He'll do anything to keep Rocky happy, and I need something to save me from death by tedium." He looked at his sick friend in the bed. "You had better get up, Rocky, or else my sister might get scooped up by her brooding, stable-lad if you do not get back on your feet. Especially with the mysterious Lady Clara being noticeable only by her absence, and with my sister prone to flights of sympathy for the downtrodden."

When she left the room her brother's harsh laughter followed her down the stairs, echoing against the old, damp stone, until the door thudded shut above her, cutting out the wretched sound.

Her brother's spiteful remarks had not bothered her for years, but a bored Lindley was the very worst and when he had information he could use to bring somebody grief he was at his most dangerous. He was certainly fixated on the story of Lady Clara Beauspur. It seemed to make him angry.

Beauspur. It was strange for her brother to remember a young lady's full name. Yet he knew this one from somewhere. So was that tale of her seduction true?

She couldn't believe that Caulfield was the man responsible, even though he had acted very oddly— even guiltily— whenever she mentioned Lady Clara.

Then there was Rochfort's confession about the stolen carriage and horses. What to do about that? How like her brother to make such a wager and entice his new friend into villainy. Rochfort was not clever enough to see that he'd been used.

As she arrived at the bottom of the winding staircase, she found her father waiting in his chair.

"Well, my girl, you had better not let this one get away."

Weary suddenly, she pressed her palm to the cold stone. "What do you mean, father?"

He jerked his head impatiently. "Rochfort has taken a liking to you, girl. So don't waste your time gawping and giggling over that other fellow— the one with the face like a sad, confused bulldog. Rochfort has a fortune and a house in London. Your brother says he's well set and a prize catch, but that other fellow has nothing."

She was supposed to be flattered and grateful, of course— that was what her father thought. Rochfort was a gentleman of means and she had very little to tempt a man into marriage. It was her duty, as her father would tell her, to make a good marriage, no matter what she felt, or did not feel.

As if she could ever stand to marry a man who kept a box at the opera merely so he could take his new walking cane there and show off to his equally shallow friends. Rochfort was not evil or mean-tempered like Lindley, and she might never want for pin money for the rest of her life, but she would shrivel up and die married to such an empty fellow.

Melinda thought then of Mr. Caulfield. A sad, confused bulldog, her father had called him. That was a very unkind description, but typical of her father and he was right in that there was a sadness lurking. She'd seen it herself and so had Hattie.

Mr. Caulfield looked nothing like a bulldog. He was more of a...oh, she couldn't think how to describe him.

That surly police officer had asked her once, "What do you want?"

Nobody else had ever asked her that.

Sir Ludlow, of course, would say that what she wanted didn't matter.

"That other feller is naught compared to Rochfort, girl," he exclaimed. "Why, he's nothing more than a government inspector for fruit."

No, father, she wanted to say, *he is an officer of the police.* But what else was he? What did she really know about him?

Lady Clara had been hesitant to accept that bonnet at first, as if fearful of something. And Caulfield did not like to talk about her. He slipped away from Melinda's questions like a fish wriggling out of a net, seldom answering anything directly.

Miss Goodheart, I hate to disappoint you, but I am a very ordinary, uninteresting, humdrum fellow.

Melinda couldn't breathe for a moment. She pressed a hand to her side where she felt a stitch, as if she'd been running again.

"What's amiss with you, girl?"

She straightened up. "Nothing, father. Growing pains, I think." Yes, she suddenly felt much older.

"Well, I've no objection to Rochfort, so I'm sure you cannot have any. His may only be new money, but as long as he's got plenty of it I don't care when it were minted. Old blood like ours needs new money, and new money— like yon Rochfort— needs old blood to make it legitimate. Aye. It'll work out well enough. You don't even 'ave to like the feller. You've got an imagination, so use it on your wedding night. I daresay it won't last more than a minute or two, from the looks of the dopey feller."

Incredibly they all thought she would throw away her dreams for the first man who agreed to take her. They were that desperate for money. She was heartily sick of the whole sordid business. All of it.

"And from now on, keep Rochfort out of harsh winds and cold rain. We need that weaklin' feller alive. For a while at least. Just to get him to the altar."

Chapter Twenty-One

After his afternoon on the lake, young Samuel had a basket of fish to show off. Some of it they left in the kitchens at Kingsthorpe to be smoked or salted. The rest Harriet told them to carry home to the inn. Since it was raining again by then, and there was no chance of getting more work done outdoors, Heath decided he had earned an afternoon off. The last thing he wanted was to work inside the house and hear Rochfort ringing his bell every five minutes.

Tipsy Rimple was always eager to share a mug of cider with his most important guest and would forget anything else he was meant to be doing whenever Heath returned to the inn. Today he greeted the returning fisherman, admired the catch with all due amazement, and sent his son into the scullery to wash his hands.

"Young Samuel speaks very highly of you, sir," he said. "Says you're teaching him all sorts."

"I hope so. He's a good lad. Eager to learn."

"Aye. I'm grateful to you, sir. I seldom have the time to take him fishing. I've not had much time to spare for him at all, and it must be hard on the lad, being the eldest."

"I can see you must be busy." And yet Tipsy, despite running a forge and an inn, and having lost his wife two years ago, still managed to show all his children love. If only other men, other fathers, could have acquired that skill, Heath thought. "Your children are lucky to grow up here with you," he said. "They will have wonderful memories to carry them into adulthood. A fine example to follow."

"Do you think so, sir?" Tipsy beamed, the apples of his cheeks blushing with ripe color. "I am sure of it."

"That's kind of you to say. And Miss Melinda says you don't give compliments for the sake of it."

"Indeed I do not." He rubbed his thigh. Wasn't going to ask, but he did. "What else has that menace mentioned about me?" She probably chattered a great deal.

"Not much else that I can recall."

Oh, well, he supposed that was.... "Good." Not in the least disappointing.

"Although that might be more dangerous." Tipsy chuckled. "Don't know what she's thinking when she's not talking. It's not usual in her case, and that's all I know."

Heath nodded and stretched out his boots to feel the warmth of the fire on his feet. He was getting accustomed to the bite of Tipsy's cider. It set his body into a comfortable mood after a hard day's work and on this afternoon, with the rain chasing him indoors, its qualities were especially soothing.

'Tis a good life, this is.

He'd have to see about taking some of Tipsy's cider back to London with him.

Back to London. He sighed. To the crowds, the noise and the stench. To the loneliness of his usual evenings. Odd how one could feel alone, even in the midst of a bustling place like Covent Garden.

The thought of leaving all this behind did not bring him much pleasure today, so he put it out of his mind. That was another thing to which he grew accustomed in the country— putting unpleasant things out of his mind and distracting himself with the good. Making a swift note of that, he mentally chastised himself. But not very crossly. He'd deal with that problem later.

"Another cider, sir?"

"Well...just one more, perhaps." It would do no harm.

Suddenly two figures crossed in front of the rain-dashed window and a moment later the door opened and they blew in.

"Miss Goodheart!"

At least she had an umbrella this time and she was with Hattie, not Rochfort. He could, therefore, forgive her for being out in the rain. In fact, she looked fetching. Very fetching.

"Good afternoon, Mr. Caulfield. I am glad to find you here, for I wanted to ask you about the horses. They are well, I hope?"

The horses. She came to ask about the horses.

What on earth had enticed him to think she came there to see him? Even if it was only a fleeting thought. A fancy.

No. He didn't have those.

He nodded. "Better now. Well looked after in these stables."

She closed her umbrella and set it by the fire. "It seems you've taken a liking to that cider, sir. Tipsy is a bad influence on you. Did you catch many fish today?"

"Master Samuel caught the most." He was conscious suddenly of the strong fish smell floating up from his shirt. "Then it started to rain again."

Having looked around to be sure that Hattie had gone into the kitchen with her brother, she said, "I have something to tell you about the horses."

He squinted. "Do you?"

Her entire body seemed to heave with one deeply inhaled breath. "They were...borrowed from the house of another gentleman. In London. Apparently there was a wager involved. He thought it was a game of sorts."

Heath scratched his cheek slowly. "He?"

She lowered her voice further. "Mr. Rochfort."

"He told you this?"

"Yes. I think he was feeling sorry for himself and brow-beaten by his cold. Perhaps even guilty too. It was my brother's idea, you see."

"Was it?"

"Oh, yes," she replied glumly "Lindley loves his games. The owner of the horses must have irritated him somehow, so he prompted his friend to take them."

"To steal them."

She blew out another breath and crumpled into the seat facing his. "That is why you came here, isn't it? You were following the stolen barouche and the horses."

With one swig he drained his tankard. "What makes you think that?"

"Did a gentleman named Hastings hire you to find them?"

He pressed his lips together.

"Surely you know you can trust me now! I came here to tell you what I knew and I could have stayed silent."

258

But there was too much she did *not* know and he wanted Rochfort for more than four stolen horses and a broken barouche.

"I came here," he said carefully, "for my health."

She glowered across the little table. "Ugh! You're impossible! And you stink of fish."

Slowly he smiled. Couldn't help it. When annoyed and frustrated she was quite delightful.

"Are you in your cups?" she muttered crossly, as if she read his mind.

"Perhaps."

"Did she tell you there's going to be a dance at the manor house?" Hattie cried, reappearing with cups of cider for herself and Melinda, her excitement apparently bubbling over. "It's been many years since the last one. Not since Sir Ludlow's wife were alive." She looked at Melinda and patted her arm. "I was a girl then, and I can still remember how jolly it was. How happy your mother was when she danced. The music and all the flowers. I never thought to see another like it. Not at Kingsthorpe Park. Not with your father the way he is. I did not think he'd agree to it."

"My father will do whatever Lindley and his friend want," she replied sullenly, "and they want entertainment."

"Then we shall make it a wonderful evening for everyone."

"I suppose so."

"You like to dance, Miss Melinda," said Hattie. "You know you'll enjoy yourself. You can dance with your handsome Mr. Rochfort."

Heath felt his mood darken. He toyed with his

tankard.

"You will come, of course, Mr. Caulfield."

Surprised, he looked up into Melinda's bright eyes. "I'm not much for dancing, Miss Goodheart."

"Oh, but you must. I know Lady Clara isn't here, but you must join in."

"Why?"

With a sigh of exasperation, she leaned across his table and assured him earnestly, "Because we have too many females and a shortage of gentlemen, especially those fit for dancing. Besides, surely you do sometimes seek enjoyment, do you not? You cannot be all work, Mr. Caulfield."

He watched a curl by her cheek. "Why can't I?"

"Because I believe Lady Clara would not be in love with you, if you were always so somber and disagreeable. She must have seen you merry, once at least."

"You know a lot about my—" he lifted his tankard and found it empty, "Lady Clara, do you? Despite meeting her only once?"

"I know about women."

"But you do not know about men. Not this one, in any case."

She huffed. "You take pride in that. Being so secretive."

"I do not dance, Miss Goodheart. Even if Lady Clara were here, I would not dance." He had not attended a dance since his university days and of those experiences he had very few good memories. Just a line of pale faces peering up at him, some openly disappointed that he was only a younger son, others making the best of it, waiting for something

260

better to come down the dance and catch their eye. He did not have the knack of chit-chat or the desire to charm. No woman remained long in his thoughts.

Until this one fell from a drainpipe into his arms and hadn't left since.

"How terrible for Lady Clara that you won't dance!"

"She would understand it. We are, neither of us, the sort who like to be the center of all attention."

"Now, you leave the gentleman alone," Hattie said, stirring up the fire and throwing another shovel of coal onto the flames. "He doesn't need you pestering him. Leave him to rest after all his hard work. He deserves an afternoon of peace. I daresay he came back here to get away from you."

"I'm not pestering, Mr. Caulfield," she replied defiantly. "I'm offering him my advice. Which he may take or leave, as he chooses. But if he is ever going to win his lady he must soften his temper. And take a chance, once in a while. Be bold and seize the moment." Leaping up out of her chair, the chatterbox took Tipsy by the hand, curtseyed and began to lead him around the small parlor in a minuet, humming a tune as she did so.

Tipsy merely looked befuddled, but amiably went along with the dance, shuffling his feet and periodically apologizing for stepping on her toes, until she swapped his hand for that of young Samuel who, having heard the ruckus, came downstairs to see what it was all about.

"She's always full of advice, is that one," Hattie murmured, standing beside Heath's chair. "Pity she doesn't listen to any in return."

"Ah, she is young. Means no harm."

Hattie gave him a sideways look and he realized that he had, once again, spoken his thoughts aloud.

"Mr. Caulfield, you must learn to dance," Melinda called out. "Lady Clara is a young person of refinement and accomplishments. If you do not dance, the next time you see her, she may dance with somebody else."

She was teaching Samuel, turning him around in a slow allemande, and Heath sat back to enjoy the sight of her figure in the firelight. She might not be the most graceful of dancers, but she was the most cheerful and energetic. It made a man want to smile, just watching her. Until he caught his reflection in the tankard.

Suddenly suffering an image of Melinda dancing with Rochfort, Heath could no longer sit still. Standing so swiftly he almost knocked his chair over, he captured her free hand in his and held it firmly. Startled, she came to a halt, dropping her grip on the young lad, who gratefully stumbled to a stool by the fire.

They had no music because she was too shocked to keep up her humming, and the others stared in a similar state of surprise.

* * * *

It was his right hand. She realized this at once, but he, apparently, had not thought about it until they were dancing. Then it was too late. She saw a flicker of worry in his eyes, but he blinked and it was gone.

Melinda knew how privileged she was to be given that hand, to be entrusted with it.

262

"Mr. Caulfield, you *can* dance!" Very well too.

"I did not say I could not dance," he replied softly. "Only that I do not."

But he was now. With her.

"We had better stop then," she murmured, suddenly lost in his gaze. But Hattie began tapping her feet to keep time and Caulfield would not release her hand. Before she knew it, he was spinning her around in a merry country dance, their small audience apparently enrapturedHis lips moved as if he counted the steps, but this afternoon he looked different, his face easier, less tense. He might almost be handsome.

Hastily she pulled away, covered with confusion, her feelings twisted into knots.

She had gone there that afternoon in hopes of seeing him alone to talk about the horses. Although she didn't want to get anybody into trouble, she knew he had to be told that they and the barouche were stolen from a London house party— if he did not already know. And if he did know, why had he done nothing yet?

But then he held her hand and she could not think. Nothing else seemed terribly important.

"Well, he showed you again, didn't he?" Hattie rocked in her chair, chuckling. "I don't think there's much you could teach Mr. Caulfield, young lady."

"Perhaps not." She sat, feeling breathless.

"I did not think you would give up so easily," he remarked wryly.

Melinda shook her head.

"You wanted me to dance, Miss Goodheart, and now you sit."

"Perhaps I have decided that *I* do not care to

dance."

* * * *

Strange. In the blink of an eye, she had gone
from lively laughter to a solemn, pensive demeanor
which was not like her at all. Perhaps it was just as
well, but now he was left standing and feeling stupid.

"Mr. Rochfort's constant bell-ringing wore you
out, did it?"

She turned to glare at him. "I simply did not feel
much like dancing anymore."

"With me. That is what you mean to say. You did
not care to dance with me."

"Yes," she snapped crossly.

"I see." He stood for a moment, listening to the
crackle of the fire, then he took his hat from the table
and went up to his chamber.

* * * *

Did he not know how it felt to hold his hand?
How it made her heart stumble over itself, her tongue
feel clumsy?

No, he did not mean for it to effect her that way,
and she had teased him until he got up to dance, so it
was partly her fault.

But now she wanted to cry. She was, by turns,
angry with herself and then with him. The only
person she could not be angry with was Lady Clara,
who knew none of this was happening.

When he had gone up to his room she and Hattie
discussed food, decorations and music for the ball.
There were Rimple cousins who played the fiddle and
the flute most nights at *The Willful Goat* and they

could be called upon to assemble a few other musically inclined friends from Castlebridge, as long as they were promised refreshments enough. Tipsy, of course, could provide beverages.

As Hattie chattered away, Melinda found her mind wandering to the man who had left them. She heard a few creaks across the low, timbered ceiling and now all was quiet up there. What was he doing? It was surely too early for bed. Was he sulking up there? Reading one of his precious books?

His tankard remained on the table where he left it, a wet ring showing where it had stood before the last time he lifted it to sip. There was the handle he had held. Probably with his left hand as the stiff wooden fingers would not fit easily in the curve.

But he had held her hand with his right.

She looked down at her fingers in her lap. They looked very small and insignificant tonight. Silly, childish hands.

"What's the matter with you, Miss Melinda? Are you day-dreaming again?"

She sighed. "No, just tired."

"I should think so too. The fellow Rochfort has had you running up and down all day, fussing over him. And that wretched man Moone does nothing but eavesdrop and then report it all to your brother."

She forced herself to pay attention. "Yes, apparently."

"Always whispering in Master Lindley's ear. Never has much to say to his master."

Melinda was thoughtful. There were a few occasions when she'd seen her brother and the manservant together, usually talking in the passage when nobody else was around. They always separated hastily when they saw her approach. Moone paid no heed to anybody else and treated Rochfort with the same thinly veiled disdain as he looked at *her.*

When she asked Rochfort if he had employed Moone for long, the gentleman said they had only been together for a few days.

"*But Moone always hears the most useful things,*" her brother had said. "*Worth his weight in gold. Astounding what he's found out for me in servants' halls over the years. That's where all the gossip can be found.*"

She should have realized that Moone was her brother's friend, not Rochfort's valet. For some reason they had decided to hide the truth. Another of her brother's pranks?

"You've gone pale now. Are you sure you're not coming down with that cold? If nursing that dandy Mr. Rochfort has made you ill, I shall—"

"No. It's not that." She stood, feeling unsteady on her feet, but resolved in her heart. "I must speak with Mr. Caulfield. There's something I forgot to warn him about."

Hattie looked shocked. "You cannot go up there now. Not to a gentleman's bedchamber."

"He has not gone to bed, has he? Besides, it is a matter of urgency and I think we both know I'll be safe with him. He's not the sort of man to ravish a woman against her will, is he?"

"That's beside the point, young lady."

"Actually, it is the very point. He's a gentleman."

She knew he would never have taken advantage of a lady to seduce her away from his family, whatever Lindley had tried to suggest. She'd known that all

266

along and to even wonder about it— however briefly— was ridiculous.

Not pausing to argue longer with Hattie, she raced up the stairs, stood for a breathless moment in the narrow hall outside his door and then raised her hand to knock.

Chapter Twenty-Two

Before her knuckles made contact, it swung open and there he was, barefoot. And bare-chested. "Melinda! I wondered what the devil was coming up the stairs! I thought the house was afire!"

Down in the parlor Hattie was yelling at her, but she ignored it.

"My brother knows that her name is Lady Clara," she blurted. "Moone heard us in the kitchen and now Lindley is making up wicked stories. I had to warn you." It all flew out of her in a rush and then she felt better, relieved. "It wasn't that I didn't want to dance with you. I just had too much in my head. I couldn't remember the steps."

He didn't seem to know what to say for a moment.

Trying not to look at his chest simply made her look more, so she might as well get it over with. He wore only his breeches. Had even removed his gloves. Her gaze skimmed his wooden fingers, where they held the door open, and then she let her perusal flutter down over his taut stomach.

"I was changing my shirt," he managed finally.

"So I see."

"It stank of fish."

"Yes." *Stop looking, you wicked, wicked woman.*

"I thought that was why you didn't care to dance with me."

"Oh."

He had gone up there to change shirts, just for her. But this wouldn't do at all.

She panicked. "Lady Clara," she said again, her throat tight. "Did you hear what I said? Lindley knows about her. He has some unpleasant gossip about a Lady Clara Beauspur."

Without waiting for any invitation, or protest, she ducked under his arm and walked into the room.

The beams were low; he must crack his head a lot, unless he was cautious. And he would be cautious, of course. Not like her— crashing into everything and falling from drainpipes.

"Unpleasant gossip?" he murmured, turning to watch her.

"That she fell in love with a man of whom her family did not approve. That he seduced her, ruined her reputation, and abandoned her."

In the corner of her eye she saw him go very still, arms at his sides. "And you thought I was this man."

"That's what Lindley seems to think. I warned you it would do you no favors here to be secretive." Melinda walked around the small, candlelit chamber, taking it all in: the open trunk full of unremarkable clothes. So plain and dreary that one might think he made a study of it. No fashion, but all well made and good material. No patches. Everything very neat and folded just so. "I *could* imagine that you are repentant and try now to win her back. There is, it must be said, something very sad in your face at times, and it would explain your nervousness— why you act so mysteriously when she is mentioned. There is also the young lady herself, closeted away with her guardian in that little cottage. But who keeps her there? Is it her family, who hide her from the world and from you? There is definitely something or someone from whom

Lady Clara hides. So you see, I *could* imagine all that."

His precious books sat upon the writing desk under the window, which was open. The rain had ceased now, and a cool, damp breeze, honeyed with autumnal scents, whispered between them, tickling her cheek, disturbing the thick air of his room. A remnant of burnt sausages seemed to cling to the very walls and beams.

"But I know you better than Lindley knows you," she said softly. "I know you don't ruin women. You rescue them. You rescue them whether they like it or not."

Slowly he scratched his chest.

When she looked at his eyes they were narrowed, fixed upon her. She felt, in that moment, as if she faced down the rifle barrels of a firing squad.

Had she made the wrong conclusion? Perhaps he was not so safe, after all.

"Tell me, madam," he growled, "is this visit to my chamber entirely proper?" He remained in the doorway, one hand keeping the door ajar.

She put her chin up. "As you said, my propriety has ephemeral qualities."

For a long moment he stared and then, abruptly, he laughed. It swept out of him, a gale of good humor. Leaving the door open he stepped into the room and the shy afternoon light touched his face with a gentle hand, suddenly giving it more expression than usual. More tenderness. His face looked less sad and tired today, but his eyes were still wary and ready to flinch. No, he was not like a bulldog, she thought, remembering what her father had called him. He was a bull mastiff, his build quietly powerful, his manner patient, dignified and courageous.

"Besides we are friends now and you must trust me," she added, relieved by his laughter. "Will you tell me now why you came here?"

Slowly he folded his arms, feet apart, looking a little too pleased with himself. "Since you're so clever and perceptive, Miss Melinda Goodheart of The Wayward Imagination and Desperate Bonnets, should you not have uncovered this mystery yourself by now?"

With a groan, she reached into his trunk, took out a shirt and tossed it at him. "Kindly put that on."

He caught it with his left hand. "I thought you were unmoved by the sight of a male chest."

"I think I might have obtained Mr. Rochfort's cold and it has weakened me. Any awful sight could set me over the edge."

"I see. We wouldn't want that, would we? Miss Goodheart *on* the edge is dangerous enough."

"How very amusing!"

As he began pulling the shirt over his head, Melinda turned away and surveyed the books on his table again, flipping open the first one. Dull, stuffy books on the outside, complicated and dense with words inside. They were the sort of books she would usually pass over in favor of a gothic romance with a sensational title. Or she would have, in the past. She was beginning to appreciate the old adage about not judging a book by its cover. But before she could open the last tome, he stopped her, his hand resting over hers.

"Curiosity, Miss Goodheart, killed the cat."

She pulled her hand from under his, feeling as if

it had scorched her. "What's in the book then?" Her thoughts raced with ideas. "Is it your diary? Is it full of torrid stories? No, I daresay it is a list of your expenses and how many pairs of stockings you've lost in the laundry, or some other dreary thing."

He looked perplexed and then laughed, tucking the book under his arm and away from her prying fingers.

"Do you mean to arrest Mr. Rochfort for stealing the horses?" she demanded.

"Why would you care what happens to him?"

"My brother is just as much to blame for setting such a wager. He is thoughtless and cruel. Mr. Rochfort is merely... easily led."

He gave a snort. "He acts the part well enough. But as I said to you earlier, he's well beyond the age when he might deny responsibility for his actions. He cannot escape the consequences by feigning stupidity. Thievery is thievery. We do not have one rule for a poor man and another for the idle rich."

"You took a dislike to him from the beginning. I think it has colored your view of his actions."

"*Damn you, woman,*" he roared suddenly, making her jump. "Open your eyes for once and see what is really before you, not what you want to imagine!"

His hair was rumpled, calling out for fingers to comb through it. She quickly looked away again, ashamed of herself. Oh, why did he suddenly have to look so attractive when angry? Was it because she knew she could not have him? That would be just like her, of course. Contrary!

* * * *

"Well, really. There is no occasion to raise your voice."

Much to his bemusement, having barged her way into his room, the woman suddenly made her way out again, keeping her back to him and bumping into the beams, murmuring about work to do.

"I hope you don't mean to run back to Kingsthorpe Park and warn your gentleman friend," he muttered.

She stopped in the doorway, her curls twitching with irritation. "That is just what you think of me, is it? Oh yes, an absurd chatterbox."

"That was your interpretation of my words," he replied tightly. "But far be it from me to correct you."

Spinning around on her heel, she walked up to him, stopped a few inches away, poked him in the chest with her finger and said, "Mr. Rochfort has been led into trouble by my brother. He is not a wicked man. I have an instinct for these things. If there is a trial when you haul him back to London in chains, I will speak on his behalf."

Yes, he could see she'd like that. The drama of it. She probably already had one of her bonnets picked out for the event. He smirked. "The average trial at the Old Bailey lasts eight and a half minutes. They don't have time for the ramblings of flighty young women."

"Flighty? I'll have you know, sir, that Mr. Rochfort thinks me refreshing and artless. He values me as an independent soul!"

"Congratulations, you too have fallen victim to a handsome face and a few well-placed compliments. Like so many addled young ladies." He paused. "And

I thought you might be different. I'm disappointed."

Her eyelashes swept down and her lips moved uncertainly. For once silently.

Before she could turn away he caught her wrist in his left hand. When she tried to pull back, he kept it in his fierce grip and felt her quickened pulse.

"I must inform you that Mr. Rochfort is not who or what he pretends to be. He is more than an amateur horse thief. Much more dangerous than that. I would advise you to stay well away from him."

"How do you know what he is?" she demanded.

"Because I followed him here."

"I knew it," she cried, trying once again to pull away from him. "So you *are* here on a matter of business, after all. You lied to me."

"I had no choice. I did not know if I could trust you, Melinda. All I knew of you then was that you like to dispense your own forms of justice and take matters into your own hands. I couldn't have you getting —"

"In your way?"

"Getting hurt. I told you I would cause you no harm while I was here. Nor would I allow anyone else to harm you."

"You didn't like Mr. Rochfort from the first. I suppose because he is handsome and—"

"William Rochfort, as he currently calls himself, is a crook, a thief, a charlatan. He survives by pushing his way into the lives of the idle rich, befriending them and, like a leech, bleeding them of all their wealth and property until they are depleted and he is sated. Whereupon he drops away, changes his identity, and slithers off in search of another plump

274

victim. Your brother appears to be his latest. And now you."

She closed her eyes, briefly disrupting the dance of the fireflies. "Then you used your acquaintance with me to gain admittance to my father's house and keep an eye on a man you believe to be a villain? You put on a sad face so that Hattie and I felt sorry for you."

"Yes," he ground out between gritted teeth. "I do love to be a creature of pity."

"Clearly you played us both for fools. She's been feeding you and I've been...all this time..." She swallowed hard, her pulse fluttering even more wildly under his fingers. "All this time I have thought of you as a kind and generous man."

"I am. I hope. I try."

"But meanwhile you used us for the opportunity to spy on Mr. Rochfort. How could you take advantage of me? Of my family? To worm your way in—"

"I did not know who you were when I first came here. I never knew your name." He lowered his voice, mindful of the people below in the parlor. "Only when I arrived here did I learn that you were Lindley Goodheart's sister. It was not planned that I should *worm my way in* through my very slight acquaintance with you. In fact, I did not want to. You invited me to dine, if you recall, madam, and you were very insistent. When I saw how Rochfort had his eye on you, naturally, I had to stay close. For your own good." He paused, steadied his voice again. "I wanted only to protect you."

"Because it's your duty, as a gentleman?"

He nodded.

For a third time she tried to pull away, but he held her adamantly. There was, suddenly, nothing duty-bound, or gentlemanly, about the way he felt. It tore out of him on a spitting breath of frustration.

"I won't let him have you."

The unbearable desire to kiss her rocked through his body, a hot, hard tension tightening every muscle and sinew.

Her lips were slightly parted, her eyes wide and suddenly fearful, as he had never seen them.

What had he done? What was she turning him into?

"Forgive me." His fingers loosened and flexed, releasing her wrist.

Slowly she backed up toward the open door. Then, without another word, she ran out of his chamber and descended the creaking stairs with the same clattering noise as she came up them before.

He heard Hattie chiding the young woman for "bothering that nice Mr. Caulfield", to which she replied haughtily, "I'm sure I couldn't *bother* him if I tried. The man has no feelings. He's the most uninspiring slab of mutton I ever met."

Walking to his window, he looked down in time to see her running across the yard. She stopped to look up at him and when she saw him standing there she was obviously surprised.

Naturally, she stuck out her tongue.

Heath laughed, the tension dissolved. But he knew that for all her bold chatter and claims of fearlessness, he'd frightened her. When she thought he was going to kiss her, she didn't know what to do

276

with herself.

Not that she would ever admit her fear of his kiss. She was as likely to confess a weakness, as he was to ever admit how much he wanted to kiss her.

Chapter Twenty-Three

The prospect of a ball was much talked about by the kitchen staff at Kingsthorpe Park, and with Rochfort being Sir Ludlow's unofficial guest of honor it was unlikely the villain would go anywhere until after the event. He was too closely watched by the old man and his son. But Heath had no doubt that, having found little worth stealing at Kingsthorpe Park and bored of lying low, Rochfort would take his chance to leave soon after the ball, or during it— while everybody was distracted. The "Cuckoo" always came and went suddenly, which helped him to vanish and re-invent himself so often. Sometimes he left his temporary nest with a trunk full of stolen goods; sometimes he took coin or banknotes, or plate and candelabra that was later sold in Town. Sometimes he took women, whether for money or simply his own malevolent pleasure. To feed the insatiable beast of his greed and profligacy

But he would take Melinda over Heath's dead body.

She had, much to his relief, held her tongue about the information he gave her. Whether or not she believed him, he could not tell. Perhaps he should have told her everything— including Rochfort's part in his sister's troubles— but that was a matter that tended to make him even angrier when he spoke of it. Who knew what he might have done if that came out too?

No, there was no need to make her privy to all that. His sister would certainly prefer as few folk as possible to know about it and Heath had told nobody the full story, not even the kindly Mrs. Oliver. Instead he kept it in his own breast and suffered in silence.

Meanwhile, the villain who caused all this could play malingerer no longer, his illness probably cured quicker than expected by the fact that Heath took the bell out of his room and buried it in the garden. It was only his second choice of where to hide the thing, but he decided to be content with that. For now.

With no other way to summon his nurse, the "Cuckoo" had no choice but to get up. A physician arrived to look him over and provide medicine, but by then his services were hardly required. Heath, who had never had much patience for illness, wondered if there had ever been any cold at all.

"Seems to me the fellow just wanted to enjoy a few days in bed, being waited on," he said one day in the kitchen at Kingsthorpe.

Melinda, naturally, insisted that Rochfort had been very sick. Just as she insisted that her own nursing was responsible for curing him. "Certain men think that certain women are nothing more than meddling busybodies who cannot be trusted and never know what they're doing. That they are not mature enough to be of help."

Bemused, he looked at her. *Where did she come up with these ideas?*

"They cannot believe," she continued, "that certain women are not utterly useless and a mere inconvenience to men in general."

"Certain women," he muttered, thinking of those wide, startled eyes, "are all talk."

"Certain men don't talk nearly enough when they

should."

"Certain women talk enough for the both of them."

The debate ended when Hattie set a bowl of potatoes down for Melinda to peel and Heath remembered his list of jobs.

* * * *

He was outside, mending the rose arbor, when Lindley Goodheart slipped into view between the bushes and planted himself firmly in the grass, knuckles on hips, his very posture one of arrogance and conceit.

"I hope you know, sir, that you waste your time here every day. My sister is far out of your reach, and it is something of a mystery to me why you continue this pursuit. Moone assures me you are nobody and have nothing to offer the lady."

"Moone assures you?"

"He hears and sees a great deal."

"I'm sorry, Mr. Goodheart, I do not have the pleasure of understanding you." He continued twisting wire around the thorny branches, eyes on the task at hand. "Perhaps you have caught your friend's fever?"

"I can see you must be a rather thick-headed fellow."

Heath kept his expression blank.

Goodheart strolled around the arbor, smacking his gloves into his palm. "My sister is a generous, somewhat naive, woman and seems to consider you with some *kindness*," he said the word as if it tasted bad in his mouth. "But that is all there is to it.

Sympathy. If she has misled you in any way—"

"She has not misled me. I don't believe she could if she tried."

"Then you must know you are far below her. Why are you here?"

"To look after Miss Goodheart. Why are you here?"

Lindley stopped, his nostrils slightly flared. "I brought William Rochfort here for my sister, and you will not get in his way."

Heath paused his work and glanced at the other man. "What do you know of your friend?"

"I know he is perfect for us."

"And your sister?"

"Will do as she's told."

"I would not wager on that. Even if I were you."

Outrage caused a vein in Lindley's forehead to bulge ominously and his lips strained over his teeth. "I hear you have some connection with a Lady Clara Beauspur."

"Yes, Melinda told me you've been spreading the gossip about—"

"*Melinda*? How dare you address her so informally?"

It was a slip. Quickly he returned to his work, twisting the broken branches together. One particularly large thorn stuck right through his glove. He cursed under his breath.

The agitated man continued. "I demand to know at once whether there has been any intimacy between you and my sister— anything to obstruct her marriage to William Rochfort. I sensed a connection of some sort from the first, and it has made me increasingly

281

uneasy."

"Oh, I would hate to spoil your plans."

"I don't like your manner, sir. Or your face."

"Yes, I've been told its bothersome, but it's adequate for my purposes."

Lindley stepped back, holding his gloves tightly. "Where are you from?"

"Here and there."

"You will tell me, sir, how you came to be acquainted with my sister. This nonsense about rescuing a bonnet—"

"There is nothing more than a friendship between your sister and myself, Goodheart." He almost felt reluctance to admit it. And then he couldn't resist annoying the fellow by adding softly, "I tore her gown a few times and that is all there is to it."

"I beg your pardon?" The fellow had turned puce.

"By accident, of course. She is somewhat reckless, as you know."

"Why are you smiling, sir?"

Hadn't realized he was, and it took longer to curb than usual.

He thought of the time she swept a stray horse hair from his face. The touch of her fingertips to his lips. Of the way she smiled so easily at him. Of the way he had wanted to kiss her by the water pump and how he was interrupted by Rochfort's window opening above.

"You're a very common sort of man, evidently, with no sense of the gentleman's code, or else you would step down and leave my sister alone, knowing that William Rochfort has more to give."

"Leave her alone and unprotected, a victim of your mercenary motives and your questionable friend's morals? I've seen what *Mr. Rochfort* can do to a young lady, and I'm here to see to it that it doesn't happen again. By the way, you are quite mistaken if you think you know anything about him. I realize you think you've found the goose that lays golden eggs, but Rochfort will take you for every penny and be gone before the wedding bouquet has wilted. If the *marriage* even gets that far."

"How dare you? You're nothing more than an ill-mannered groom, who does not know his place."

Heath looked at the fellow and said steadily, "I will not let you or him cause Melinda any hurt."

"Again you call her by her first name."

"Oops. So I do. You'd best put a stop to me before I do it again. We common men have no social graces. Not like a pompous dandy."

Goodheart moved swiftly, hand ready to slash his gloves across Heath's face, but he did not get that satisfaction. Moving even faster, Heath blocked the other man's arm with his right and then sent a sound punch into that soft, arrogant belly with his left.

It was remarkably pleasing, a release.

Lindley Goodheart doubled over, wheezing and spitting.

"Keep your big head down a while until the pain eases," Heath muttered, before striding away into the house.

* * * *

"Miss Melinda...may I call you that?"

She was barely listening, too busy stretching up to fix a bower of greenery to the wooden crest above the fireplace. "Could you pass me a nail, Mr. Rochfort?"

"Oh...of course." He looked around for the box and passed one up to her. "I wondered if I might have a word with you. A matter of some delicacy."

Melinda aimed her hammer. "Yes?"

"I spoke to your father this morning, Miss Melinda, and he made it clear to me that I have his blessing to—"

"Blast! I dropped the nail. Could you pass me another? What were you saying?"

He handed her another nail and she readied her hammer again.

"Sir Ludlow is amenable to the idea of—"

At that point another expletive, far worse than the first, escaped Melinda's mouth, due to the fact that the business end of her hammer had contacted not with the head of the iron nail at which it was aimed, but at the end of her own finger. Blood instantly ran from the fingernail and Mr. Rochfort stumbled for the nearest window, unable to complete his sentence.

For which she was grateful.

* * * *

She was sat alone in the priest's hole with a candle, her box of Grandmother Ethelreda's treasures and the remains of a rhubarb pie. The candle, marked with lines at every inch to tell the hour, had burned down almost two inches, and she had come to a somewhat remarkable discovery by the time the door to her hiding place creaked open.

"Are you not supposed to be dressing for the ball?"

"Why did you have to be the one to find me?" she exclaimed, fraught, gripping her box of treasure to her bosom.

"I followed the trail of pie crumbs. I remembered that rhubarb was your favorite."

She scowled. "How could you know that?"

"I listen more than I speak. Try it occasionally and you will be surprised by what you learn."

"Well, there is no room for you in here." Melinda tried to shut the door again, but Caulfield squeezed his way in, ignoring her protest. "Mind the candle! For pity's sake, what are you doing? This is not—"

"Hush, before everybody hears you." The candle flame fluttered wildly, pummeled by his breath and then the draft as he pulled the hidden door shut behind him.

"There's no pie left." That must surely be the only thing he wanted from her.

"What or who are you hiding from in here, Miss Goodheart?"

"I have much to think about. I suppose it shocks you that I do think."

He looked grim. As usual. "It does rather alarm me," he admitted.

She licked her lips and forged ahead. "Mr. Rochfort is about to propose marriage."

At once his face paled. He looked down at the crumbs on the platter between them. His jaw tightened. "I see."

"At least," she added, "he has my father's

permission already, and soon he will ask me." Holding up her bandaged finger she explained, "I escaped the subject temporarily."

He exhaled a slow breath, like a kettle letting out steam after it was removed from the fire.

"If he is really the villain you think he is, I could help you capture him," she whispered.

His head bowed. She waited, forcing patience for once.

The walls of that hiding place were thick, letting no sound in or out, but occasionally there was a distant rumble from somewhere within the walls, a slow drip, or a mysterious flutter that made her think of ghosts. A house this old must have plenty, but she'd never met any.

Ghosts of Goodhearts who had not made the most of their lives and now bitterly regretted it. Ancient Goodhearts and Bon Coeurs who missed opportunities and overlooked treasures of greater value, because they, like their hapless descendant Melinda, was a noisy blunderer. She looked down at her grandmother's box of jewelry.

At last he spoke. "I appreciate that you want to help, but I must keep you safe."

She sensed that he'd struggled hard to find the right words this time. To not get angry again.

"I do not need your protection. But I thank you for finally telling me the truth about your own purpose here. Perhaps now you will leave me alone to make my decision about Mr. Rochfort."

"What is there to decide?" he exclaimed. "You cannot marry him. You know you cannot."

She smiled brightly and innocently. "Why ever

286

not?"

"I would have thought that was obvious, as you like to say."

Her throat was dry, her heart pounding. "You are so sure he is the man you seek?"

"Yes." There was no equivocation.

"But Mr. Rochfort doesn't seem evil to me, just rather full of himself, not very clever and not very industrious. Which can be said of most gentlemen I know."

"He's a thief, a seducer, and a charlatan. Most criminals do not look as you would expect, Melinda."

"Yet Lindley takes more from him than *he* has taken from us."

"What about your dowry?"

She laughed softly. "Counterfeit pearls. As he well knows. If there was anything of real worth, Lindley would have taken it from this box already. He has no qualm about taking anything he thinks he should have, even from my dinner plate at times, so he would take the pearls too if they had value." Melinda knew that her brother must not have discovered the secret, velvet lined drawer hidden inside the bottom of the box. If he had it would have been empty when she, just half an hour before, accidentally stumbled upon it. Now she knew why her grandmother had commissioned a special box to be made, and why the dear old lady had advised Melinda to look beyond the obvious. Ethelreda was clearly not so eccentric as they'd all thought. Knowing, all too well, the greed of her son and grandson, she had cleverly misled them by placing worthless pearls inside the box, and concealing the real necklace in a hidden compartment beneath.

Grandmother Ethelreda had loved her secrets and her games— particularly hide and seek.

Melinda flirted now with the idea of telling Caulfield about her discovery, but why should she? He had not been very forthcoming with his own secrets, to put it mildly. And now that she suddenly held real treasure in her hands, she wanted to relish the sensation awhile before anybody else knew about it. Representatives of the male gender would, undoubtedly, try to take it away from her. Caulfield, being the suspicious type, might think she'd stolen it.

"And Rochfort?" he demanded. "Does he know these pearls of yours are worthless?"

"Certainly. He has heard my brother say it many times and he looked at them himself before giving them back to me. If he was an unscrupulous thief, as you suggest, would he not have taken them and left, rather than proposing marriage just to get his hands on them?" Melinda knew the secret drawer had not been opened in years. The mechanism was rigidly stiff and the velvet lining still as bright and plush as it must have been when first nailed inside.

They were quiet for a while, the only sound that of her puttering flame, dancing in their breath.

"I do not know what Mr. Rochfort wants with me," she said.

He scowled. "Not all inducements take monetary form, Melinda."

She looked askance. "What else might anybody want from me?"

His eyes warmed and his lips, usually so reticent to make any movement, bent very slightly. "He could simply want you."

"What for?"

He scratched the side of his nose. "Oh, you have certain qualities a man might want."

It puzzled her that he would say such a thing. Fortunately she was already inside a cupboard, or else she would have had to find one.

And when he raised his hand to thrust frustrated fingers back through his hair, she suddenly realized the dreadful, gruesome and inescapable truth.

I'm falling in love stupidly, blunderingly, with a man who belongs to somebody else.

It was another stiff, secret drawer suddenly opening in her hands.

Yes, after all this time she was falling through mid-air again. Falling for a real man, and the furthest thing from a highwayman he could possibly be.

And yet he had Lady Clara. Or Lady Clara had him. Again she was appalled by the emerald streak of wicked jealousy that burned through her like lightning.

Damn him.

When he had told Melinda that he was disappointed in her it had cut her pride like one of those vicious thorns on the rose arbor. At the time she was vexed, not knowing why it upset her so, but now she knew.

"I wish you had told me about your suspicions from the beginning," she said solemnly, trying to ignore the heat in her face, "but I understand that you could not trust me then. I suppose you thought I would try to capture him myself, then take all the credit and reward." She paused, licked her lips. "*Is* there a very great reward for his capture? There must be."

He looked at her, his eyes dark and heavy in the glow of her flame. "Do not get any ideas, Melinda."

"Me?" She smiled as cheerfully as she could. "I never get any ideas."

"Melinda, these matters must be handled with caution. I know what I'm doing."

"Well, naturally. And I'm the sort of girl who blunders about, speaking her foolish mind and getting her heart crushed." Short of breath, she bit her tongue. "I am a silly thing, just as you said." She tried to make light of it now, the laughter skipping out over her tongue, but she saw in his dark fathoms of his gaze that he was sorry.

If only things were different.

Yes, she had finally learned to read his expression.

He put his left hand over hers, steadying the candle. "Melinda, I forbid you from getting involved in this."

"But I already am." More than he knew. Much more.

How ironic that she had once playfully picked him out as her future husband, not realizing she would soon trip over her own feet and fall in love with him. Or that he belonged to another woman already and therefore was not hers to choose.

When they were this close she was terribly conscious of his strength and stature. The scent of him filled her. The merest brush of his shirtsleeve to her hand was enough to make her skin shiver and sing shamelessly. And he didn't even try.

What would happen if he did? It didn't bear thinking about.

Chapter Twenty-Four

Melinda's eyes were wide open, the fireflies exceptionally lively today in the light of that solitary candle.

What had she just said? Something about her heart being crushed? Who was responsible? He would take the blackguard's teeth out.

His own heart clenched like a fist. "Melinda—"

"I know," she interrupted hastily. "You are in love with Lady Clara and she with you, but I hope...I hope you think of me as a friend to you both. I would like to be your very good friend." She blinked, and some of the fireflies disappeared. "That is all I can...all I wanted to say."

It was not, however. He knew at once there was more. There always would be with Melinda. A young lady was supposed to flutter her fan and feign disinterest, but Melinda was incapable of cunning tricks and fakery. And she never ran out of words.

She was pulling back, trying to take her candle, but his left hand was still around hers and he did not want to let her go. His fingers tightened their grip.

"I knew you wanted to keep your distance," she whispered, "but I could not respect your wishes. I have no one to blame but myself for this pain."

"Melinda—"

"Please say nothing," she gasped, the flame dancing wildly between them.

"But I must."

"Think of Lady Clara."

"I am. I think of her every day."

292

"Yes."

"Because she's my sister."

* * * *

She thought she must have misheard, but when he repeated the sentence there was no mistaking it. Fortunately, trapped in so small space, she could do nothing but sit still.

"How can that be?" she snapped. "How? How can Lady Clara Beauspur be your sister? I don't understand." Confused and anxious, her emotions heightened, pulsing across her skin, Melinda waited for his answer.

"I am the third son of the Duke of Ormandsey, for all that is worth."

The candle trembled and then steadied again as his hand tightened gently around hers.

Shivers tickled up her spine. She ought to be furious with him for not telling her, all this time, that Clara was his sister. Apparently he agreed.

"Are you going to slap me across the face now?" he asked.

Of course that was what he expected, thinking her a silly woman "*prone to acts of impulse*".

"You did say you would warn me in advance," he added, half turned away in preparation for her strike.

Melinda exhaled a sigh and shook her head. "I cannot see the point of it. The deed is done and although a certain cleansing satisfaction might be achieved from my point of view, it won't teach you anything, will it? I'm sure I would not be the first wounded lady to administer a stinging hand, nor will I be the last, if you continue this deceitful way of life."

"Ah. So you will get your vengeance in some other way and drag out my torment."

She smirked. "Precisely."

After a moment he relaxed his shoulders a little.

"And you work as an agent of Bow Street, despite being a Duke's son?"

"You think I should waste my life doing nothing?" A sharpness returned to his voice, and his eyes narrowed, flinching. Anger simmered not far beneath his surface, as if this information he'd been forced to give her, was a poisonous draught that changed him from one man to another. One more dangerous.

"I didn't mean that," she said carefully. "I am merely surprised. You don't act like a Duke's son at all."

"I take that as a compliment."

"And I meant it as one."

Suddenly the fluttering flame expired, leaving a curling wisp of grey smoke. Then darkness. Had he blown it out deliberately, or was her startled breath the last zephyr to catch that flame's twisting edge and devour it?

The blackness enveloped them both, and she could hear her heart beating in her ears. Gradually reality was catching up with itself, the spinning wheel of her mind churning steadily. "Then your name is not Caulfield?"

"It is my middle name. I don't use the Beauspur. I prefer to be my own man." He added crossly, "What else do you want to know?"

"Well, gracious, I believe I have some right to be curious, since you lied all this time and let me believe

294

Lady Clara was your sweetheart."

"I let you believe what you wanted. I simply went along with it and did not correct you. I wouldn't dare."

"Then tell me the truth now, you wretched man! All of it!"

In the dark he sprouted prickles and spikes. She felt them growing out toward her, their cold tips trying to keep her at bay. He spoke icily as he told his story.

"My sister and I were the youngest in the family. We always took the brunt of my father's temper. Clara because she was born deaf. In his eyes it was unacceptable, an imperfection that could not be borne. A blot on the family. She was shut away like a dark secret, and he hired no tutors for her, just a stern old nurse. He made no marriage plans for her future. I think he simply wanted to forget she had ever been born."

"How...how dreadful. And you? You said you both took the brunt of his temper?"

"I stood up for Clara...for anyone or anything he abused, and to my father that showed disloyalty. I tried to teach my sister to speak, but her attempts horrified and frustrated my father so much that he forbade me to continue. The duke, you see, had to have everything in its place. Everything had to meet his standards of perfection or else it was inadequate, rotten, a shameful blemish in his sight. Nobody outside the family and the house staff was ever to know of her deafness. We lived with the secret. It was never to be spoken of. Even Clara herself was never to be spoken of outside that house."

Melinda shook her head, horrified.

"After university, I received a letter from my father, informing me that he had chosen a wife for me. Rather than submit to his plans, I went into the cavalry. He was shocked by my defiance, furious. When I was discharged due to my wounded hand, I returned to find that Clara had...she had run away from my father's estate, the only life and home she had ever known. She was in trouble and lost." He stopped. "I had to find her, so I—"

"Clara was one of *his* victims, wasn't she?"

He groaned softly, and she could feel the anger simmering in the dark. Anger he tried to hold in.

"The man you hunt is the one who seduced her?" she whispered, her heart aching. "That story Lindley told me—"

"She thought herself in love. She knew nothing of life. It was not her fault."

"Of course it was not!"

He cursed. "I shouldn't tell you this. It is a private matter."

"You don't need to tell me," she replied sadly. "I can guess what happened. Your sweet sister was an innocent who had never even been away from your father's estate. The fellow took advantage of her."

She heard him inhale a deep breath, felt the air move as he fidgeted. "Perhaps he would have married her, had my father agreed to provide the dowry he expected. Perhaps. But his history suggests otherwise. In any case, His Grace, the Duke of Ormandsey, does not submit to blackmail, not even for the sake of saving his only daughter's reputation. Once the villain—who then called himself John Croft—

296

realized that the Duke would sooner disown his daughter and cut her off completely than accept her with such a husband, he left her for richer quarry. Our father turned his back on Clara, refused to help her. She was abandoned on the streets of London, unable to explain anything to anyone, unable to hear."

His words licked around her in the dark, hard and angry, flicking at her, as if trying to make her squirm, to scare her away.

"That is the monstrous family into which I was born, Melinda. People who would rather abandon a young girl to the degradations of the workhouse, or the gutter, rather than risk their name being tainted by scandal. This is why I do not use the name, the title, or any of that meaningless drivel." She heard his breathing slow. "Thankfully, I found my sister in Whitechapel, terrified and alone. Of course, no one living in that hovel knew who she was or anything about her. She could not have told them, even had she wanted to. I hired Mrs. Oliver to take care of her. Now I know she is safe and she has learned to speak with her hands. As you, no doubt, saw."

She nodded.

"As far as I know, our father thinks us both dead by now. Many outside our family never even knew the Duke of Ormandsey had a daughter. If they knew, or remembered that a girl was born at Beauspur Rising, they knew only that she was an invalid of some sort. To this day, only Mrs. Oliver, my family, that old spinster nurse sworn to secrecy, and a man who once called himself John Croft, know that Clara can neither hear nor speak. Such was our father's desire to hide my sister from the world, to deny her existence and erase, what he felt to be, his one imperfection."

Slowly the picture was made complete. Tears pricked her eyes, dampened her eyelashes. "And John Croft is William Rochfort?"

"Those are but two of his incarnations. He is known to Bow Street as The Cuckoo."

Even when the snuffed candle had fallen from her grip, their hands had remained joined, but now he began to remove his.

"So you see now why I felt the need to become a police officer. I had to do something, make something useful of my life. Help others less fortunate."

Oh, yes, she understood that desire.

Melinda was grateful that he had told her all this. Allowing her a peek into his life must have cost him, for she knew how reserved he was and how he valued his privacy. Not only his, but that of his sister too.

His sister.

She was his sister.

Her heart whispered the words, and they echoed around her head. Suddenly she reached beyond those unfriendly prickles with which he tried to fill the darkness and found his right hand. She heard his gasp as she lifted the fingers to her lips and kissed them, one by one, through his leather glove. Even those he tried to hide from her.

Then, with both hands, she felt for his shoulders, his face, his lips.

How cold his life must have been, she thought.

And they only had one life to live.

Life without risk was no life at all.

So she leaned forward, plunging into the ebony

298

depths, and kissed him. It was awkward and clumsy and oafish as anything she'd ever done, but desperate situations required extreme measures.

* * * *

He couldn't stop her any more than he could have turned back the tide by raising his hand. And very quickly he knew he didn't want to try.

There was too much stifled passion and desire, and he was, after all, just a man like any other. He held her waist and then moved his left hand to her hair, tentative at first, unsure of what he meant to do. Closing his eyes, he pictured the brilliant bronze and copper— as it was in daylight— floating around him.

He had to remove his gloves, needed those heavy, silken locks against the bare skin of his hands.

Why would anybody, he wondered distantly, ever feel the need to decorate that natural abundance with foolish flowers. Melinda Goodheart was a force of nature herself and required no embellishment. He would never, for the life of him, understand her love of extravagant bonnets to cover that hair.

Then, even as he kissed her back with greater fervor, and let his bare hands touch her, relishing the softness, a stern voice in his head tried to remind him that he liked his solitary, well-ordered life. Heath Caulfield could certainly not afford a wife and should not be kissing this woman in a dark cupboard.

Footsteps.

She pulled back, slipping out of his grasp. He heard the hitch in her breath before she held it. His own pulse thumped so hard he felt it in the balls of his feet.

The steps passed.

"We could have been caught," she whispered, accusatory. "What a pretty picture that would have been."

"You kissed *me*, madam," he reminded her. "I thought you said I would get fair warning whenever you planned to assault me."

"That was for when I planned to punch you or poke you in the eye. Perhaps you would rather I did that."

"It might have been less shocking, madam!"

"There is no need to adopt an uncivil tone, Mr....your lordship...oh, I don't know what to call you now."

"Caulfield will suffice. Plain Mr. Heath Caulfield. Forget the Beauspur and the bloody lordship. I have."

"Very well then," she whispered. "I am in love with you, Heath Caulfield forget-the-beauspur-and-the-bloody-lordship."

He didn't know what to say. It was like being landed on again, crushing the breath out of him. He reached for her and found a shoulder, a sleeve, a wrist. Her own pulse was surprisingly steady compared to his.

"I doubt I'm supposed to tell you," she added. "It is probably not the done thing, but you must have guessed already and I'm not very accomplished at playing coy. Not even in the dark."

"Really? This had escaped my notice."

"I tried to flirt once, and the gentleman thought I was having a fit of hysterics." There was a pause and a wistful sigh. "Well, you told me your secrets so I must return the favor and tell you mine. I didn't expect to

300

be in love with you. You're not at all what I imagined."

"Sorry to disappoint."

"Oh, it's not that at all. It's just that I was looking... in the other direction. I might have missed you completely."

It was so easy, apparently, for her to say all this, to express herself fearlessly.

"But I recently remembered my grandmother telling me to look beyond the obvious," she whispered, a smile evident in her voice again. "She was a remarkably clever lady."

Heath struggled to tell her what he felt, but it was not in his nature and he'd never been taught. If anything it was ingrained in him to hide his emotions, not to feel anything at all for fear of recrimination.

At that moment he was grateful for the dark.

* * * *

"I will protect you," he said, so softly and hoarsely it was barely above a whisper.

"Still you ignore my ability to take care of myself, Caulfield."

"Let me do that much. It is all I can offer you. I have nothing else. Not now, at least. I cannot afford a wife, Melinda. but if I could..."

Slowly she lifted his right hand and kissed the wooden fingers he had tried to conceal from her and the world. "You're a dreadfully practical, know-it-all sort of person, aren't you?" she said, as she had done before.

"I have to be."

But she didn't, did she? She was the naive,

gullible, unsophisticated Miss Goodheart, and she was very accustomed to the role. Everybody believed it.

She'd been in many a pickle before and survived. She would find a way out of this one too.

"I suppose, even if my dowry pearls were real, you would not want to marry me," she said crisply. "You would protest the indignity of a wife using her own riches to help you." He was the painfully noble type.

And he proved her correct when he muttered darkly, "When I marry it will be because I can afford to keep my wife. Not because she can keep me!"

"Oh, lord. If only you weren't quite such a gentleman."

Again she felt her grandmother's gentle pat and heard her whisper, as she passed the box of treasures into young Melinda's sticky hands. "*You must look beyond what is apparent. Turn your eye to the unexpected. That of most value often goes unnoticed.*"

Grandmother Ethelreda was right. It almost had.

* * * *

She slipped out into daylight first and Heath waited a while before he too left the hiding place. For them, he mused, it had been something of a Confessional. Appropriate, considering it had once hidden Catholic priests from Harry Tudor's temper and Good Queen Bess' recriminations.

A weight was gone from his shoulders now that he knew how she felt and he had revealed the truth about his purpose there. But there was soon another worry to replace those, for as he had told her, he could not afford a wife. It would be selfish to make her wait until he could, and who knew how long that would be? He expected no inheritance from his father and Clara was now solely his financial responsibility. Above all this, Sir Ludlow Goodheart would never approve such a suitor for his only daughter.

Best to put that out of his mind for now and concentrate on the job at hand.

Chapter Twenty-Five

The music had already begun in the great hall. Melinda, with her window open as she sat at her mirror, could hear Salty Rimple's fiddle weeping its first tune. Villagers were arriving in little clumps and clusters, carts rumbling up the drive, hooves clomping steadily across the gravel. Children laughed and shouted as they ran across the grass to peer in at the dancers, pull faces at the windows, hide under the tables and steal sips of punch from the bowl or cider from one of Tipsy's barrels.

Her father must be going spare, she mused. Sir Ludlow had no liking for children or villagers, but he must grin and bear it tonight and put on a good face to impress his wealthy guest.

She pinched her cheeks and studied her face in the spotted mirror. Well, she didn't look any different, but inside she felt older. Wiser. And that smile on her face was a new sort of happy, less mischievous, more... knowing?

Today she had kissed a man passionately for the first time. Surprisingly, he lived.

Yes, he had survived without being bowled over, kicked in the shin, or sustaining a black eye. He had even, she ventured to guess, enjoyed it.

And she was desperately in love.

She'd had no idea it would feel like this. Wretched man!

Once she'd calmed down somewhat she must write to Emma and Georgiana and let them know all about it. All about *him*. But where to start?

Some romances might be described as whirlwind...

She closed her eyes, thinking back to the three of them standing around one of Mrs. Lightbody's globes of the world, sticking pins in all the places they one day planned to visit. Georgiana always had a plot bubbling away in her mind, and Melinda was depended upon to put the plan into action, because she did not care about being punished. Little Emma would come along merely for the company and— so she always claimed— to ameliorate the damage.

But this adventure was all Melinda's.

She got up and went to the window.

A stiff breeze blew it wider open— silently, since her quiet hero had oiled the squeaky hinge— and she gazed out at the cool, creeping dusk.

Ethelreda Goodheart had often stood at this window, brushing her grand-daughter's hair and entertaining her with a tale of the infamous highwayman known as John 'Swift Nick' Nevison. An action-packed story, probably much embellished, and not truly fit for the ears of little girls, which is, no doubt, why Melinda loved it so and begged often to hear it.

Grandmother Ethelreda had a lot to answer for.

Suddenly, as she stood looking out, a lusty drum-roll of horse hooves thumped across the damp lawn toward her. Melinda squinted until she saw the dark shadow of that wicked highwayman emerge into the flickering torchlight that, tonight, maintained a welcoming glow over the crumbling facade of Kingsthorpe Park. In a cloud of dust and gravel, he halted before her and swept his cloak over one shoulder.

"Well, madam, shall you flee with me now, or keep me waiting again?"

Her fingers curled around the rough edge of the stone window ledge. "You're just a fantasy," she whispered.

"That is not the spirit of a true adventuress, madam! Where is your gumption? Commit those luscious lips to me now and I will carry you far away from here. We will ride forth together and carve our names in infamy."

As her friend Georgiana liked to say, "*If one must go down in something, it may as well be infamy.*"

She blew out a tense breath and watched her highwayman as his horse skipped in restless circles.

"You are tempting, sir," she whispered. "But one does have to grow up eventually."

Besides, she had another villain to catch tonight.

"Do not get any ideas, Melinda."

"Me? I never get any ideas."

"Melinda, I forbid you from getting involved in this."

"But I already am."

Forbid her, would he? He ought to know, by now, exactly how that would turn out.

* * * *

Heath found his path blocked by three large men, one holding a broken cricket bat and a torch, one with what looked to be the blade of a scythe, and one with a knife.

"Mr. Lindley Goodheart does not care for your presence at the ball," the tallest one growled, waving the lit torch. "He wants you gone from this 'ouse and away from 'is sister."

"I don't doubt it."

"And you ain't to come back."

"I can quite understand his concern," he replied politely. "Chilly evening, isn't it?"

The three brutes exchanged confused glances.

"Perhaps you'd join me for a drink before I leave?"

One of them looked as if he might agree, but the other two raised their weapons in readiness, expecting a fight.

He tipped his hat back and scratched his head. "Why should you miss out on all this just to see me off? I doubt Master Goodheart means to pay you much for your inconvenience, eh? I know what these fancy London gents are like. I suppose he promised you some reward, but look around the place. He's naught to give."

The torch was slightly lowered.

"Listen," he added with a casual shrug, "I've no urge to fight. I was on my way out in any case. Why not just enjoy a jug of Tipsy's cider with me? Master Goodheart will be none the wiser." Walking up to where they stood, he took off his hat and held it to his chest, smiling. "I've no quarrel with you gentlemen."

The man with the knife spat onto the path and said, "Goodheart will have plenty when his sister weds that other feller."

Heath chuckled, shaking his head. "Is that what he told you? I'm afraid his expectations are greater than the reality."

At that moment Tipsy Rimple came down the path behind him. "Mr. Caulfield! What are you doing out in the cold? Sammy said you were out here."

The three hired thugs evidently knew Tipsy for they lowered their weapons immediately.

"What's amiss here then?" the genial fellow exclaimed. "Hal Dawkins, is that you? Does your mother know you're out? And with her best carving knife? And Bob Tulley, mind you don't cut yourself with that rusty scythe, or you'll get lockjaw, knowing your luck." He laughed. "Look at all of you out here with grim faces when there's cider aplenty to drink and pretty maids waiting for partners. When I were your age, I know where I'd be."

The weapons were, somewhat guiltily, put aside. Tipsy ushered them all down the path and gave Heath a quick wink.

"Not that I'll expect you to remember this when it comes time for the cider judgin'," he whispered.

Once again Heath had the distinct impression that he was missing part of the story, but that had happened to him ever since he came into the country.

* * * *

About to leave her room, Melinda was startled by the arrival of Lindley at her door. Having kicked it open, he leaned against the frame and glowered at her with a blistering rage. "Father sent me to fetch you down. Rocky is waiting for you in the hall. I suggest you make haste and do your duty for this family at last, before some bosomy Rimple wench catches his eye. I didn't put up with that idiot for the last six weeks just for you to let him slip away again."

She was pulling on her evening gloves and now she slowed the action, carefully straightening every wrinkle, her gaze darting discretely sideways to her reticule on the dresser. "Is he really so very rich? It's not like you to go to this much effort."

"Yes," he spat. "He is richer than you can possibly comprehend. Or he will be, once he fulfills his grandfather's wish and marries."

"Sounds like a gothic romance. Is Rocky's grandfather on his deathbed high up in a castle turret somewhere?" She laughed lightly, still floating a little on The Illicit Cupboard Kiss. There were some things, so she'd found, that one could enjoy in a cupboard and which did not come in one of Hattie's pie crusts. "Was it a family feud between the old man and Rocky's father that separated them all these years and marriage is the only thing that will appease the dying fellow?"

"No, his grandfather resides in Antigua, on the sugar plantation he owns, and by all accounts he isn't dying quickly enough. He disapproves of young men leading a life of leisure and keeps a stern hand on Rocky's finances all the way from over there. I believe it's time he loosened his grip."

"I will never cease to be amazed by how you always know best for everybody else and their finances, brother. Considering you fail so miserably at your own."

"Do I?" He laughed curtly. "Just because I choose not to pay a debt, doesn't mean I couldn't. You needn't worry about me, sister, I do very well for myself, and the fact that everybody dismisses Lindley Goodheart as a wastrel, merely getting by in life by the skin of his teeth, actually works very well in my favor."

With a sigh she closed the window and checked her reflection in the mirror one last time. "How exactly do you intend to help Rocky's grandfather loosen his grip on the finances?"

"Do follow along, sister. You're going to help our dear, witless Rocky change his idle ways— at least, on the surface. He is about to become a fat, settled, married man, soon to be a father, and a god-fearing, charitable gentleman. Especially charitable to his good friend," he swept a sarcastic bow, "yours truly."

She stared at his reflection in the mirror as he came up behind her. "So you really did bring him here, expecting that he would marry me?"

"Why not? He's not terribly discerning and loves female company. I knew that if I could keep him here, away from more sophisticated, prettier petticoat for long enough, he was bound to latch onto you sooner or later. And, as I said to him, marriage to you doesn't have to end his fun, does it?"

"*His fun?*"

Lindley rolled his eyes and adjusted one of the seed-pearl pins in her hair. "If you are sensible, after the first piglet to please his grandpapa, you'll let him go his way and you can go yours— with that odd little hat shop of which you are so inexplicably fond. These days a married couple does not even need to live in the same house, as long as you keep up appearances whenever it's necessary."

"Lindley, you are the very end!"

"You ought to be grateful to me." He scowled hard into the mirror. "Somebody, sooner or later, would have snapped the plump boar out of the sty

310

and butchered him for the Christmas sideboard, so why should it not be us who gets to feast?"

It was clear that her brother had no idea of his friend's true identity. He must have been fooled, like everybody else, by Rochfort's act of a fashionable, not very bright, but affable gentleman. In all likelihood, the story about the grandfather in Antigua was entirely false. Lindley had swallowed it whole, unable to resist the promise of a fortune waiting for him to help spend it.

"You're wearing Ethelreda's pearls," he exclaimed, just noticing them around her throat and hanging from her ears. "Rocky gave them back to you?"

"Yes, I decided I might as well wear my dowry tonight, even without the stone in the clasp." A scarlet silk poppy had been requisitioned from one of her bonnets to replace the missing stone. It added a jaunty new look to the old counterfeit pearls, she thought.

"It looks ridiculous," he snapped. "You look like a dancer in a Parisian supper hall."

"Well, Mr. Rochfort apparently appreciates my independent soul and my own peculiar style. My *joie de vivre*." She laughed and realized, too late, that it sounded thin and hollow.

"You're in an odd mood this evening." He walked over to the window and looked out, his eyes suddenly suspicious as they scanned the darkened lawn. "You needn't think your Mr. Caulfield will be there tonight. We've seen the back of him. Off he's trotted, back to Lady Clara Beauspur no doubt. Unless he's found some other woman to ruin since then. I shouldn't imagine he stayed with *her* for seven years if he could get nothing from her family."

Melinda touched the false pearls at her throat. "What makes you so certain that he is the man in that terrible story?" she asked nonchalantly.

"Whether he is or not, I didn't like him. There was something odd about the fellow." He gave an exaggerated shudder. "We are better off without him hanging about, drooling after you. He had nothing to offer, and he was just getting in the way. No, let him go back to sad, silent Clara. At least she will never be able to nag the fellow." He punctuated this remark with one of his lazy, snide chortles.

With two sharp tugs he drew the heavy old tapestry curtains across her window.

Melinda stared at his back and the dark curls of his hair where they rested on the high collar of his evening coat. Lindley had his hair cut in London. He refused to have it cut anywhere else. Likewise, he insisted on having his coats made by a particular tailor on Old Bond Street and his boots made by none other than Hoby in St James Street.

Her brother was a man who grew up with expectations and tastes he couldn't afford. Or should not be able to.

Just because I choose not to pay a debt, doesn't mean I couldn't. You needn't worry about me, sister, I do very well for myself.

"What do you mean— *silent* Clara?" she asked, aware of the pearls in her ears trembling, her heart pounding until her veins seemed to vibrate under her skin.

"She's a pretty girl, but a deaf mute. If only you

312

had been born thus, sister. We could have been rid of you much quicker."

"I daresay," she squeezed out. Somehow.

"There is much to be said for mute wenches," he muttered, still fussing with the pleats of the curtain, sticking his finger through a moth-hole. "Look at the state of this place. Rochfort's money doesn't come a moment too soon."

You have no inkling. You never did. You're all so damnably stupid.

Yes, they had been. She had been.

With shockingly steady fingers Melinda took her reticule from the dresser and hurried out of her room.

* * * *

A quarter of an hour later she swept into the kitchen and announced to Hattie, "I'm going to marry Mr. Rochfort."

"You what?"

"He wants to help me with the hat shop and is content to take me even with so little dowry. You know my five hundred pounds is lost, and now there is only this old jewelry of Grandmother Ethelreda's," she said loudly. "As Lindley says, it could be my last chance, Hattie. Be happy for me."

"Have you taken leave of your senses, young lady?"

"Not at all. In fact, I'm being practical for once."

"And you think Rochfort will make your life complete?" Hattie cried. "He'll be off with the first pretty face he sees and before Christmas, no doubt. This is not what you want, my girl. And not what I ever wanted for you!"

She laid a hand on the good woman's arm and gave her a deeply meaningful look. "Trust that I know what I am about, dear Hattie. You've taught me well and you know I can look after myself."

Before Hattie could protest, Melinda embraced her in a tight squeeze and whispered in her ear, "Moone is listening. Do play along."

The poor woman did not know what to say or do, so Melinda lengthened the hug for several minutes, exclaiming, "In any case, we leave tonight. Immediately."

"But what about—"

"Mr. Rochfort will surely apply for a special license and we'll marry in London at once. Better that than wait three weeks here for the reading of the banns. I'm certain he will agree."

Hattie whimpered uncertainly, "But this is all so sudden."

"You know how I am when my mind is made up."

Still confused, Hattie followed her to the door into the kitchen garden. "But I don't know what—"

"Oh, do not fuss, dear Hattie," she exclaimed loudly. "Of course I am ready for marriage. I know all that. Four years at a lady's academy, and the occasional sighting of a chimney sweep's biceps, opened my eyes quite sufficiently to the potential horrors of the marriage bed, but I feel adequate for the task." Planting a quick kiss on the good lady's cheek, she added, "Now do stop weeping, Hattie. You'll make the blancmange salty. Here, take this." She slipped a folded square of linen into her friend's hand. "For your tears."

Even as she stepped out into the night air, she heard Moone get up and dash out to find his master. His real master.

Now to locate the perfect bonnet for this escapade, then find Mr. Rochfort and tell him the full story. This was his chance to be brave at last.

Chapter Twenty-Six

Heath had looked all over the house for her. When he realized the "Cuckoo" was missing too his heart sank. Then Hattie found him.

"She left with that dandy, Rochfort, and gave me this." She passed a folded square of linen into his hand. "There's a message inside, but I can't read."

At once he recognized his own handkerchief—the one he gave her after she was caught in the rain. It had had been washed, ironed and folded. When he opened it and found a scrap of paper inside bearing a hastily written message surrounded by ink blots.

Amor Non Praecepi

Love cannot be commanded.

It was a message for him, obviously.

That damnable woman!

He was furious. Had he not told her, in no uncertain terms, to leave this matter to him? He should have known she would try to take this into her own hands and apprehend the "Cuckoo". Never should have told her. Never should have given in to her wide eyes. Of course she could not resist the adventure.

Just wait until he got his hands on her again....

"How the devil did they leave?" he demanded. "Rochfort has no coach, no horses at his disposal. I saw to that."

Hattie wrung her hands together anxiously. "They must have taken one of the carts brought up here tonight from the village. She said they were going to London, so they need only get as far as the crossroads to catch the stagecoach. One is due to pass tonight, and Miss Melinda will know that."

Why, in God's name, would she leave now, this very minute? What was she up to?

The dance was in full swing and the cider flowed. Was she expecting everybody to be too drunk to give chase? What then was her plan?

"*I suppose you thought I would try to capture him myself, then take all the credit and reward. Is there a very great reward for his capture? There must be.*"

Surely she didn't think she could disarm Rochfort and hand him over to the magistrate herself to collect the reward.

Even Melinda would not be that reckless. Would she?

He saw again the image of her dangling from a drainpipe. And that was only to rescue a bonnet for a friend.

Sir Ludlow rolled his chair into view, not caring whose foot he mowed over in his path. "Where's my blessed daughter?" he demanded of Hattie. "Where's she gone off to now? I'm supposed to make an announcement about this bloody engagement, and neither she nor that daft bugger with the fat purse are anywhere in sight."

"She's run off," Hattie exclaimed, fraught and clutching her apron. "She's run off to London. Eloped! I always knew that girl would get herself into trouble one day."

"*Eloped?*" Sir Ludlow roared, thumping his bandaged foot upon the flagstones. "She can't elope!

She's got to be married here at the church. Proper
like! There's arrangements to make, papers to sign."
He scowled fiercely. "Bills to be paid and money to be
'anded over by that primped popinjay. He needn't
think he can just take my beloved daughter off and
not pay for the privilege. Ours is one of the oldest
family's in the country. He can't just take our pedigree
to raise 'imself up a rung. New money needs old
blood, and old blood needs new damn money!" The
old man twisted around in his chair. "Where's my
son? Fetch my son. He'll know what to do."

Lindley already approached, his face dark with
fury, the sullen manservant Moone in tow. "She's
gone off?" he yelled. "Moone tells me she's flown off
to London with Rocky. How could this happen? I
know it must be her bloody idea, because Rocky
wouldn't have the gumption to defy me. He wasn't to
leave until the wedding was done."

Heath stepped back into the shadows behind a
thick stone pillar, but Lindley was too angry to see
him there in any case. He shouted at his father, "If
she gets him back to London she'll have him pouring
his money into that shop of hers and we'll never get a
penny. The damned idiot is too easily led, too easily
influenced. We can't afford to have him out of our
reach. I've gone to a lot of trouble to get him here
and arrange all this. She needn't think she's taking it
all. Oh no, that wasn't the plan. That was *not* the
plan!" He paced beside his father's chair, one hand to
his head, cursing and spitting.

All around them the dance continued and this
seemed to make the man even more irate. Finally he
screamed at the musicians, tore down a bower of

greenery and marched across the hall, shoving people aside. Again, Moone followed in his wake, muttering in his ear.

It was evident by then that Moone was not Rochfort's manservant at all. He was clearly in Goodheart's employ. Interesting. Puzzling.

Why the masquerade? Why would Sir Ludlow's son not want anybody to know he kept a valet?

But almost immediately Heath understood. Moone could spy a great deal more efficiently for his master if nobody knew who his master truly was.

Lindley Goodheart possessed greater cunning than Heath had so far attributed to the fellow.

* * * *

They rode for the crossroads in an old dogcart borrowed from Salty Rimple.

Rochfort had spent the two=mile journey expressing, in varying degrees of concern, his foreboding about the enterprise. "Miss Goodheart, I cannot help but think this departure hasty. Should we not have said goodbye at least to your father?"

"Oh, my poor, dear Mr. Rochfort, do you not see? The haste of our leaving is necessary because it gives my brother no time to plan. He must act. And he will act rashly as a consequence. We cannot allow him time to think. Men are the very worst when they think."

But the gentleman still failed to understand why it was essential to leave before he could pack all his garments. She had allowed him only one trunk and that was tied very precariously to the back of the dog cart. Apart from that he had only his coat, hat and walking cane— the latter almost dropped every time they went over a bump or a deep puddle.

"Do have a care, Miss Goodheart," he cried, one hand on his hat.

Melinda laughed as she urged the horse faster. "Do not fret. You will get your fine clothes back, Mr. Rochfort, as soon as all this is over." In the meantime, he made a splendid hare with which to catch a predator.

"And... we are not going to be married, you say?"

"No, Mr. Rochfort. I am so very sorry, but I am not the woman for you. I would like us to be friends, however. Real friends, that is. Not like you and my brother."

"But what has Goodheart done to bring about this mad chase to London?"

"Many things, I fear. Many bad things. And I have been stupidly blind to it, as he actually pointed out to me recently. Unfortunately I never paid much heed to Lindley— what he does or says. I have learned to block it out from my mind. Had I paid more attention I might have realized before now."

They arrived at the crossroads and she fed the horse a carrot, then tied him to an oak, knowing Salty would find him there before too long. The alarm must have been raised by now. Moone would have run instantly to Lindley with the news of her unexpected departure with Rochfort, and everybody should be looking for their carts and horses to see whose had been taken.

She checked anxiously down the road in both directions and asked Mr. Rochfort for the time. He glanced at his fob watch in the moonlight.

"Ten minutes to midnight, Miss Goodheart."

Good. The stagecoach should be along soon. As long as they had not missed it. One could never be sure, of course. It was a risk she took. And Melinda was no stranger to risk.

When she lifted the veil of her best hat— a necessity when one was on a desperate mission— her excitable breath made a curling cloud of fog before her mouth.

"What if your brother does not follow us, Miss Goodheart?"

"Oh, he will. He won't want you and your money to get out of his reach."

Why go to the trouble of capturing a villain when she could make him chase her all the way back to London, doing the work for her? He had embarrassed their family enough. Getting him away from Kingsthorpe now was imperative. And Lindley never chased anything as recklessly as he chased money.

There was also, she must admit, more than a little wicked pleasure to be had in seeing whether she could race Heath Caulfield to this reward.

* * * *

He borrowed a horse from Tipsy Rimple, took his pistol from its hiding place inside the hollowed out book in his room, and rode at speed for the crossroads.

That redheaded woman was not getting away with this. He was quivering with anger. But more than that even, he worried for her safety. It rattled through him, stirred his blood.

This, he vowed, was the last night she would ever

321

be out of his sight again.

He couldn't afford a wife, but he was in no mood at that moment to think practically as far as she was concerned. One way or another, she was his. She'd been his since the first time she fell out of the sky and landed in his arms, and he was never letting her go again.

* * * *

"Gracious, Miss Goodheart, is this really how other folk travel?" Crammed into a corner of the stagecoach, clinging to his walking cane with one hand and the greasy strap above the door with the other, Mr. Rochfort endured an eye-opening experience.

"I'm afraid it's how *most* folk travel," she replied with a little smile. "Including me."

The moonlit carriage interior held six passengers and a bad-tempered lapdog which had already made its feelings known about the two latest additions to the un-merry band.

"At least we don't have to ride on the outside," Melinda added brightly. "Think of that. Could be worse."

He gave her a woeful look. Leaning toward her he whispered faintly. "But I believe I just sat...on a tooth, Miss Goodheart."

"One must laugh, Mr. Rochfort. In the direst of moments, one must laugh." And so she did.

Suddenly a shadow shot across the coach window, hiding the moon and temporarily casting them all in darkness. The little dog barked. Her heart leapt a beat. She clutched her reticule tighter.

Jayne Fresina

The carriage suddenly shuddered and bounced, bumping them all out of their seats, and the door was wrenched open.

"Ladies and gentlemen, I beg patience for the interruption, but with your kindly cooperation this shall not take long." A wide-shouldered figure stood there, a black shadow against the moon.

Oh, Swift Nick, this is no time for you! Her highwayman had come after her, it seemed. With a handkerchief masking the lower half of his face, he looked into the stage coach. "You, madam." He pointed with a pistol. "Out you come, if you please. You and I have some business to tend."

She groaned softly. This was the worst time for her imagination to go off on one of its adventures, but surely it wouldn't last.

Holding her reticule, she apologized to the other passengers, and to Mr. Rochfort, who was still trying to locate the tooth upon which he thought he sat.

As she stepped out, the highwayman gave her his left hand to help her down.

"I haven't anything of value about me," she assured him. "I'm afraid you'll be disappointed."

"I beg to differ. I happen to know you have something in your possession that I want, madam." He lifted her veil, folding it back over the crown of her hat, getting his fingers momentarily tangled in the silk flowers.

"I'm busy. Make haste and get it over with. Mind my hat!"

Leaning over her, he tugged the kerchief from his mouth and smiled. "Always impatient."

Melinda stared. It was not 'Swift Nick', her

323

naughty highwayman.

It was Heath Caulfield, the dullest man that ever lived.

What was he doing in her daydream?

His gloved hand swept slowly along her jaw, and then lifted her chin. "You thought you could beat me to London and that reward?"

There was no chance to reply, because he lowered his lips to hers and stole away the answer.

She shivered. The chilled night air blew against her and somewhere nearby an owl let out a sultry hoot. She could smell the horses, the dead leaves, the smoky air— residue of burning in the fields. It was all too real.

And she tasted his kiss. It slipped into her like warm mulled wine and made her dizzy.

This was no fantasy, Here before her was a real hero.

"You're much too sensible and practical to chase me in the dark," she gasped out. "I didn't expect you to follow us so soon."

"Caulfield! Is that you? What the blazes are you doing here?" Mr. Rochfort peered out of the coach window. "Unhand Miss Goodheart at once!" But he couldn't get the door open and was left fussing indignantly with the handle.

"Does my brother come?" she asked, ignoring the rocking carriage.

"I have a strong suspicion he does. He and Moone have no doubt found a vehicle by now."

"Then there is no time to waste. You must let us go on to Castlebridge where the stagecoach changes horses. Lindley will no doubt go there looking for us."

324

Heath frowned down at her. "Are you mad, woman? Who cares about your brother? I'm not letting you go in that coach," with one arm curled around her waist, he pointed his pistol at Rochfort, "with *him*." Instantly the other man stopped trying to open the carriage door, his entire body frozen at the other end of the muzzle, hands raised in the air.

"By the way, you've got the wrong man." Drawing Heath away from the coach, she reached up and patted his chest over his heart with a loving hand. "My darling, protector," she whispered, "trust me this once. You're quite wrong about Mr. Rochfort. He is not the man you've been seeking."

"Melinda, I told you not to get involved—"

"You said that nobody other than your family, a few servants and John Croft ever knew the truth about your sister's deafness, because your father hid her away."

He nodded, his lips tight again.

"Well, there is someone else who knows," she added somberly. "My brother."

His eyes narrowed in the moonlight.

"My brother knew the name Clara Beauspur and yet he never remembers any young lady's name. He knew the whole story. Even that your sister is deaf and mute."

Still he stared.

"My brother," she said firmly, "is the scoundrel you know as the 'Cuckoo'. And I would wager on it."

"Wager?" His eyes flared with interest, but she could tell he still didn't quite believe her.

"I'll wager my dowry on it."

"Your dowry?" He trailed his gloved finger over

the pearls at her throat. "These old, counterfeit things?" He gave a wry smile that made her want to kiss him again. And not stop.

"Do you want them or not, Caulfield?"

"What use would they be to me? Hardly practical."

"What if I come with them?"

"Even less use to a prudent, logical fellow like me."

"Very well!" She put her chin in the air and said grandly, "I know Mr. Rochfort wants my pearls."

Before she could get two steps, he had hauled her back to his side, tucked his pistol away inside his coat, and yelled at the coachman to drive on.

As the stagecoach rattled off down the road toward Castlebridge, he leapt up onto his borrowed horse and offered Melinda his left hand.

"Come with me before I change my mind and leave you here, wretched, meddling woman."

"You wouldn't do that," she replied archly. "You're a gentleman."

"I fear I might not always be so," he grinned, "where you're concerned."

What else could an adventuress do, especially with that promise whispered through the trailing shadows and with his kiss still warm on her lips?

So she took the hand of her highwayman and let him pull her up onto his horse. As his warm arms closed around her to grip the reins she felt a new kind of excitement in her heart. It was possible perhaps, after all, to find a good, reliable man who could also give her a wicked thrill once in a while.

Certainly there was nothing dull about the kiss

with which he now dampened the side of her neck.

"I hope you don't have plans to take advantage of an innocent lady," she managed on a breathy gasp.

"Madam, I am on a matter of business. And I never take advantage of innocent ladies. Only the wicked menaces." He whispered in her ear. "Especially those in desperate bonnets."

She laughed.

He paused in the process of *not* taking advantage of his captive to say, "Kindly remove your hands from inside my coat, madam."

"I was trying to keep them warm," she muttered, blinking.

"You were trying to steal my pistol. I may be in love with you, Melinda, but you needn't think I'm that distracted."

* * * *

When they arrived in the busy market town of Castlebridge it was almost daylight. She knew her brother had probably taken short cuts across fields to get there. He would be too angry and impatient to take the turnpike road. Nor would he want to pay at the toll-gate. Lindley never had a qualm about trampling anybody's fields.

Yes, she knew him too well. And yet, on the other hand, she didn't.

At that last moment, as she rode with Heath into the yard of the "Fox and Hound" coaching inn, she felt a tremor of sadness that it had come to this.

If her brother truly was the villain known as the "Cuckoo" he deserved punishment, of course. He must face justice.

But he was still her brother.

She remembered running after him through the stable-yard when they were much younger, begging him to let her ride upon his shoulders, where the unsteady tilt gave her a thrill and made her squeal with excitement. She remembered picking blackberries with him for one of Hattie's pies, both of them eating so many that they were sick.

Simpler times, now long gone.

The stagecoach pulled in not long after they arrived and Mr. Rochfort was the first one out, brushing himself down and severely outraged by the roughness of his journey.

"I would have leapt out to save you, Miss Goodheart. I do hope that man Caulfield has not compromised you."

"Not completely as yet," she muttered. "But I have high hopes."

* * * *

He had taken a seat just inside the tavern doorway, but partially hidden by a beam. From there he could watch for the arrival of Lindley Goodheart who, according to Melinda's prediction, would arrive not long after them. If he was not there already. Meanwhile she and Mr. Rochfort sat across the room with their breakfast, playing the part of an eloping couple.

Melinda, he suspected, was enjoying every minute of the performance. She wore, he had noted last night, a very colorful bonnet, complete with veil. Probably the sort of thing she imagined a woman running away with a lover might wear. He had to agree that she did indeed have a peculiar sort of style. One all of her own.

Across the tavern her gaze met his. He took off his hat, dropped it to the table and raised his pewter tankard. She smiled, lifted her own drink to her lips and let her coppery eyelashes flutter against her cheeks.

Merely watching her was enough to heat his blood again, to think of when she would next be in his arms.

And then in his bed.

He had never felt like this before. The anticipation of claiming the reward she offered, was greater even than the anticipation of capturing the infamous "Cuckoo" and bringing him to justice at last.

Beside her, Rochfort seemed very confused, or else he had indigestion. Clutching his walking cane, he looked at the black pudding on his plate and looked as if he might lose the contents of his stomach.

Just then the door opened and several passengers from another stagecoach entered the premises. Among them were two women, one looking around eagerly, the other, an older woman in a widow's bonnet, following closely with a worried look on her face.

Heath almost dropped his ale. "Clara!"

He flew out of his seat and Mrs. Oliver clasped her charge's hand, drawing her around and pointing. His sister's face lit up and she went to him, embracing Heath and kissing his cheeks before he could shout at her.

"Mrs. Oliver," he exclaimed angrily, "kindly

explain to me what my sister is doing here?"

The lady shook her head wearily. "She would not be told, sir. As soon as she received your letter she said she could tell there was something amiss and she must go to you at once. We were on our way to Kingsthorpe and the coach stopped here to change—"

"Horses, yes I know. But what the devil are you doing on the public stage coach? You know the rules, Mrs. Oliver. My sister is not to venture out like this."

Clara reached up, grabbed his face in both her gloved hands and made him look at her. Then she signed quickly and Mrs. Oliver interpreted, "I insisted that we must find you, brother."

"Clara, this is absolutely not—"

"I wanted to explore the world just a little. I am tired of being kept indoors."

"It is for your safety, Clara! For your own good. What if something happens to you again? What if you get lost, or—"

"Are you ashamed of me too? Like our father?"

He took a step back. "Of course not."

"Then why hide me away?"

"You could be hurt." He couldn't bear the thought of it. Seven years ago he had not been able to save her from pain and anguish, but now he could.

Even now he was aware of people in the tavern turning to watch with curiosity, wondering what all the gesturing was about.

Clara looked at him with her head on one side, and then she signed slowly so that he could understand. "I love you, Heath, but you cannot keep me a prisoner. You must let me live in the world, or else why did you rescue me?"

He swallowed and bowed his head, running hands through his hair. Again she made him look at her while she signed with her quick lithe fingers.

"I am not afraid of life anymore. After everything I lived through, I am stronger than I look. Thanks to you, I survived. Now, please, *please,* let me see more of this world than one cottage garden." Since he had begun to get lost trying to follow, Mrs. Oliver stepped forward again to translate. "I need something new to paint. I am tired of painting ..." the elder lady blushed and scrambled for a word, "devilish...hollyhocks."

He tried to maintain a good scowl. "*Devilish* hollyhocks won't hurt you or mock you."

"If I go out in the world," she insisted with adamant gestures, "it will teach people that there is nothing strange about me, or others like me. You are not the only one, brother, who wants to make a difference for the better."

He could hardly argue with that point, and she knew it.

Her final thrust was then delivered with pert determination. "I am older than Miss Goodheart, and she travels *alone.*"

Her face took on the twitchy countenance of one who knew she was victorious and yet wanted not to seem not too pleased with herself.

"Lady Clara, how lovely it is to see you again!" Melinda Goodheart had wisely waited until the storm abated before hurrying across the tavern to greet his sister. "And wearing one of my bonnets too!"

The two women embraced and Heath looked on feeling oddly relieved. Although he should still be furious with his sister, she had made too many good arguments. She knew she had won. As he looked at the two young women chattering together, with Mrs. Oliver interpreting for them, he began to feel...outnumbered.

Then, to his horror, he remembered Rochfort. The fellow had got up and followed Melinda. Now he stood a few feet away, still looking befuddled by the proceedings in general.

Heath was about to intercept, when Melinda suddenly turned and introduced his sister to Rochfort.

There was not a glimmer of recognition on either face. The two politely greeted one another and then, after one self-satisfied smirk in his direction, Melinda resumed her conversation with his sister. Rochfort went back to being bewildered. Perhaps that was his habitual state, Heath mused.

"Do come and have breakfast with me, Lady Clara." Melinda took his sister's arm and was leading her back to the table, when a chill draft blew more people into the crowded tavern.

Something caused Heath to swing around, but not fast enough to draw his weapon from inside his coat.

"Sister! Did you really think you could get away with this?"

It was Lindley Goodheart with pistol drawn, aiming at Melinda. He must not have seen the woman at her side at first. Or else he merely was not interested.

Only when both women turned to look at him, did he see Clara.

Chapter Twenty-Seven

The crowded tavern suddenly went quiet, the only sound being that of the fire cracking and wind howling around the corners of the low, squat building.

Lindley's dark eyes were pinned to Lady Clara's face, and his cheeks hollowed as he sucked in a breath of surprise. Suddenly he looked many years older and several inches shorter.

Watching her brother, Melinda saw him as he would be in another decade, a sad, miserable, discontented fellow with a round belly, a red nose, and shoulders rounded after so many years of rolling through life with that slovenly posture, waiting for other people to do his work, expecting riches to fall into his lap.

There was denying that he knew the woman at her side. Lady Clara had let her arm slide away from Melinda's and stood now with her clever hands— those little doves usually so busily expressing her thoughts— stilled at her sides. Melinda remained close to protect her.

"Well," Lindley finally muttered, "is this not an interesting reunion?" But his eyes glittered with frosty anger, his gaze darting from side to side, as he tried to make sense of seeing them all there together. He still, of course, did not know that Heath was Clara's brother. "Rocky," he shouted. "You disappoint me by running off to London with my sister. Leaving me to explain away Hasting's property and possibly take the blame for it? Not paying the considerable gambling

333

debt you owe me?"

"I say, old chap, I didn't mean to——"

Melinda placed a firm hand on Rochfort's sleeve, and his sentence burbled away to nothing.

Her brother continued, "I told you the wedding was to take place in Kingsthorpe, within the eyes of the local peasantry. The pomp and circumstance does them good, keeps them in their place. And it's what my father wanted. Why would you suddenly flee in the night? Not thinking to seduce my sister and abandon her, surely? I know she's not worth much in the way of a dowry, but——"

"It was my idea to leave," Melinda interrupted. "I didn't want you to take money from Mr. Rochfort, and I don't care to be sold like an old chair."

"I see my sister still labors under the impression that her opinion counts. I ought to shoot her where she stands. The devil knows how she's tried my patience in the past."

And he would do it too. She knew, from that hard look on his face, that there was no little boy left in him. Their past was gone, popped like a bubble on the surface of a fast-moving stream. They were now two strangers with nothing in common.

"I'm not going to marry Mr. Rochfort in any case," she said. "Sorry to disappoint, but you'll have to find another way to fund your excesses."

Lindley took a step forward, pistol still aimed at Melinda. "Then why this masquerade of running off together? I know you enjoy the drama, sister, but really this——"

"I know what you are, Lindley, what you have become and all that you've done."

He stared arrogantly, his lips stuck in their usual sneer.

"How could you?" she demanded. "Have you nothing to say." She supposed, in the end, she had hoped for some sign of contrition, some apology to show that he was not completely lost to evil.

But there was none. "Come then, Rocky, we shall go about our business and forget this trollop." He glanced at Clara. "I see from the company she keeps, that she is nothing more than a cheap hussy, a strumpet, every man's leavings."

That, of course, was when Heath sprang.

A ruckus quickly ensued as the two men fought, spitting curses, tipping over chairs and crashing into tables, tankards and dishes falling with a clatter. All around them, folk scattered, screaming and yelling. For a moment it was all confusion. Lindley's gun went off, firing into one of the thick wooden beams, and then Heath knocked it out of his hand. The two men went down, still wrestling. Somehow Lindley managed to get Heath's gun, but that too was wrenched from his grip. Heath threw a final punch and Lindley's head flopped back as he crashed into an upturned table. The gun flew across the floor and Melinda picked it up.

For some reason the tavern guests flew for cover again, women and men alike screaming in terror when they saw that pistol in her hands— as if she might be more dangerous than the villain of this piece.

"Well, really," she muttered, quite put out. "I know how to handle a weapon."

Fortunately, she had experience, and she was a far better shot than her brother. As Lindley well knew. When he opened his bleary eyes, peered up at his sister and saw her standing there with pistol in hand, he daren't move, not even an inch. Not even to wipe his bloody nose and lip.But all was not yet over.

Heath was just picking himself up when Moone entered the place with another pistol drawn. In all the excitement, the grumpy manservant had been forgotten about until that moment, and he must have been outside arranging fresh horses.

He was, as always, bloody inconvenient.

Melinda groaned under her breath and aimed Heath's pistol at the fellow. "Be still, sir, or I shall fire!"

Moone sneered.

It would, possibly, be the last time he underestimated a "chit of a girl", because this one fired her pistol and shot his own weapon clean out of his hand. He screamed like a stuck pig, clutching his bloody fingers and falling to his knees. The air was certainly rendered colorful by his curses and Melinda worried that she ought to cover Lady Clara's ears.

But she need not have worried. The vulgar fellow was silenced shortly after, when Mr. Rochfort came up behind him with that lovely walking cane in his hands and sharply cracked the ivory bulldog handle down upon the back of Moone's head. Her brother's accomplice went down— as Melinda described it later in a letter to her friends— like the proverbial felled oak.

* * * *

Lady Clara Beauspur formally identified Lindley Goodheart as the man who had seduced and abandoned her seven years before. Following her lead, several other victims came forward and recognized the man who had eluded arrest for so long.

Braver now, than she had been before, Lady Clara was prepared to face him, without flinching, when he was brought to trial.

In fact, Lady Clara grew bolder by the day, so much so, that her brother frequently worried aloud that she had come under a bad influence.

Especially when he saw some of the subjects she was painting these days.

And the reward for the capture and arrest of the notorious blackguard known as the "Cuckoo" was, according to a dramatic story in *The Gentleman's Weekly*, (penned by Lady Thrasher), shared equally by an engaged couple who wished to remain anonymous. Although one of them wished it to be known that she had very fine taste in "desperate bonnets."

* * * *

"Since I won the wager, I suppose I don't have to give you my dowry, or myself, after all," Melinda remarked pertly.

"On the contrary." Heath splashed water on his face from the washbasin and examined his bruised cheekbone in the looking glass. "We're sharing the reward for the capture of the villain. We both won."

"The wager was made upon his identity, sir, not which of us would ensure his capture. I was right. You were wrong."

He turned, wiping his face on a towel, eyeing her thoughtfully. "Who the devil taught you how to fire a pistol?"

She grinned. "I taught myself. You men make such a fuss over everything. It's really not that hard." Perching on the bed she began to remove her bonnet. "And don't change the subject. Can you not admit that I was right? Is it so painful to your masculine pride?"

"What are you doing?" he demanded warily, watching as she removed her gloves too. "This is my room."

"But with your sister and Mrs. Oliver in my room it's rather crowded, and Mr. Rochfort took the only other vacant chamber in the inn." She paused. "Perhaps you'd rather I be locked up in the landlord's meat cellar with the captives until our carriage arrives?"

He grimaced. "Not a bad idea. Might keep you out of trouble for an hour or so." But his pulse was racing, his heart hammering in his chest. Melinda Goodheart was always up to something. This time, apparently, she planned to make Heath Caulfield her mischief.

"I was hoping you could do that." Head tilted, she looked up at him. "Isn't that what you're supposed to do? Keep me safe and away from trouble?" She blinked. "You never know what I might do if you let me out of your sight."

"The coach will be here in under two hours." He strode over to the bed and tossed his towel to the floor. "How much mischief could even you get up to in so short a time?"

"It doesn't bear thinking about." Melinda knelt before him on the bed, grabbed his shirt with both

338

hands and whispered, "I can't wait for you to show me."

And so he did. With the very thorough attention to detail in which he prided himself.

"Mr. Caulfield," she exclaimed at one point, "you are really quite wicked, after all."

"That's your fault, Miss Goodheart. You bring out the worst in me."

But she, no doubt, considered that her crowning achievement.

* * * *

They dressed in a hurry because they had quite forgotten the time and when the carriage arrived, they were still in bed, wrapped in each other's arms.

"See," he complained, "you're a distraction already!" But he gave her another kiss. "A very lovely one."

"I'm glad to hear you say it, otherwise I might have assumed you were after my dowry."

He laughed and Melinda delighted in the sound of it. She secretly vowed to make him laugh more often from now on.

Later, when he was not so busy, she would show him Grandmother Ethelreda's treasure— the genuine necklace. For now she kept it in her reticule, relishing the pleasure of being the only living soul who knew of its existence. Her determinedly and proudly impoverished lover was in for a surprise when he discovered that she was quite rich after all.

Hopefully he wouldn't be too disappointed.

Pinning her hat securely in place, she took one last look around the tiny room that had served as the scene of her final corruption. She had entered the place a maiden and was leaving as a woman. It felt a little like falling through the air.

Thank goodness she had found the right man to catch her.

Epilogue

Lady Bramley looked around the small, tidy parlor and gave it one of her reluctant nods of acceptance.

"It is, of course, not decorated to the standards of my style, but then it is...adequate." She smiled at Melinda, who passed her a tea cup.

"I'm glad you approve, Lady Bramley."

"And you mean to live here as a companion to Lady Clara Beauspur, is that so?"

"Yes, your ladyship. Of course, I will still manage the shop. Lady Clara, in fact, has expressed an interest in helping me. She has an artist's eye and may be extremely helpful."

"I see. I must confess, I never realized there was a daughter in the Beauspur family. I thought they were all boys."

Melinda sipped her own tea. "Really?"

"Yes, there were three or four boys, as I recall. All of them very competitive for their father's attention. One of them went rather bad, I understand. Defied his father and went into the cavalry."

"Goodness."

"But these things happen, of course. One brings children into the world and hopes for the best." The Lady sighed heavily, clearly thinking of her own sons and her nephew, who was somewhat eccentric and now married to Melinda's friend Georgiana.

They heard the sound of the front door opening, followed by heavy footsteps and a male voice. Melinda glanced anxiously at the clock, for Heath wasn't due home for another hour. She'd thought it would be quite safe to entertain Lady Bramley until four. Alas, he had taken to coming home early lately, putting his feet up and enticing her into his lap as they sat by the fire together.

"'Tis a good life, this is," he liked to say, with one of those very naughty grins.

Fortunately, before he could reach the parlor he was intercepted by Mrs. Oliver's gentle voice in the hall and then his footsteps retreated.

Melinda gave a quiet sigh of relief, grabbed a slice of Tipsy's special fruit cake from the platter and quickly took a bite.

"Was that a man's voice?" Lady Bramley asked. "There are no men in the house, are there?"

Melinda took a moment to swallow. "Oh, it must be Lady Clara's suitor." Then she added hurriedly, in a much quieter voice, "Or her brother. He calls in occasionally. To visit."

As she had hoped, her ladyship was more interested in the first option. "Her suitor?"

"Yes. Mr. William Rochfort." Melinda smiled broadly. "He's a very keen fellow and quite sweet really, although I am not certain Lady Clara feels the same for him as he does for her. He can be a little...well, a little much. It may all come to naught. But he is trying so hard to win her over, and I think she very much enjoys somebody making that effort for her. The friendship is good for them both, I think."

"Does her father approve?"

Melinda chuckled. "I fear Lady Clara Beauspur does as she wishes these days and whether her father approves or not will neither encourage nor deter her affections."

Lady Bramley shook her head as she tossed another lump of sugar into her tea and stirred violently. "You young girls these days. How much bolder you are than I was allowed to be. I wonder what the world is coming to."

"Hopefully, it is becoming a happier place." She knew *her* world was much happier.

"And how is your father these days?"

"Much the same as always. He writes to me, but his anger over my brother's arrest and trial is still bitter. He blames me, of course, as usual. One day I will visit him." But it would not be for a while, she knew. He did not want to see her. The only child he had ever wanted was Lindley. Even now that he knew what Lindley was, he still talked of his son in glowing terms. Like his daughter he was a dreamer. In his case, it might be for the best if he never woke from his dream. The reality would be too hard for him to bear.

"But what about a suitor for you, Miss Melinda Goodheart? When I saw my nephew's wife recently she laid a few heavy hints that you may be in love. And behind my back! What do you have to say to that, young lady?"

Melinda licked her lips. "I would say..." she reached over and lifted the cake platter under the lady's nose, "have a slice of cider cake. It's made with that lovely award-winning cider from the village where I grew up."

Lady Bramley could never resist a good slice of cake.

* * * *

When their visitor was gone, Melinda found her lover in the library at the back of the little house.

"You decided not to introduce yourself to Lady Bramley then," she teased, sliding into his lap behind the desk and wrapping her arms around his neck.

"Since the last time I saw her she decided to beat me around the head with a parasol, I've decided to wait before I show her my ugly face again." He kissed her. "Besides, you surely are not ready to let her know we live together in this house. Isn't that supposed to be a secret until we can marry?"

"When I'm in love, I'm terrible at keeping secrets." She ran her fingers slowly through his lovely hair and inhaled the spicy scent of his soap. "And since your sister lives here too, it could be quite acceptable."

"Your Lady Bramley is no fool. She'd see through that in the blink of an eye. If she hasn't already."

"Then we'd better hurry up and make it respectable."

He reached for her hand and carefully entwined her fingers with his. Even the wooden ones. "I should have been a gentleman and waited before I took you to bed."

"I'm glad you didn't." She laughed. "I've told you before, no woman wants to feel safe all the time. Every girl wants a little danger, something naughty in her life."

He nodded solemnly. "I see. Well, I have something naughty for you. Right at this moment in fact." His eyes sparkled up at her as she used her free hand to stroked the hair back from his forehead. "Do you want it now?"

"Yes, " she cried. "Take me upstairs now. At once."

"Always impatient." He shook his head, his lip quirked. "Menace. Look in the drawer."

She squinted. "What is it?"

"For pity's sake, look in the drawer. It's not going to bite." He licked the side of her neck. "Although I might."

So she looked. There, inside a velvet-lined box, sat a simple gold ring.

"I think it's time I made you my wife. I've enough money saved now and another promotion—"

Before he could spoil it all by being too practical, she kissed him, almost pushing the chair over in her passionate desire to thank him for this gift.

When she let him breathe again, he laughed and kissed her fingers. "You don't think the ring is too plain?"

"It is utterly you, my darling."

"How flattering."

"Oh, I did not mean it that way!" She squeezed his chin. "I love it."

"And I love you, Melinda of the Desperate Bonnets and, one day, I'll take you somewhere very grand, where you can wear your grandmother's pearls and show them off."

"Who needs pearls when I have you?"

"You're a woman." He sighed, shaking his head. "And I know you like pretty things."

"If I wanted filthy riches and a handsome face,"

she exclaimed dramatically," I could have had Mr. Rochfort."

"So why take me?" He looked up at her, his eyes wide, wondering.

"Because I like the way you hold my hand." She felt tears in her eyes and didn't need to shake them off this time, for they were good, happy tears.

He nodded slowly. "And that's all it took?"

"Well, there are other things you do that I like..."

"Are there indeed?"

"If you take me upstairs, I can show you what they are." She wanted to be sure he kept doing them, of course.

"Strumpet." With that, the lusty highwayman lifted his mistress over one shoulder and carried her up to bed.

* * * *

On the eve of their wedding, she wrote to her friend,

"So now you know my story and how many years have gone by since it began.

I always thought that I would be the one of us who would never marry. Who would want this graceless clodhopper?

Then he came into my life— the most unexpected of heroes— and piece by piece he laid claim to my heart.

To think that it all began with Emma's lost bonnet.

How little I knew, when I stepped out onto that ledge, that the arms of love were waiting for me to fall."

COMING SOON

Pumpymuckles
(The Deverells – Book ∞)

Damon Undone
(The Deverells - Book Five)

Also from Jayne Fresina and TEP:

Souls Dryft

The Taming of the Tudor Male Series

Seducing the Beast

Once A Rogue

The Savage and the Stiff Upper Lip

The Deverells

True Story

Storm

Chasing Raven

Ransom Redeemed

Damon Undone *COMING SOON*

Ladies Most Unlikely

The Trouble with His Lordship's Trousers

The Danger in Desperate Bonnets

A Private Collection

Last Rake Standing

ABOUT THE AUTHOR

Jayne Fresina sprouted up in England, the youngest in a family of four daughters. Entertained by her father's colorful tales of growing up in the countryside, and surrounded by opinionated sisters - all with far more exciting lives than hers - she's always had inspiration for her beleaguered heroes and unstoppable heroines.

Website at:
jaynefresinaromanceauthor.blogspot.com

Twisted E Publishing, Inc.
www.twistederoticapublishing.com

63309789R00210

Made in the USA
Middletown, DE
31 January 2018